Praise for *Treason*:

"Plenty of action. . . . David [is] in perfect form and readers will laugh and cry as he takes them on an emotional adventure. . . . Difficult to stop reading. . . . David has shown again why he is arguably the best *Star Trek* author."

—TrekMovie.com

Praise for Peter David and *Star Trek: New Frontier*®:

"Peter David mixes wry humor . . . with tense drama. . . . [His] narrative is populated by a vast array of previously minor characters from the screen incarnations of *Star Trek,* all vividly fleshed out into well-rounded personalities."

—Sci-Fi Online

"Peter David is the best *Star Trek* novelist around."

—*Starburst*

"A new *Star Trek* novel by Peter David is always a good bet."

—SF Site

Star Trek: New Frontier novels by Peter David

In chronological order:

STAR TREK
NEW FRONTIER®

TREASON

PETER DAVID

**Based upon
STAR TREK: THE NEXT GENERATION®
created by Gene Roddenberry**

POCKET BOOKS
New York London Toronto Sydney

Pocket Books
A Division of Simon & Schuster, Inc.
1230 Avenue of the Americas
New York, NY 10020

™, ® and © 2009 by CBS Studios Inc. STAR TREK and related marks are trademarks of CBS Studios Inc. All Rights Reserved.

This book is published by Pocket Books, a division of Simon & Schuster, Inc., under exclusive license from CBS Studios Inc.

This Pocket Books paperback edition March 2010

POCKET and colophon are registered trademarks of Simon & Schuster, Inc.

For information about special discounts for bulk purchases, please contact Simon & Schuster Special Sales at 1-866-506-1949 or business@simonandschuster.com.

The Simon & Schuster Speakers Bureau can bring authors to your live event. For more information or to book an event, contact the Simon & Schuster Speakers Bureau at 1-866-248-3049 or visit our website at www.simonspeakers.com.

Cover design by Alan Dingman; cover art by Jerry Vanderstelt

Manufactured in the United States of America

10 9 8 7 6 5 4 3 2 1

ISBN 978-1-4391-6627-7
ISBN 978-1-4391-2339-3 (ebook)

STAR TREK
NEW FRONTIER®

TREASON

The blackness beckons to hir. It is cold and inviting, and s/he is greatly tempted to lay down hir burden, as hir local religious leader used to say. Yet s/he is reluctant to do so, because s/he cannot shake the belief that there is something else for hir to do. S/he just cannot seem to remember what it was, or is.

S/he tries to haul hirself over to the ship's control console, but hir body refuses to acknowledge hir brain's commands. This is not a development s/he readily accepts, and s/he continues to shout, and then to scream, within hir own head for hir pain-wracked body to do something useful rather than just lie there. Hir body ignores hir.

S/he would not have thought it possible that every cell could hurt, but that appears to be the case. S/he tries to think of it as a cleansing pain, one that will strip hir of all worldly sins—of which there are quite a few—and prepare hir for the next plane of existence.

And still s/he refuses to acknowledge that it may be time to cross over. "Too much to do," s/he says, and is surprised by how strangled hir voice sounds.

S/he looks up at the screen just in time to see something massive appear on it. S/he thinks it may be a ship, and s/he finds the timing most remarkable. S/he cannot wait to *comment upon the timing to whoever is aboard it, and then the blackness that will not be denied seizes hir.* "Not fair!" *s/he cries out within hir mind.* "I was thinking about something else," *but the blackness ignores the protest and drags hir down and away.*

Starship Excalibur

i.

"Burgoyne propositioned me."

The announcement took Mackenzie Calhoun, captain of the *Starship Excalibur,* by surprise. Seated in his ready room, he put aside the ancient Xenexian battle axe that he had recently acquired and looked up with a quizzical expression at Tania Tobias. The conn officer was standing just inside the door, shifting uncomfortably, fiddling with the trailing ends of her hair.

"S/he did?"

Tobias nodded.

"I apologize," he said, "if hir doing so made you feel uncomfortable, Lieutenant, and I assure you that—"

"I wasn't offended, Captain."

"Oh." Calhoun took pride in his ability to react

quickly and authoritatively to any situation. It was that resourcefulness that had enabled him and his crew to survive many hazardous situations. Yet he occasionally found himself disoriented when talking with his eclectic crew members, and this was one of those occasions. "So this is not something I should be concerned about?"

"I think you should be, yes."

He leaned back in his chair, resisting the temptation to throw his hands up in surrender.

His bewilderment must have been evident to Tobias, because she said apologetically, "I'm sorry if I lost you, Captain."

"I wouldn't say you've lost me, Lieutenant," he said, without adding aloud, *I was never following you to begin with*. "I am a bit unclear on what the precise nature of your complaint is. Do you see this as a disciplinary matter?"

"I see it as cause for concern."

"Why? Burgy has always been rather licentious by nature. Granted, s/he curtailed that when s/he became involved with Doctor Selar, but they never actually married and the relationship seems to have gone by the wayside. So I don't see that there are any moral issues in the mix."

"It's nothing like that, Captain. I'm sorry, I haven't been making myself clear."

No kidding. He forced a smile, which caused the edges of his mouth to hurt from the unaccustomed muscle strain. "Well, then, perhaps clarification might be in order at some point within our lifetimes."

She gave no indication that she noticed the gentle dig. "The problem is," she said, "that when s/he propositioned me, hir heart wasn't in it."

"I don't understan—" But then his voice trailed off as he comprehended her meaning.

Tobias, still in that gentle obliviousness that was her foremost characteristic, didn't realize that further explanation was unnecessary. "When Burgoyne makes hir interest known to people, s/he's very enthused. S/he . . ." Tobias paused, trying to determine the best way to put it. "When hir attention is on you in that way, s/he makes you feel as if you're the only person in the entire galaxy. That there's nothing else s/he would rather be doing than gazing into your eyes." Her voice was soft and languorous, and she was looking dreamily off to the side as if she had mentally departed the ready room several minutes earlier. "That's how s/he does it. S/he just makes you come alive. Appeals to sensuous aspects of your personality that you hadn't dreamed could possibly—"

Calhoun cleared his throat loudly, and the interruption snapped Tobias from her reverie. She looked momentarily confused, as if she had forgotten where she was. Quickly composing herself, she said, "At least that's what I've heard."

"Obviously heard and thought about a good deal."

"The point is, s/he wasn't that way with me. S/he just seemed to be—"

"Going through the motions?"

"Yes!" she said excitedly as if Calhoun had just produced three doves from his sleeve. "Yes, that's exactly it. Going through the motions. S/he was doing it because s/he thought it was expected of hir, or maybe because s/he felt maybe s/he could make hirself feel a certain way."

"And your concern is that if s/he's off hir game in this manner, it could negatively affect the way s/he carries out hir duties as first officer?"

"I hadn't even thought about that, to be honest. My concern was that a friend was in trouble." She tilted her head and looked at him with open curiosity. "That wasn't your concern, Captain?"

"Of course it was," said Calhoun, who was a bit disturbed that it had not, in fact, occurred to him. "I just . . . I hadn't noticed anything that 'off' about

Burgy. Then again, since Burgoyne has never propositioned me, that could be why it slipped past."

"Well then," she said briskly, "I've done what I needed to do. I'm sure you can handle it from here, Captain."

"I appreciate the vote of confidence, Lieutenant."

Tobias walked out of the ready room. Calhoun watched her go, and wondered what the best way was to proceed on the matter. Mackenzie Calhoun, one of the foremost strategists in all of Starfleet, couldn't conceive of how to handle it. What was he supposed to say? He could have found a means of addressing it if he had noticed some sort of deterioration in Burgy's performance of hir duties, but that had not been the case. Calhoun had been caught off guard by Tobias's concerns specifically because he had not, in fact, noticed anything wrong with the way Burgoyne 172 was conducting hirself. "How am I supposed to approach hir on this?"

"Have you considered doing so as a friend?"

Calhoun was startled, which was not something that happened often. When it did occur, though, Morgan Primus was more often than not involved somehow. This time was no exception, although one would not have known at first glance that it was, in fact, Morgan, because she had assumed the exact likeness of Mackenzie Calhoun. His clone might as well have walked into the room.

"Ask how things are going in a general way," the duplicate Calhoun said, "and see if s/he presents an opening. Doesn't that seem practical?"

"Change back to yourself, Morgan." He did nothing to keep the irritation from his voice.

"It's just that you are the only person you ever feel comfortable consulting. Except, of course—" and abruptly Elizabeth Shelby, Calhoun's wife, was in front of him.

"Morgan—"

To Calhoun's surprise, "Elizabeth" sauntered toward him. Every movement, every aspect of her appearance was indistinguishable from the original. She even had Elizabeth's smile down. Calhoun was standing behind his desk, and the image of his wife came around the desk and cradled his chin in her hand. "Morgan . . ."

"I can be her, if you wish," said the mouth of Elizabeth Shelby. "It would benefit you tremendously."

"Would it?"

"You're becoming isolated and increasingly frustrated, Mac, because you're here and your wife is off commanding Bravo station. It's not fair to either of you, but it's particularly unfair to you. You could use the diversion. Release all manner of endorphins. Put you back on your game."

"I was unaware I was off it. You need to step back, Morgan."

She rested a hand on his chest. "I am simply trying to—"

Calhoun grabbed her wrist and, gripping it firmly, said, "Step. Back."

Morgan did so, pulling her hand free. Her appearance rippled and the holographic form of Morgan Primus changed back into her normal image. "Burgoyne isn't the only one who could use a little intimate time, is all that I'm saying."

"I know what you're saying. Now listen to what I'm saying: I'm going to order Tobias and Xy to run a complete diagnostic of your operating systems."

Morgan smiled. "I don't see that that's necessary, Captain."

"I say that it is. And since I'm the captain, I have to think that my feelings on the matter take precedence over yours. Are you disputing that, Morgan?"

"No, but—"

"There's no 'but' involved in this, Morgan. Obviously you don't realize it, but you haven't been yourself since you rebooted."

"And here I thought you were happy to see me return from the dead."

"I was. We all were. Even though I'm not entirely certain that what happened to you counts as 'dead.' But your behavior has become increasingly erratic in recent months."

She drew herself up, fixing him with a stern glance. "Have I been less than diligent in fulfilling my duties as ops officer? To say nothing of being the heart of this ship's operating systems."

"No, you have not."

"Then I do not understand the reasoning behind a full diagnostic. It is an intrusive procedure and the prospect makes me uncomfortable."

"You're a computer entity, Morgan, whatever else you may have been in your previous life. The fact that you would find it uncomfortable alone should tell you something, shouldn't it?"

She paused, not having an immediate response, and then shrugged as if the matter were simply not worth pursuing. "As you say, you're the captain."

"Thank you for that acknowledgment," he said, trying not to sound sarcastic and only partly succeeding.

"By the way, you'll probably want to get out onto the bridge. Something new is about to start."

"Something new? What are you—?"

His comm badge beeped at him. He tapped it, never taking his eyes from Morgan. "Calhoun, go."

The voice of Zak Kebron, security chief, came back to him. "Long-range scanners are picking up something, Captain. A ship floating."

"Derelict? Or survivors?"

"Impossible to determine from this distance, sir."

"Then let's cut that distance down, Mr. Kebron. On my way."

Calhoun strode toward the door as Morgan stepped aside. "Captain," she said.

He turned toward her and froze.

She had reassumed the image of Elizabeth Shelby, and she was stark naked. She was also smiling in a come-hither manner. "In case you change your mind, just call my name. Or hers. Never underestimate the power of a good endorphin rush." Morgan vanished before he could say anything further.

"*Grozit,*" he murmured.

ii.

Commander Burgoyne arched an eyebrow upon seeing Calhoun emerge from the ready room. "Captain, are you all right?"

"I'm fine, Burgy."

"Because you're walking rather oddly—"

"I said I'm fine," Calhoun said impatiently. Moving quickly, he sat in his command chair and crossed his legs. Burgoyne considered this a bit odd, since Calhoun tended to stand or move about the bridge like a caged cat. "What have we got?"

"Single-pilot vessel drifting at 325 mark 4. Looks to be," and s/he studied the readouts from the sensors, "a reconfigured freighter of some sort."

"Smuggler?"

"Or an explorer. Such reconfigured ships are popular among those who fancy themselves wandering adventurers who might stumble upon valuables and want to have a convenient means of hauling them."

Calhoun glanced toward Kebron. "Any life readings?"

"One. Sensors indicate . . ." The massive Brikar stopped. If he had an eyebrow to raise, he would clearly have done so.

"Indicate what?"

Kebron addressed Calhoun, but was looking at Burgoyne as he said, "The pilot appears to be . . . a Hermat."

"What?!" Burgoyne could scarcely believe what s/he was hearing. S/he moved toward the science station. "Xy, double-check those readings."

"A less confident officer," Kebron said with just the slightest hint of annoyance, "might take offense at your lack of trust. But I do not. I understand your reluctance to—"

"Later, Kebron," said Calhoun.

Not for the first time, Burgoyne found hirself nostalgic for the days when Zak Kebron was a detached, foreboding individual who rarely strung more than three words together at a time.

S/he stepped in next to hir son, Xy, who was studying the sensor information that Kebron was feeding through to him. Slowly he nodded. "Definitely Hermat. Kebron is right." Kebron did not offer much beyond a smug "Hmmf" in acknowledgment of Xy's announcement. "You don't see many Hermats out this far."

"You don't see *any*," said Burgoyne. "Trust me, I know my people. One of the reasons I was such an aberration was my desire to explore the galaxy. That mind-set was considered . . ." S/he paused and then, for want of a better term, said, ". . . rude. I was practically an outcast even before I chose to exile myself—"

"As fascinating as this litany of Hermat social mores is," Calhoun said, "might we focus instead on the derelict that is in possible need of our help?"

"Sorry, Captain," said Burgoyne, abashed.

"Condition of the pilot?"

"Life signs are low, even marginal, but steady," said Xy.

"Have hir beamed directly into sickbay," said Calhoun, rising from his chair. "Inform Doctor Selar she's about to have a new patient."

Inwardly, Burgoyne flinched. Speaking to Selar was not a task that Burgoyne welcomed these days. It was actually painful to hear her voice, detached and emotionless beyond even what was typical for a Vulcan. For an instant s/he considered ordering Xy or Tobias to do it, but then s/he rallied. S/he was, after all, the first officer of the *Excalibur*. S/he shouldn't fob off an order from the captain merely because carrying it out was going to make hir uncomfortable.

Burgoyne tapped hir comm badge. "Bridge to sickbay."

"Sickbay, Selar here."

"We've found an injured Hermat in a derelict. The captain wants hir beamed directly into sickbay."

"That is against procedure," her voice came back. *"S/he should be sent to the transporter room to undergo triage while hir transport signature can be studied in the buffer and properly screened for any harmful bacteria or germs."*

"Those are the captain's orders."

"One would have thought that, as chief medical officer, my desire to see regulations followed would have been accorded some consideration." Her tone was flat and even, as if she were speaking about the feelings of someone else entirely. *"Do as you see fit. But have hir beamed into the sickbay quarantine area rather than into the main section. That way, if s/he has some sort of infectious disease, only the immediate personnel in quarantine will lose their lives because of the captain's orders. If you require further interaction with me, I will be in quarantine. Selar out."*

Burgoyne could sense the captain's gaze upon hir and could not bring hirself to meet it. Instead s/he said, "The CMO is prepping sickbay for the new patient."

"Good," was all Calhoun said in reply.

Xy exchanged a sympathetic look with his father. Burgoyne smiled wanly. Over the past months, they had both been trying to deal as best they could with

Selar's smoldering rage and frustration hidden behind an impenetrable wall of stoicism. If she had been something other than a Vulcan, it would have been much easier to cope. But she was what she was, and they were simply going to have to live with it and pray that eventually things would improve.

Unfortunately, Burgoyne had very little hope of that.

iii.

What do I do with my anger . . . ?

The odd question crossed Doctor Selar's mind, and she was astounded by it. However, being what she was, and who she was, she did not permit either the fury she was feeling nor her surprise at feeling it show upon her face. Instead she busied herself with the task of preparing for her new patient.

She entered the quarantine area and, in total defiance of proper protocol, wore absolutely no protective gear. This had drawn confused comments from several of her medical technicians. Selar had told them curtly that her Vulcan physiology would permit her to withstand just about anything that an incoming patient—even an infectious one—might have to throw at her. The truth was that she simply didn't give a damn if something happened to her. Should that occur, and should she die, then the positive aspect was that she would no longer have to deal with such inconveniences as inner turmoil.

Selar glanced around at the medtechs. They were watching her, commenting to one another in low voices that her sharp hearing would have been able to discern were she not already in the quarantine area, sealed off from the rest of sickbay. She was reasonably sure she knew what they were talking about, though. They were going on and on about how she had become unconscionably cold, even for a Vulcan. *Even for a Vulcan.* That was the exact phrasing she had overheard when they thought she wasn't listening.

They had no idea. They had all bought into the notion that Vulcans were emotionless beings rather than what they were: a race that labored every single day to keep emotions in check lest they lead to endless strife. They were relentlessly rational by choice, not by design. Would that the lie were the truth and that emotions were never a consideration for her.

If she ever allowed the emotions roiling within her to display themselves, it would be a sight that would terrify her coworkers. They would run screaming from the sickbay.

She waited calmly with her instruments at the ready. She still believed that beaming the patient directly into sickbay was the wrong way to proceed. But if they were determined to ignore her advice, then she was perfectly entitled to ignore protocol as well and wait for the patient without wearing any protective gear. That would show them.

Selar knew that her attitude was, at best, petulant, and at worst, unprofessional. It was, however, *her* attitude, and she believed she was perfectly entitled to have it.

She remained where she was as the quarantine area filled with light and with the building hum of energy that heralded the transporter beams. Credit Transporter Chief Halliwell: her aim was precise. The incoming patient materialized, supine, atop the diagnostic table. Selar immediately moved toward the Hermat—for such the patient clearly was—and proceeded to apply the various scanning devices to get readings on hir.

She did not require the scanners, however, to make an instant assessment of the patient's main problem: radiation poisoning. The cellular damage, the skin deterioration, were both consistent with that diagnosis.

Selar worked quickly. Bioskin could be applied to heal the surface wounds easily enough, but how she would deal with the poisoning itself would depend upon the extent of the damage. The first thing she needed to do was stabilize her patient, and she did so with her customary brisk efficiency. Within minutes, she had the Hermat's vital signs at levels that were low but acceptable.

She became aware of a familiar presence behind her. She didn't even have to look to see hir there; she just knew it. The fact that they still had that sort of connection was troublesome, but she resolved not to let it impede her ability to do her job.

"Why are you here?" Selar asked.

Burgoyne, standing on the other side of the quarantine partition, said, "The captain wanted to know hir condition."

"Then the captain could easily have asked me himself. I am correct in assuming the comm unit is still operational, yes?" She did not look away from her instruments.

"Yes, but considering the species of the patient, I thought I would come down personally to . . ." Burgoyne's voice trailed off and then s/he said softly, "I'll be damned."

Selar made no comment as to how likely it was that Burgoyne would be consigned to the flames of perdition. It didn't seem especially relevant to the situation at hand. "May I correctly assume you know this individual?"

"Rulan," said Burgoyne. "Rulan 12. I remember hir all too well."

For the first time, Selar looked toward Burgoyne. "A former lover of yours?"

"No. Not for want of trying," said Burgoyne. There was no shame or embarrassment in hir voice. Burgoyne was impossible to shame when it came to sexual exploits. "We were educated together. Our teachers despised both of us. Said we were bad influences on each other."

"Then I am surprised you did not, in fact, have sexual relations, if you were that much in accord with each other's sensibilities."

Burgoyne gave her a curious glance. "You seem rather intrigued by my romantic history all of a sudden."

"I have a patient dying of radiation sickness and no idea how s/he became this way. Anything and everything in hir background could be germane."

The first officer appeared skeptical, but then shrugged. "We did not become lovers because Rulan prided hirself on hir chastity."

"Really?" She arched an eyebrow, which was the most she typically allowed in her reactions. "Why?"

"S/he never said."

"Hmm. Unusual for a Hermat."

"Very much so."

"And did s/he share your wanderlust as well?"

"No. In that s/he was as conservative as the rest of our race."

"Obviously something changed."

"Obviously," said Burgoyne. "Is s/he going to be okay?"

"It is too early to know for sure. I have managed to stabilize hir vitals and have commenced a biocellular regeneration process."

"That sounds positive," s/he said hopefully.

"The problem is that the process takes time. Up to seventy-two hours. Any time during that period, when the damage is this catastrophic, vital organs could give out from the strain. Should that happen, I may be unable to save hir. If s/he is alive three days from now, hir chances are good. Otherwise . . ."

"I know you'll do your best."

"Your confidence is most uplifting."

Burgoyne opened hir mouth as if s/he wanted to say something more. Selar waited. Burgoyne remained that way for some seconds, looking—in Selar's opinion—perfectly ridiculous. It was clear to Selar what Burgoyne wanted to do. S/he wanted to bring up their relationship, or lack thereof, yet again. But everything that could be said had already *been* said, at length, repeatedly, and to no real effect. What could possibly be the point of wasting both their time yet again?

She must have managed to convey her thoughts, or at least her state of mind, to Burgoyne, because eventually s/he closed hir mouth, nodded as if everything that needed to be said had, in fact, been said, and then walked out of sickbay. Selar noticed that others were staring at her. They quickly looked away, like voyeurs who had been eavesdropping on the personal matters of other people. Which, Selar supposed, they were, though she didn't especially care. She had matters of far greater importance to worry about. Let them listen in if it amused them. Let them draw whatever inferences they wished to from all that was left unsaid.

She had work to do.

iv.

Burgoyne stared into the contents of the glass before hir on the table as if the answer to all life's questions could be found within the amber liquid. Unsurprisingly, none seemed to be forthcoming.

S/he had gone off shift an hour earlier and had wound up in the Team Room, the informal name for the crew lounge. On a typical day, Burgoyne was one of the more accessible senior officers. Anyone from a lieutenant commander on down to the lowliest ensign did not hesitate to approach Burgoyne, and socialize with hir.

However Burgoyne was equally capable of conveying through attitude and body language that s/he felt like being left alone. It wasn't all that often, but on those rare occasions when Burgoyne wanted to discourage company, s/he had little trouble doing so.

So it was that Burgoyne was sitting alone at a table toward the back of the Team Room, nodding in acknowledgment to any who walked past hir, but otherwise enjoying solitude. Or, if not enjoying it, at least being relieved that s/he didn't have to interact with anyone.

A shadow fell across hir table. S/he glanced up, although s/he had an idea who it was going to be before even looking. S/he turned out to be correct. "Hello, Xy," s/he said softly.

"Dad." Xy indicated the other chair at the table with a tilt of his chin. "Mind if I join you?"

Anyone else would not have even thought to ask. They would have given Burgoyne hir space. Xy, on the other hand, didn't need to ask, but did so anyway out of politeness.

"Go right ahead," said Burgoyne.

Xy sat in the chair opposite his father. He was already holding a drink. Burgoyne recognized it immediately and said, slim eyebrow arched, "Romulan ale? Isn't that still illegal?"

"Only technically," said Xy. "Since the war, it's been a lot easier to acquire."

"Still, rules are rules. I'll have to file a report about this . . . unless, of course, something happens to impede my memory . . ."

Without a word, Xy switched his glass with that from which Burgoyne had been drinking. Burgoyne picked it up, sipped it, and sighed contentedly.

"Well?" said Xy.

"My mind's a blank."

"I thought that might be the case. So I understand

you know the Hermat that mother is working on."

Burgoyne inclined hir head slightly. "Hir name is Rulan. We've had passing acquaintance. Although," s/he said, sounding chipper, "Selar seemed extremely interested in learning the details of whatever relationship I may have had with hir."

"What do you mean?"

"I mean"—and Burgy paused for effect—"she sounded jealous."

"Jealous." Xy repeated the word. The skepticism was evident in his tone.

"Yes. Jealous," Burgoyne said again, more insistently, perceiving the doubt in Xy's voice.

"I just . . ."

"You just what?"

"I just don't see it. I mean, jealousy is an emotion. She isn't exactly brimming with emotional depth. You know what I'm saying?"

"Yes, I do. You're saying that I'm imagining it. That I made it up."

"I'm saying," Xy said softly, "that you're trying to force yourself to believe it because you're so anxious to do so."

"Is it so impossible . . . ?" But Burgoyne knew the answer to the question before s/he even asked it. Xy didn't even have to respond. Burgoyne knocked back the rest of the contents of Xy's glass and muttered, "You don't have to look at me that way."

"What way?"

"Sympathetically. Sadly. As if I were pathetic."

"I don't think you're pathetic."

"Why don't you? I do."

"Dad . . ."

"It's all your fault, you know."

"*My* fault?" Xy didn't sound angry at the accusation; he was more amused than anything. "How is it *my* fault?"

"You know why."

"Because I'm aging so quickly," Xy said patiently. "Because, thanks to the combination of my Vulcan and Hermat biology, I'm speeding through my life. Except I didn't create my metabolic processes, Dad. I didn't ask to be the way I am. I didn't even ask to be born. All things considered, I could be the one going around pointing fingers at you and Mother for getting together in the first place without regard for what the results of such a union might be."

"Your mother didn't have all that much choice."

"I know." Xy looked uncomfortable for the first time. "And we shouldn't really be talking about that."

Burgoyne smiled at hir son's streak of provincialism. Topics such as *Pon farr,* the Vulcan mating drive, were generally considered inappropriate matters for discussion. Usually that applied only to outworlders. Burgoyne was hardly any outworlder, having mated with Xy's mother. And Xy was, naturally, not a full Vulcan himself, although he shared Selar's delicate pointed ears and arched eyebrows. Yet he was respectful enough of Vulcan traditions to balk at talking about such delicate subjects, even with his own father.

"All right," said Burgoyne, not desiring to press it. S/he leaned back in hir chair and sighed deeply. "You know . . . for someone who purports to have no emotions, your mother is one of the most passionate creatures I've ever met."

"Do we really need to talk about that?" said Xy, shifting uncomfortably in his chair.

Burgoyne laughed, displaying the edges of hir pointed teeth in doing so. "I'm not referring to *that* sort of passionate. I mean that she can become so fixated on something that it can—well—consume her."

"Are you thinking of anything specific?"

"You know I am."

"You're thinking about me," said Xy. "And her obsession with trying to find a way to 'cure' me. Rather than appreciating the time she has with me, she can only obsess about the time when I'll be gone."

Burgoyne nodded.

"In fairness to Mother, the latter span is going to be so substantially greater than the former that it cannot help but weigh on her mind. Plus they were her— impulses," he said for lack of a better word, "that set the events into motion that led to my birth in the first place. So it's reasonable that she would feel the greatest sense of responsibility."

"Yes. It's reasonable. It's just tragic that it has to overwhelm every aspect of her life so that she can't take any joy in anything else."

" 'Anything else' meaning, specifically, you."

Burgoyne chuckled in spite of everything. "Certainly that's one aspect of it. There's this as well, though: just the sort of interaction you and I are having now. I'm egotistical enough to think that your mother is missing out on a lot by wanting to have nothing to do with me. But I know for a certainty that she's missing out on even more by having nothing to do with you."

"I don't take offense, if that's any consolation," said Xy. "She doesn't keep me at a distance because she dislikes me. It's simply that it hurts her too much to interact with me for long, and someone like my mother doesn't do especially well with feeling hurt. Or feeling anything."

"So I should feel sorry for her like you do, is what you're saying."

"I wouldn't have put it that way . . ." Xy hesitated, then said, "Yes. I guess I am saying that."

"What if she knew that we feel sorry for her?" said Burgoyne.

"Honestly? I doubt she would care very much. Or at all."

"Or at all," agreed Burgoyne.

V.

Selar did not care that she hadn't slept in more than thirty hours. She knew what her body was capable of enduring, and her need for rest was not as great as a human's. Various technicians would come and go on their shifts as the hours progressed, but Selar remained where she was and monitored Rulan's vital signs. She told herself that she was doing so because she was the logical individual to take on such a sustained duty.

Selar had not left the quarantine area the entire time that she had been monitoring Rulan's status. She had consumed a small amount of food, taking care not to exceed the minimum her body required to continue functioning, and had been likewise sparing with drink. Her assistants had offered to relieve her from time to time during the first twenty hours. She turned them down flat every time with the slightest shake of her head, not even bothering to reply. After that they had stopped asking.

It was during the thirty-first hour of scrutinizing Rulan's healing process that she began to notice something odd. She checked and double-checked and triple-checked the results, and she was still having trouble understanding or even daring to believe what she was seeing.

She had been standing while going over the results of the cell monitoring. She was surprised to now discover that she was sitting. Selar didn't recall actually sitting down in a chair; one moment she was on her feet, and the next, on her backside. It was an indication of just how stunned she had been that she had momentarily blacked out, for there was no one on the *Excalibur* who was more aware of her surroundings, and of the passing of every moment, than Selar.

Focus, she told herself. *Focus on procedures. That is the only way to function.*

"Medical log, supplemental," she said. Her voice sounded distant, alien even to herself. "Although the bio-regeneration process is proceeding, the results are surpassing expectations sufficiently to warrant further study. The cellular damage sustained by subject Rulan 12, particularly the damage to the internal organs, is healing forty-three percent faster than my original estimates would have allowed. Since my estimates were based upon documented previous results of applied bio-regeneration, this is clearly some manner of aberration. The question to be pursued is whether the aberration can, in some manner, be replicated. Could, for instance . . ." She paused. To her internal shock, her voice was bordering on being choked with emotion. An outside observer would have been unable to determine such a reaction, but she was all too aware of it. An expert after long years of self-control, she managed to bring her emotions in check so that on her log there was only the briefest of hesitations, as if she were calmly pausing to select the right word with her customary precision. ". . . an individual such as Xy, who is essentially suffering from accelerated cellular deterioration, be aided by some manner of controlled application? An infusion of Rulan's DNA into his own genetic makeup? The notion would have no practical application if Xy did not already have Hermat biological markers in his own DNA. The further matter to be investigated is just how Rulan came to have such attributes. If s/he underwent some manner of procedure that enabled hir to regrow cells at an unusual rate, then Rulan's genetic components may not be necessary for further research; I could go straight to the source. As long as Rulan remains insensate, however, I cannot determine the—"

She stopped talking, suddenly aware of Mackenzie Calhoun's presence.

Calhoun stepped up to the partition that separated the quarantined section from the rest of sickbay. He studied the unconscious Hermat for a moment, then shifted his attention to Selar. "Please don't allow me to interrupt, Doctor. Feel free to complete your medical log."

"I can do so later, Captain."

"Doctor, seriously, you shouldn't allow my presence to—"

"I do not believe it is within your prerogative to dictate when and where I choose to perform my duties, Captain. Now, did you have something specific you wished to discuss?"

Calhoun did not reply immediately. Instead he stared at her for a time before saying, in a formal tone, "What's the prognosis?"

She hesitated. She had told Burgoyne that it would be seventy-two hours before she knew for sure whether Rulan would survive. But she knew now that Rulan would, in fact, be just fine. Selar couldn't determine when s/he would recover consciousness, but she knew s/he was going to survive the radiation poisoning that might well have killed anyone else. The problem was, if Selar gave the more optimistic assessment of Rulan's chances, then Calhoun might start asking what aspect of Rulan's condition had changed. And if asked directly, then Selar would naturally have to tell him . . .

Why not tell him? He is your commanding officer. He has a right to the information at your disposal.

Selar opened her mouth to tell him all about the Hermat's condition, about the amazing cellular regeneration properties that s/he was displaying, about what it could possibly mean for her son. Instead, as much to her own surprise, she said, "Hir prognosis is positive and proceeding on schedule." She had no idea why she said that, and worse, didn't wish to figure out why.

Calhoun's purple eyes flickered, as if he had some idea that she was being less than forthright with him, but wasn't positive enough to call her on it. Then he inclined his head slightly and said, "That's excellent news. However, I think you should know that we have a medical emergency on our hands."

"Any of my personnel could handle it, Captain, whatever it is."

"I'm sure they can, but your presence has been requested and I am inclined to honor that request."

"Sir, I am monitoring a patient who is at a delicate state in hir recovery," Selar said insistently. She realized she was fighting to keep her voice even and passionless. Fighting to do something that ordinarily came as naturally as breathing. "To take me away from hir at this point . . ."

"No one is taking you away from hir, at least not immediately. You have another few hours with hir. We have to reach our destination before your services are required. After that, no promises."

"I do not understand. Our destination? This is not a shipboard emergency?"

"No. It's non-Starfleet personnel, actually."

"Then I do not understand why my involvement is required at all."

"Because the mother-to-be requested you."

"The . . ." Then she understood. "Robin Lefler."

"That's right, Doctor. Robin Lefler is giving birth to the son of the late Si Cwan on New Thallon, and you are the only person she trusts to do the job."

I do not care. All I care about is my own son. Leave me alone, you arrogant bastard.

"Please inform me as soon as we reach New Thallon," said Doctor Selar, "and I will naturally do all within my power to deliver the male heir to the House of Cwan into the world."

New Thallon

i.

Kalinda, the sister of the late Si Cwan, sat on the floor in the far corner of the room. Her legs were drawn up, her chin resting on her knees, and her arms were wrapped around her legs, pulling them tightly against her. She rocked back and forth slowly, repeatedly whispering the same sorts of aimless comments that she had been muttering over the past months.

Tusari Gyn, the Prime Arbiter of the New Thallonian Protectorate's Council, could not help but feel pity for the girl. Or, more accurately, could not help but look as if he did. Tusari Gyn was extremely good at feigning such emotions. Whether he truly felt anything at all would have been difficult for anyone to know for sure. Some days he wasn't even all that certain himself.

Tusari Gyn had not been the Prime Arbiter when the Protectorate had first been formed. That honor had fallen to the late, lamented Fhermus of the House of Fhermus, a most worthy and brave Nelkarite. A Nelkarite who had fallen to the blade of the Lady Cwan in vengeance over the death of her husband, the equally late but most unlamented Si Cwan of the House of Cwan.

At least, he was unlamented as far as the Council was concerned. Unfortunately, Si Cwan's legend had grown in the retelling and he was gaining power and influence in his martyred state. There was a certain irony to the fact that Cwan was becoming more popular dead than he was while alive, but it was not unprecedented. Tusari Gyn had always been a student of history, and he was impressed by the staggering number of people who accomplished great things long after they had passed away.

The problem for Kalinda was that she obviously had yet to acknowledge her brother's passing.

It seemed only yesterday to Tusari Gyn that he had been among the Protectorate Council, arguing over whether Kalinda's betrothal to the son of Fhermus should be allowed, since such marriages were typically affairs arranged by others. Kalinda had been a different girl in those days, smiling and upbeat, happy, nearly ethereal in her presence. Although Tusari Gyn had spoken in opposition to the concept, secretly he could not help but adore the girl and feel envy for Fhermus's son.

How long ago that dispute was. Now both father and son were rotting in the Fhermus House's crypt, Si Cwan was dead as well, and the creature that had survived all the trauma was Kalinda in appearance only. The poor girl's mind was totally gone.

"Is she like that all the time?" The question was put to him by Norkai, the new Nelkarite ambassador whom Tusari Gyn had taken under his wing, seemingly out of a sense of altruism, but actually so that he could influence—if not control outright—Norkai's vote on all Council dealings.

They were a study in contrasts, Norkai's muscular build and golden skin standing in sharp opposition to the sallow appearance and the distended bone ridge on Tusari Gyn's forehead that made his eyes almost impossible to see. Tusari Gyn preferred it that way, and was grateful to the evolutionary happenstance that had caused his race to develop in that manner. Eyes tended to give away far too much. They betrayed the inner thoughts of their owner, so the less visible they were, the better.

Norkai had whispered to him, but Tusari Gyn did nothing to modulate his voice in response. "More or less all the time, yes."

"Shhh! She'll hear you."

"I wouldn't be too certain of that. Kalinda!" He raised his voice. "A fine day, is it not?"

Kalinda didn't reply. She continued to mutter at nothing.

Norkai looked tremendously uncomfortable. "Shouldn't she . . . be somewhere else? Somewhere not so out in the open for all to gawk at?"

"No one *gawks,* Norkai. At least, not anymore. The Thallonians used to try to keep her sequestered in her room, but she always managed to get out, even when they locked her in. I think her keepers have just given up. So she's allowed to wander the manor whenever and wherever she sees fit. People can become accustomed to just about anything."

"So it would seem." Norkai tilted his head as if he could better grasp what he was seeing from a marginally different angle. "She acts as if she is speaking to someone directly rather than muttering to herself."

"She believes she is speaking to her dead brother," said Tusari Gyn. "Pathetic, is it not? She simply cannot let go of him. Some people find death impossible to cope with."

"I . . ." Norkai once again lowered his tone nearly to a whisper, despite the fact that Kalinda obviously wasn't hearing him. "I hear rumors that it is more than that. That she supposedly can see spirits. That she has vision directly into the afterlife."

"Yes, I have heard similar things. Nonsense. All nonsense. I find it astounding that such an intelligent individual as yourself would believe such absurdities."

"I didn't say I believed it," Norkai said quickly. "I just said that was what I had heard. That is all."

"Well, thank you for clarifying that. Come, then . . . let us look to matters of greater importance."

Tusari Gyn strode forward with the air of someone obsessed with his own significance. Norkai followed quickly, casting one last glance in Kalinda's direction. He thought he heard her say, "They're going away, we're alone now," but he wasn't certain.

The two council members made their way to the private chambers of the Lady Cwan. There was a frustrated-looking Thallonian doctor outside, calling through the door, "Lady Cwan! Lady Cwan, this is absurd! You are in need of medical attention!" Standing on either side of the door were two Thallonian guards, both of whom looked increasingly uncomfortable with the situation as it was developing.

"Not from you, you quack!" Robin Lefler shouted from within. The irritated protest was followed by another moan.

"Quack?" said Tusari Gyn in confusion.

"I looked it up," said the doctor, "after the first ten times she called me that. It appears to be an onomatopoeia for the noise made by an Earth fowl called a 'duck.' "

"What does that have to do with the practice of medicine?"

The doctor shrugged.

Tusari Gyn glanced at the guards. "This is insane. The woman is in need of medical assistance. If you have any loyalty to the New Thallonian Protectorate, you will let this good doctor in immediately so that he may attend to her."

The guards glanced at each other. The taller one said, "It is not up to us, sir. She's sealed the door. Even we cannot override it."

"Really." Tusari Gyn was unimpressed. Then he called through the door, "Lady Cwan! Or, if you prefer, *Prime Minister*! That is your official title, you know, inherited from your husband . . . even if you have been lax in your duties."

"Drop dead, Tusari!"

"It's nice to know that labor pains have not dampened your basic spirit," he said.

"Lady Cwan," said the doctor imploringly, "you will do neither yourself nor your child any good by this isolation you have insisted upon. You cannot deliver the infant yourself."

"That's my business!"

Tusari Gyn was about to reply when she unleashed an ear-splitting screech from within. The guards winced upon hearing it. Reasoning that she wouldn't be in any shape to hear what he had to say until it ended, Tusari Gyn waited patiently for the latest wave of pain she was experiencing to subside. When her agonies eventually tapered off, he said, "I beg to differ, Prime Minister. You are giving birth— or at least endeavoring to give birth—to the last heir of the House of Cwan, the most respected family in Thallonian history."

"So respected that your predecessor murdered my husband!"

"That was regrettable."

"You endorsed it!"

"Yes, but now I regret that I did so. You have no idea of the hold that Fhermus had on the hearts and minds of the Council. Had I sided against Fhermus, my head might well have wound up next to Cwan's."

"You think I give a damn?"

"Truthfully, I do not. You have the luxury of not caring. I, however, do not. I must reiterate that you are trying to bring the last heir of the House of Cwan into the world, without any sort of medical aid or anyone by your side. You are displaying a shocking lack of concern about both your health and that of your child."

"My concern is letting one of you bastards in here! The first thing you people did when you found out I was pregnant was tell me that you wanted to take my baby away!"

"That was handled badly, I admit . . ."

"Handled badly? They came in here with a knife to Kally's throat and threatened to kill her unless I did what they said!"

"I must remind you that I was not a part of that group, nor do I endorse their actions." This, of course, was not strictly true. Tusari Gyn had known all about what his colleagues were doing. He had distanced himself from it, not because he disapproved, but so that he could act shocked. Tusari Gyn was very experienced at playing both sides against the middle. It was the Boragi way. "Frankly, I think they handled it abominably. I should point out, though," he added, "that when they threatened to kill Kalinda, you invited them to do so."

"I was calling their bluff."

"Were you? Or did you simply not care? And are you now ashamed of your actions in the matter? It seems that all of us, Prime Minister, do things that we later regret."

She screamed again. Tusari Gyn glanced at his timepiece. "That," he said, "was rather close to the previous one in terms of intervals."

"I know," said the doctor worriedly.

"Then I think we must do something about it." He reached into his long, sweeping coat and removed a metal cylinder. "Prime Minister," he informed her very carefully, "it is my belief that you are not thinking clearly. Because of that, and because of my position as Prime Arbiter, I'm afraid I must take matters into my own hands."

"Meaning what?"

"Meaning that I have a cutting tool in my hand that I am about to employ on the door's locking mechanism. I will cut a hole in the door and manually override the dead bolt seal. We will be in there inside of five minutes unless you open the door willingly."

"Don't you dare!"

"You're giving me no choice."

"Guards! Stop him!"

The guards moved automatically to do as she commanded, but Tusari Gyn did not back down. "Is this how you're going to fulfill your responsibility to the house of Cwan?" he said. "By standing by and allowing this woman, who is obviously not thinking clearly through the pain, to condemn both herself and the last heir to death? You took an oath to Si Cwan. Do you think it would have been his wish to see harm befall his wife and child?"

Once again the guards exchanged looks. Then, as if in unspoken accord with each other, they stepped back. One of them, the taller one again, called through the door, "Lady Cwan, I would not violate my oath to the House of Cwan for all the world. I would lay down my life for it. But I am not willing to lay down your life or the life of the child."

"I'm holding a phaser in my hand!" shouted Robin, clearly unimpressed by his claims of fealty. "Anybody who sets foot in here, I'll blow you to atoms!"

"She's bluffing," said Tusari Gyn.

"You are undoubtedly right," said the doctor. "However, in the event she's not, might I suggest you go first?"

To Tusari Gyn's surprise, Norkai stepped forward. "Prime Minister, you are embarking upon a suicidal course," he said sternly.

"Go to hell, Norkai. Why should I listen to you? Your cousin killed my husband!"

"Distant cousin," he corrected her.

"I don't give a damn! Cwan's blood is on your hands."

"And if I stand by and do nothing, then the blood of his child will likewise be on my hands."

"I have everything under contr—!"

She screamed again, this one louder and longer than ever. As this happened, Tusari Gyn said, "Enough's enough," and immediately switched on his torch. He brought it up to the side of the door and started cutting into the metal. The guards stepped aside to give him room.

"Don't you dare! *Don't you dare!*" she screamed from within, clearly able to hear the whining of the torch above her own outcries. The frantic sound of her voice led Tusari Gyn to believe that she had been bluffing about holding a phaser. She might well have weaponry at her disposal, but it was likely nowhere near the bed and she was hardly in a position to go and fetch it.

Tusari Gyn kept at it as the doctor and Norkai watched, the doctor with increasing nervousness, Norkai impassively. "Almost there," said Tusari Gyn. "Almost there . . ."

Then he heard another noise above the sound of the torch. It was coming from within the chamber, and then the Lady Cwan moaned, "Oh, thank God! You sure as hell couldn't have cut it any closer!"

At that moment the square of metal fell away. Tusari Gyn reached in, quickly found the override, and activated it. The door slid open. Automatically Tusari Gyn started to run through but suddenly rebounded off something that amounted to a solid wall. He fell backward and hit the ground hard, landing on his tailbone with a startled yelp. He looked up. And up.

A massive being that Tusari Gyn recognized all too readily was blocking the entrance. His arms were folded across his chest, and he wore a look on his face that seemed a cross between amused and bored.

"Sorry," rumbled the massive being. "You'll have to make an appointment." Then he reached over, tapped a button on the inside, and the door slid closed again. Tusari Gyn started to reach for the hole in the wall that he had just carved with his torch, but as if capable of seeing through the door, the newcomer said, "If you slide the door open again, I'm going to be compelled to break you in half. No offense."

"None taken," Tusari Gyn said with a slightly strangled voice as he lowered his hand.

"Who, or what, was that?" said Norkai, visibly shaken from the encounter.

"That," said one of the guards, "was Zek Kebron, security officer for the *Starship Excalibur*. Which means, if I'm not mistaken, that the ship's chief medical officer is likely in there delivering the child. We can take some solace in the notion that the baby is in safe hands."

"Well, that's good to know," said Tusari Gyn. "Come, friend Norkai, let us away."

He walked briskly down the hallway, Norkai trailing behind him. Norkai looked bewildered. "But . . . what about putting it into our hands?" he said in a low voice, even though they were far enough away from the door and Lady Cwan's guards that nothing he said was going to be overheard. "Nothing has changed. The raising of the last heir of the House of Cwan is too great a responsibility to leave to an off-worlder. If she has a Brikar standing guard . . ."

"He can't stand guard forever," said Tusari Gyn. "And our own people can handle the Thallonian guards if it comes to that."

"But what if she flees with the child?"

"She wouldn't dare. It would create an interstellar incident. Who would give her shelter? The *Excalibur*? The Federation would never allow it."

"From the things I've heard, one should never underestimate what the Federation will and will not allow where Mackenzie Calhoun is concerned."

Tusari Gyn did not reply because he had heard much the same.

ii.

"Is he coming?" Kalinda said, her voice barely above a whisper.

"Why don't you go find out for yourself?" said Si Cwan. Had Kalinda been capable of listening to herself from the outside in, rather than the inside out, she would have noticed that Si Cwan's voice sounded almost exactly like hers, as if she were providing the vocalization for the both of them. But she was hardly in a position to be aware of such things.

"I thought that you could tell me."

"I could, dear sister, but what would be the point of that? You need to experience the world yourself. You can't just curl up into a ball and expect me to keep you current."

"Why not?" she said plaintively. "I don't like the world all that much anymore, Cwan. Especially with you no longer in it."

"Of course I'm in it. You know better than that." He crouched over her and gently stroked her smooth head. She sighed softly, basking in his touch. "Don't tell me that you're starting to see the world the way *they* see it? I expect far more of you than that."

"I know, I know. But it's hard to live with your expectations sometimes."

"I'm sorry."

"No, you're not."

"You know me too well," her brother said with a smile.

"Well enough to know that you've changed the subject. Why won't you tell me what Robin's condition is?"

"You tell me some things first," said Si Cwan.

"What can I possibly tell you that you don't already know? Don't you know everything?"

"Would that I did," he said with a sad smile. "It would make things much easier."

"All right. What do you wish to know?"

"Robin's mother. I would have thought she would have taken charge of the situation. Robin has a holosuite. As a computer hologram, her mother could have easily handled the delivery."

"She doesn't trust her these days," said Kalinda. "Morgan experienced some sort of—I don't know—*mishap* some months ago. She has since recovered, but Robin said that she hasn't been herself. She acts erratically at times. Plus there are technical aspects to consider. What if some sort of technological problem occurred and Morgan disappeared in mid-birth, or even had the baby in her hands and then dropped him? The only person Robin really trusts to handle her child is Doctor Selar. And that's who came."

"Then I suppose it has all worked out for the best." He looked wistful. "Does Robin ever mention me? Talk about me?"

"Oh yes, all the time," Kalinda said. "And even when she's not talking about you, she's thinking about you. I can tell when she does. She gets a certain look in her eyes. It's much the same as the one you have on your face right now."

"Is it? That is . . . nice," said Si Cwan. "It is good to know that she has not forgotten me."

"She gives birth to your heir even as we speak. I don't see how she could possibly forget you, given the circumstances. Which brings us back to my original question."

"I'm going to do you a service, Kally."

"You're going to tell me?"

"No. I'm not going to tell you."

"How is that a service?"

"Because it is going to force you to come out of yourself, at least for a little while. You need to rejoin the world, Kally."

"Why? What's in the world that holds the slightest interest for me?"

"Your nephew, for one thing. You're his only living blood relative. He deserves more than an eccentric aunt who spends her days immobile and muttering to herself."

"Is that how you see me?"

"That is how others see you, and since I have no impact on the world, I'm afraid that that perception holds a good deal of sway. And I can think of no better way to make your presence known as something other than an eccentric than by going to Robin's chambers and seeing how matters fare for yourself."

She hesitated. "What if—?"

"What if what?"

"What if they laugh at me? Or are afraid of me, or feel sorry for me?"

"None of that is going to happen," he said with assurance. "You worry too much, Kalinda."

"And you do not worry enough. Which is unfair to say since you're dead and so your worries have ceased."

"Nonsense. I worry about you and Robin all the time, and have even greater frustration since I can do nothing about it."

"I miss you."

"Yes, so you've said. And I miss you as well. But that isn't going to help one bit. What will help is you getting on your feet and acting like a proper Thallonian of noble birth. Make me proud, Kalinda."

"Very well, Cwan. For you."

Kalinda got to her feet, took a deep breath and let it out slowly. She started to take a step forward and nearly collapsed. It was only then that she realized her legs were practically numb. *How long has it been since I walked someplace?* Kalinda wondered as she braced her back against the wall and shook her legs to restore circulation. Then she headed for Robin's chambers.

Various servants or casual visitors did double takes when they saw Kalinda walking past them. She would smile or tilt her head in acknowledgment, and it amused her that people didn't seem to know how to act around her. One would have thought that she had returned out of nowhere after being reported dead for a year. They would clear their throats nervously or try to say something to her but fail. What did they think she was going to do? Leap upon them and tear out their jugular veins with her teeth?

She decided that their perceptions of her, and their discomfort, were entirely their problem.

As she approached Robin's quarters, she heard a thin, reedy whine. She quickened her pace and moments later she was at the door. Zak Kebron was blocking it, and although his face was not designed to display emotion, he still looked mildly surprised to discover her standing before him. "Kalinda," he said, acknowledging her presence in that low, rumbling way he had that always sounded like a rockslide in progress.

"Hello, Kebron. Where are the guards?"

"Robin informed them that, with me here, they could take a break. They didn't offer much protest. I don't think they were thrilled to stand here and listen to a woman screaming. Are you here to see Robin?" When she nodded, he stepped aside slightly, opening a small space for Kalinda to slide through. She did so.

Robin was lying in bed, looking exhausted but content. A child, swaddled in a white cloth, lay wrapped in her arms. His skin was pale red, evocative of his father's tone, but to Kalinda's great amusement, he had a swatch of dark brown hair on his head. Since this was a rarity for Thallonian males, Kalinda was tempted to burst out laughing. She thought, though, that Robin might take offense, so she managed to contain herself, although she did allow a broad smile to crawl across her face.

Doctor Selar was cleaning her hands meticulously with a cloth. She glanced toward Kalinda and the entirety of her reaction to Kalinda's presence was to raise an eyebrow.

"Kally," said Robin. "You're up and about."

"Yes." Slowly she approached mother and son. "He's beautiful."

"I thought you would be off put by the hair."

"He is a product of his father and mother. We accept him as he is."

"I'm pleased to hear you say that. Kally, are you . . . ? "

"Am I what?"

"Are you . . . all right?"

"Why would I not be?"

"Because . . ."

Then Robin's eyes sagged and her head slumped back. She moaned softly. Concerned for her well-being, Kalinda said to Doctor Selar, "What's happening?"

"She just gave birth. She is tired and should not strain herself in extended conversation with anyone."

"Very well," said Kalinda. "May I ask, though, if she has chosen a name for him?"

Despite her fatigue, Robin managed to raise her head from the pillow just enough to say, with a smile, "Cwansi. I'd like to think that Cwan would be proud."

Kalinda looked across the room and saw Si Cwan standing on the other side of the bed. He was smiling, perfectly beaming, down at his son.

"I very much think you are right," said Kalinda.

With that, she turned and walked out of the room. Zak Kebron watched her as she sidled past him and then slowly slid to the floor. She drew her legs up and tucked her knees under her chin, just as she had done earlier. He stared at her with open curiosity, but she did not appear to notice.

"I did as you asked," she said, her voice dropping back to its muttering tone. "I saw him. I told her he is beautiful, even if he is odd looking. All his best attributes come from you. But she looked at me pityingly. They all did. I hate when people look at me that way. Hate it."

"They weren't looking at you pityingly," Si Cwan said. "They just . . . they don't understand you, Kally. They want the best for you. They do. They worry about you."

"The only person who really worried about me is you."

"That's not true. The crew of the *Excalibur* cares about you. And Xyon. Xyon cared about you a great deal. Xyon loved you, or at least did as much as any of his ilk can love."

"You always disliked him."

"Yes, well, that's true. But that didn't diminish his feelings for you. If you find yourself uncomfortable with the attentions of others, perhaps Xyon—"

"I just want them all to leave me alone. I don't need

them. I don't need anyone but you." She reached out and held his hand and sighed contentedly. All was right.

iii.

Zak Kebron watched Kalinda as she grasped empty air and continued to speak to herself in a low, intense voice that seemed to be shifting tones. It sounded to him as if she were holding both sides of a conversation with herself.

Even as she spoke, though, one name popped out at him.

He tapped his combadge and said, in as soft a voice as he could manage—which wasn't terribly soft by human standards, but for a Brikar was positively sedate—"Kebron to Calhoun."

"Excalibur. *Calhoun here. What's the status, Zak?*"

"Mother and son are doing fine."

"That's excellent," said Calhoun, who sounded relieved.

"The aunt, however, is not doing quite as well."

There was a pause as Calhoun processed who it was that Kebron was referring to. *"You mean Kalinda? What's wrong with Kalinda?"*

"It's not so much what's wrong with her as what's right with her."

"All right," Calhoun said patiently. *"What's right with her?"*

"Nothing."

"You're going to have to elaborate."

"She's curled up on the floor about five feet away from me in what I could only term the fetal position, talking at length to someone who's not there."

"Kebron, it's been my experience that our definition of what is and is not there is not always consistent with the way Kalinda sees things."

"That may well be, Captain . . ."

"Believe me, it is."

". . . but that doesn't mean she doesn't need help coping with the world that the rest of us sees."

"I'm not entirely certain this is any of our business, Kebron, but go ahead."

Kebron laid out for him what he wanted Calhoun to do.

"No," said Calhoun.

"Don't say 'no' immediately, Captain."

"Considering I already have, that request comes a little late . . ."

"Sir," Kebron said patiently, "your instinct may be to refuse—"

"And I tend to trust my instincts."

"—but once you give it some thought, you'll realize that Kalinda is an individual in pain who needs help only you can provide."

"I intend to give this no thought at all. Calhoun out."

Starship Excalibur

i.

Twenty minutes later, Mackenzie Calhoun punched the armrest of his command chair and said with a snarl, "Damn him!" He'd been in his ready room when he had the conversation with Kebron, so no one on the bridge had the slightest idea to whom he was referring, nor did he make any attempt to clarify it. Instead he continued, "Morgan," before she'd had time to react to his unexpected outburst. "Get a message to my son."

"Do you want me to summon Moke to the bridge, sir?"

"Not my adopted son, who's barely speaking to me. My bastard son, who can't stand me."

"Ah," said Morgan, understanding. Her hand was already manipulating the ops board. "Okay. I actually have a direct emergency frequency for Xyon."

"You do?" That was news to Calhoun. "Why?"

"He left it with me in case there was a problem with Kalinda and we needed to get in touch with him quickly."

Smiles did not come easily to Calhoun, but one came now in spite of himself. "He thought ahead. I taught him well."

"With respect, Captain, you didn't meet him until he was grown. You didn't really teach him anything."

"It imprinted on a genetic level."

"Whatever you say, sir. What do you want me to tell him?"

"Tell him there's a problem with Kalinda."

"And, if I may ask . . . *is* there a problem? With Kalinda, I mean."

"Honestly, Morgan," Calhoun said slowly, "I wish I knew."

ii.

Doctor Selar strode into the ready room with a faint air of impatience. "You wished to see me, Captain?"

"I left word with the transporter room that you

should come directly here upon returning to the vessel, yes." He had been recording his log, but he turned the computer aside and focused his attention on Selar. He studied her with concern. These days she hardly seemed recognizable. She was never a warm and fuzzy individual even on her best days, but the gap between the old Selar and the one standing before him had now widened immensely.

He had toyed with the idea of relieving her of duty, but he could see no credible reason for doing so. She was performing all her duties with no diminishment of efficiency. Granted, her bedside manner was cold, even indifferent, but no one expected much bedside manner from a Vulcan anyway, so that was hardly grounds for his taking action.

"Very well," said Selar. "So here I am. Do you wish a report on the status of Robin Lefler?" When he nodded slightly, she said, "Mother and son are in satisfactory condition. The child is seven pounds, three ounces. Skin color is unusual, but attributable to his mixed parentage."

"Odd how different races can interbreed, isn't it?" said Calhoun thoughtfully. "One would think it impossible that alien species could possibly have similar enough genetic material to produce offspring. A human and a Thallonian? Or, for that matter, a human and a Vulcan?"

"Is there anything else, Captain?"

"Sit down, Selar."

"I prefer to stand. It will make taking my leave more efficient."

"Are you in a hurry?"

"I have a patient in sickbay to attend to."

"Yes. Rulan 12. How is s/he coming along?"

"No change in hir condition."

"Is s/he going to come out of it?"

"I do not know."

There was something about her, about her attitude, that Calhoun couldn't quite put his finger on. He studied her intently and said, "Doctor, is there something you're not telling me about Rulan?"

"It is my responsibility to keep the commanding officer apprised of the condition of any patients."

"Yes, it is. And I notice that that isn't exactly a reply to the question."

She pursed her lips, which was what she typically did when she was annoyed but had no desire to convey that. "There is nothing you need to know that I have not already told you."

Now Calhoun knew that something was definitely

going on. "That implies, Doctor, that you're making a judgment call as to what I need to know or do not need to know. That is unacceptable to me."

"I am the chief medical officer, Captain. If you think my judgment in such matters is not to be trusted, then relieve me of duty and replace me with someone whom you think is more reliable."

There was no challenge in her voice, or even her customary iciness. She sounded as if she were truly indifferent to the prospect of being relieved of her duties as CMO. Slowly he got to his feet so that he and Selar were on eye level. "Selar," he said with a great show of patience that didn't reflect how he truly felt, "what the hell is going on? Before you went down to New Thallon, you specifically instructed your medtechs not to breach quarantine . . ."

"In keeping with standard procedure."

"You're keeping them at a distance."

"I am limiting the exposure of my patient to others as a safety measure."

"*Grozit,* Selar, stop fencing with me. What is there in Rulan's condition that you're not telling me?"

Without hesitation, she said flatly, "Nothing, Captain. There is nothing in the patient's condition that I am withholding from you. If you do not believe me,

I invite you to have one of my technicians, or even my son, perform a detailed examination. Of course," she added, "if you do so, I will immediately tender my resignation as ship's CMO, since you will have made it abundantly clear that you no longer trust me, my opinions, or my actions."

He could not determine whether it was a stone-cold bluff or if she was simply displaying that endless pride in her abilities that so characterized her. He wished that he could somehow just flip open the top of her skull and study her brain, read her thoughts so he would know precisely what was going through her mind. Absent that ability, he felt he had no choice. "Very well, Doctor," he said finally. "I will take your word for it. May I point out that if you had simply responded in such a straightforward manner originally, we would not have had to go in circles like this?"

"My apologies, Captain. In the future I will endeavor to phrase my responses more to your liking. Am I dismissed?"

"By all means."

She turned on her heel and headed out the door. Calhoun watched her go and then sagged back into his chair, rubbing the bridge of his nose. It was one of those times when he wished that his wife, Elizabeth

Shelby, were still with him aboard ship. The isolation of command was weighing more heavily than ever upon him these days.

Selar wasn't being candid with him. The more he reflected upon their conversation, on her attitude, on all that she wasn't saying rather than what she was saying, the more convinced he became. But he wasn't pressing her on the subject. He wondered if he was making a mistake, treating her delicately because he believed she was still fragile over Xy's situation.

He wished that the Hermat's own ship had been of some use to them, but the logs had been wiped clean. Not only was there no record of anything s/he might have recorded that could have helped them, but the navigational records were also empty. The ship might as well have popped out of nowhere for all the information they were able to glean.

Calhoun intensely disliked not having all the information at hand that he felt he needed. It limited his ability to make wise decisions, and it annoyed him tremendously that he felt Selar was putting him in this situation.

"What the hell are you not telling me, Doctor?" he said.

iii.

Selar wanted to scream. She wanted to howl her frustration. She wanted to sob over her mortification because she had lied, damn it—she had *lied* to her commanding officer. Vulcans simply did not do that. *She* did not do that.

As she strode through the corridors, no one would have been able to discern simply from looking at her that her mind was in turmoil. Her self-control remained inviolate. Yet she felt as if she were viewing the world through a haze of red.

She had lied to her commanding officer.

And such a thing was inconceivable to a Vulcan.

What is happening to me? Why do I not tell him of my discovery about Rulan?

Because he might take hir away. He might recommend bringing hir to a Starbase, or might turn hir over to Starfleet. For as long as I treat Rulan as my patient, and hir condition as recovering from standard radiation poisoning, he will likely leave the Hermat in my care. But if I tell him the truth, and he informs Starfleet, they may order us to turn the Hermat over for further study. S/he will be taken from my possession. I cannot allow that. S/he may hold the key to helping Xy. If only I could dissect hir. Take hir apart, break hir down molecule by molecule. The instruments at my disposal can only tell me so much. They can provide me with details of hir current condition, but cannot tell me how s/he got that way. But if I dissect hir, I could certainly determine the origins of hir state.

S/he needs to be dead, though.

That could easily be arranged . . .

Selar suddenly realized she was standing outside the quarantine section. She didn't remember arriving there. One minute she had been in the corridor, and the next, she was in sickbay. It was the same abrupt jump from moment to moment that one would typically associate with a dream. Was she dreaming? Was that it?

Her hands were flat against the partition. She was staring intently at Rulan, and her recent thought returned to her: *That could easily be arranged . . .*

I am losing my mind . . .

But it would not be that difficult to arrange . . .

What is happening to me?

Xy has so much left to accomplish. This is some random Hermat. Hir life would be sacrificed to a greater good . . .

Stop it. Stop this sort of thinking right now. This is not you. This is insane . . .

You do not know what is you anymore. The only "you" that matters is the you who is willing to save your son. You will do anything for him. You know this to be true. Nothing else—

"Mother?"

Selar whirled. For a fraction of a second, her face mirrored the internal battle she was undergoing. Her mask slipped. Then, just as quickly, when she saw Xy looking into her eyes, she replaced her mask and was once again the picture of detachment. "Yes, Xy. What? Is this about Robin Lefler? She is well, as is her son. Anything else?"

"I have been talking to Dad . . ."

"You refer to him as 'Dad' and to me as 'Mother.' I find that interesting. Now if you will excuse me—"

"There are things he's concerned about. You, for starters—"

"I do not have time for this."

"Mother, if you would just—"

"I do not—!"

The explosion of noise from Selar stopped everyone dead. Medtechs had been going about their business but they froze in place as if their feet had been transformed into tree roots.

She pulled herself together immediately. "I do not," she said again, this time with her customary calm but nonetheless with an edge to her voice, "have time . . . for this. I have a patient to attend to, and engaging in an endless debate about your father's incessant feelings and constant reassurances that s/he is a decent and loving individual is a waste of my time. I value my time highly. As should you."

With that, she stepped through the force seal that provided the entrance to the quarantine section. It was keyed to her DNA imprint, enabling her to pass through unhindered. Since she was the CMO and in charge of the case to boot, no one else could enter the quarantine area without her permission.

This was something that Xy should have remembered, but did not. He was swiftly reminded, however, as he attempted to follow her, only to be repulsed by the field. It was not on the level of the brig's force field, designed to keep irate prisoners confined if ever they attempted to slam their full body weight against it or even open fire upon it with phasers. But Xy was rather slender, and was still thrown backward several feet. He nearly fell, but righted himself with the cat-like quickness he had inherited from his father. Selar did not bother to glance his way. Instead, her attention focused on her instruments, her back to her son, she said, "Have more care next time, lest you hurt yourself severely."

"Thank you, Mother," said Xy, straightening his uniform shirt and trying to recapture a bit of his battered dignity. "I will take that advice to heart."

"See that you do."

Xy left the sickbay. Selar listened to his receding footsteps, wanting to call to him, to explain to him all that was going through her mind, to even hold up a shred of hope for his condition.

Instead she said nothing. Not even when that same thought wandered through her mind . . .

It would not be hard to arrange hir death. Not hard at all . . .

New Thallon

The day was shaping up to be a good one for Robin Lefler.

It had been a week since the birth of Cwansi and she was already up and around. The vastness of the responsibility that lay before her of being a single mother was still a vague enough concept; she wasn't dwelling on it excessively. Instead she was far more interested in caring for her son.

She was feeling a little more secure in her position than she had been when she was in the throes of childbirth. She had met with Cawng Li, the captain of the guards, who had assured her that the guards of the House of Cwan would guarantee the safety of her and her son. "The heir is the heir," Cawng Li had informed her stiffly. "No one outside of the House of Cwan has any business raising him. Our Lord Cwan chose you as his wife, and we would be dishonoring his memory if we cooperated with those who would try to take the child for their own."

Then he had bowed deeply to her, as if she were royalty, at which point she had to remind herself that—to them—that was exactly what she was. Although the New Thallonian Protectorate had been designed to have a more equitable distribution of power than the monarchy that had once characterized the Thallonian Empire, most Thallonians still saw Si Cwan as royalty, his murder as regicide, and his widow and heir as the last, best hope of a return to Thallonian glory. At this point, who was she to disagree? Especially when it would provide a cocoon of safety in which she could raise her child.

The bottom line was that although it was still in some respects an alien world to Robin, New Thallon was Cwansi's best opportunity to be raised in an environment that was true to his roots. That would have been important to Si Cwan and thus it was important to her as well. Plus she had a stubborn streak of her own. She knew there were still people who resented her as an off-worlder and would like nothing better than to see her depart as soon as possible, preferably with her tail tucked firmly between her legs. But the

Protectorate had meant a great deal to Si Cwan, and Robin was determined to see his vision through, no matter how much some might oppose her.

The great wild card in all of this was Kalinda.

Si Cwan's sister seemed to flit in and out of sanity on an almost random basis. Sometimes she would be perfectly lucid, chatting with Robin, doting on her nephew, and being the Kalinda of old. Other times she would speak to thin air in a distracted manner, and still others she would practically collapse upon herself, curling up into a tight muttering ball. Those were the most disconcerting times, not only because she was practically unapproachable physically, but also because she sounded as if she were attempting to speak with more than one voice. Robin had no idea what to make of it. Nor did any medical practitioners appear to know how to approach the problem. Psychiatry was simply not a common discipline among Si Cwan's people, and whenever Robin tried to explain what it entailed, she received blank looks from such good-hearted but ultimately helpless Thallonians.

Today, however, was shaping up to be one of Kalinda's better days. She had seemed both clear-eyed and chipper, fully aware of not only Robin and the baby but also her whereabouts. That was all positive. It gave Robin hope that perhaps Kalinda would eventually leave those fetal periods behind and be fully restored to her normal, ebullient self. Indeed, perhaps her withdrawals were the only way she had of dealing with the loss of Si Cwan, and time—as it tended to do—would heal the wound.

Today Kalinda's mood was matched by the weather, and it seemed the right day for Robin to introduce her son to the world outside the manor. She did not undertake the outing precipitously; an honor guard of ten warriors, headed up by Cawng Li himself, ringed her and Kalinda as they moved out across the great lawn behind the manor.

For a child of only a week's age, Cwansi had displayed an almost supernatural calm. He rarely cried, and when he did it wasn't venting but instead was carefully controlled in order to get his mother's attention. Once he had it, he seemed content to allow Robin time to determine what he required. She couldn't help but observe that he was rather imperious for a newborn: If his skin tone hadn't indicated who his father was, his attitude certainly did.

At Cawng Li's insistence, Robin rode in a hover-chair. The thronelike device glided slowly along the ground on an antigrav cushion, and a simple cyber-link running along the seat of the chair tapped into her nervous system and made the chair thought-responsive. It had made Robin laugh and declare that she was now officially flying by the seat of her pants. That had prompted confused looks from Cawng Li and the other guards, and her attempts to explain the Terran colloquialism had not gone particularly well. "Lefler's Law Number Forty-two: Any joke that has to be explained isn't worth explaining," she told Cawng Li.

"Is there any particular reason that's number forty-two?" he asked.

"Yes, and it's a funny one, but I would have to explain it, so . . ." She shrugged and that was the end of that.

Robin made certain to keep the chair moving slowly enough that Kalinda could stroll along next to her. Kalinda was basking in the glory of the day. She spread her arms wide and, her face tilted toward the sun, did not actually stroll next to Robin so much as pirouette in small circles. Occasionally Robin had to cause the chair to skitter to one side to avoid Kalinda's bumping into her. The Thallonian guards were sup-posed to be keeping their attention focused on their surroundings, but every so often one or another of them would sneak a glance at Kalinda and exchange an amused smile with another.

"Nice day, isn't it, Kalinda," Robin said to kick off the conversation.

Kalinda didn't seem to hear her at first, but then she said, "Everything about it is nice, yes. How is my nephew enjoying it?"

"He's sleeping." Her infant son was cradled in her arms, his eyes closed and his little chest rising and falling rhythmically.

"He does that a lot."

"That's fairly normal for babies, actually."

"Is it really?"

"You've no experience with babies?"

"Not living ones."

From anyone else, that would have sounded remarkably morbid. For Kalinda, it was actually normal. Robin wasn't sure whether she should find that disturbing or should just be pleased that Kalinda was speaking to her in a standard interactive manner rather than to thin air.

The group wasn't all that far from the manor house, which some still referred to as the palace even though it was hardly palatial. Five hundred yards at most. Cawng Li had made it clear that he didn't want to wander too far afield. "One cannot be too careful," he had told her. "These are times that call for caution."

"Most times are," Robin had observed, and Cawng Li had agreed.

Now Cawng Li was continuing to appraise their environs. He looked as if he had vague suspicions, but nothing he could pinpoint. "Perhaps it would be best if we returned to the manor, Lady Cwan."

Robin was about to offer protest, but thought better of it. Cawng Li was simply trying to do his job of protecting her and her baby. She certainly had no intention of inhibiting him in that endeavor. "Kalinda," she said. "Kally. We're heading back home."

Kalinda had stopped moving. Her back was stiff and she seemed to be looking at something that was both right nearby them and yet also far off. For a moment Robin was concerned that her sister-in-law had picked this moment to retreat into her own little world again. "Kally?" she said tentatively.

Then Kalinda spun to face her, and there was no panic in her eyes because Kalinda was, by and large, far too composed to allow such an extreme emotion to be reflected there. But there was vast concern, and an obvious fear that things were about to go horribly wrong.

"Run," she said. Before Robin had a chance to question the order, Kalinda repeated it, and louder this time. *"Run!"*

Robin didn't hesitate. *"Get on!"* she shouted at Kalinda, and even as she spoke, the chair thrust forward and banged into her. Kalinda fell over onto her, twisting her body to avoid crushing Cwansi. The baby awoke with a start and let out an annoyed yelp, not understanding why in the world his aunt was suddenly atop him. Robin called out to Cawng Li, "We're under attack!"

Cawng Li did not question the pronouncement. "At arms!" he shouted to his men, and they started to draw into a tight circle.

The blasts started raining down from overhead.

Robin screamed, and Kalinda clutched onto her desperately as Robin's mind urged the chair to speed back to the manor and what she hoped would be safety. Her guards fell back, firing skyward even though they couldn't clearly see what was coming after them.

Cwansi did not emit the slightest cry. Instead, for the first time since his birth, his eyes focused. He looked upward and they narrowed as if he understood that he was looking upon an enemy.

Robin looked up as well and she saw it: a Boragi vessel. Fully armed, it was firing down upon Robin's people, and she saw that the shots were staying well clear of her and the baby.

Bastards . . . those unspeakable bastards . . .

She had underestimated them. She had been certain that Tusari Gyn would spend at least some time nattering to the Council about how the child should be taken into their custody. She had been certain that Gyn could be outmaneuvered, delayed, or dealt with in some manner. Unfortunately, she had been distracted by the little matter of giving birth, and hadn't accorded the problem as much attention as she should have.

This was the result. Tusari Gyn had somehow managed to enlist the Boragi, who were typically more than happy to stand to one side and allow others to fight matters out, to intervene personally.

"I'm sorry," Kalinda said under her breath. "I'm sorry I didn't know sooner."

Robin didn't bother to question how Kalinda could have known at all, much less sooner than anyone else. She was too busy focusing her attention on the chair. The chair wasn't designed for combat situations. It was made to respond to the calm thoughts of its occupant. Her thoughts now were anything but calm, and the chair bucked and veered as pulse blasts erupted around her. If it had not been for her Starfleet training, it likely would have flipped over entirely. Instead she managed to focus herself and bring it back on track.

Something went flying past her and thudded to the ground just to her right. It was Cawng Li. She couldn't determine whether he was alive or dead, but he was motionless and unable to help, and that was all that was relevant.

The ship that was descending toward them was an ambassador transport. As such, its presence had done nothing to trip the planetary defenses. *What the hell is an ambassador transport doing with armament?* The Boragi duplicity infuriated her. She wondered why they were even fleeing toward the manor; why did she think it was going to provide any shelter? It wasn't indestructible or impenetrable, didn't have any weaponry or force shielding of any kind. It wouldn't really serve as any sort of haven. But it was the only thing she could think to do.

The ground in front of Robin erupted with such

force that she was blown backward, the chair over-turned. Kalinda tumbled out of the chair and Robin followed, clutching her infant son tightly so that he did not go flying from her arms. She hit the ground hard, flat on her back, and it knocked the air out of her. The world was spinning, the air alive with the sounds of explosions. She tasted something bitter in her mouth and realized it was tears.

Cwansi still did not so much as whimper. Instead his gaze was upon her, regarding her with patient confidence, apparently certain that his mother would find a way out of this.

She had a phaser on her hip, secreted below the folds of her loose-fitting tunic. She sat up, keeping her hand upon it but hidden, counting heavily on the element of surprise.

The ground was littered with the motionless bodies of her guards. They were all down; not one of them was in any position to protect her. Kalinda was looking around, wide-eyed. She did not appear afraid; instead she seemed fascinated by the developments around her.

The ambassador transport was settling to the ground. The hatch opened and a squad of Boragi emerged. They were dressed identically, giving the impression of uniforms, and they were heavily armed. Clearly they were soldiers, which surprised the hell out of Robin Lefler because she hadn't thought that the Boragi even had armed forces. There was obviously a good deal about themselves that they had kept under wraps.

The soldiers leveled their weapons at the fallen guards, making certain that none of them was merely pretending to be unconscious. They were remaining in tight formation, but now they separated to make way for Tusari Gyn. He strolled through them as if he was on an outing in a park, his hands draped behind his back, his look imperious. He was unarmed and unarmored. This brought some solace to Robin, because he had nothing to serve as protection against a phaser blast. She reminded herself where the Boragi heart was and pictured the exact place on him so that she would be able to take aim and drill a hole right through it.

"For what it's worth, Lady Cwan, I am truly sorry about this," said Tusari Gyn. His voice was low and gentle, as if he were singing a child to sleep.

"I think you know what it's worth," she said tightly. Tusari Gyn wasn't close enough yet to guarantee that she was going to get a clear shot at him. She knew instinctively she was only going to have one chance at him, and she didn't want to blow it.

If I shoot, then they return fire. Except I'm holding the infant, which is what they came after. If they fire at me, they risk injuring or killing the baby. Which means that I'm basically using my own child as a shield, but it's not for my benefit. It's for his. It's the only way the both of us are going to survive this. Except . . . what if, for all his talk of wanting to raise the child as the last heir of the House of Cwan, they've decided that the simplest thing to do is just kill the three of us? Me, Kalinda, Cwansi, all in one shot.

"I know what you're thinking," said Tusari Gyn calmly. He had halted about thirty feet away, still farther than Robin would have liked to guarantee a killing shot. "You're thinking, why don't we just kill the three of you right here, right now and be done with it?" Robin kept her face impassive, not wanting to betray her being startled over Tusari Gyn's seeming ability to climb into her head and discern what was running through it. "It is not our first choice," continued Tusari Gyn. "The end of the House of Cwan will create a power vacuum. Such things are unpredictable, because power, like nature, detests a vacuum. The fact that you, Si Cwan's widow, were able to continue as Prime Minister avoided problems in the short term. The existence of his son will provide the long-term solution."

"As raised under the wise guidance of Tusari Gyn," she said. The Boragi's name sounded like a profanity the way she said it.

"I will expend my best efforts."

"Go to hell."

"It saddens me that you would make this so difficult, Lady Cwan. What would you prefer? Would you prefer to provoke the alternative? The tragic, untimely death of you, your sister-in-law, and your son? Because that is the only other way this is going to end."

"Maybe," said Robin tightly, "that would be preferable. Preferable to whatever you and your cronies would twist Cwansi into."

"That is your decision to make. I trust that you are not making it lightly. But making it you most certainly are. Gentlemen, take the child. If she resists, kill her. If she resists too much, kill all of them."

The soldiers advanced, filling in the space in front of Tusari Gyn. Robin cursed to herself; she should have risked the shot at Tusari Gyn when she had the opportunity. Now he was blocked from view, and she was going to have to fire through the armored soldiers to get at him.

Of course, she could also just shoot Cwansi . . . and Kalinda . . . and, for a finale, herself.

Or . . .

She thumbed a switch on the phaser, disarming the built-in safety. A sharp whine began to emerge from it, and the soldiers froze where they were. They looked at one another in confusion, uncertain what was happening. "What's that noise?" came the voice of Tusari Gyn from behind them.

"That," Robin said with grim determination, "is the sound of a phaser set on overload. In short order, this entire area is going to be a crater. At least you won't have to be concerned about your power vacuum, because you won't be alive to worry about it."

"You're bluffing," said Tusari Gyn, but Robin welcomed the uncertainty in his voice.

"Try me. Please. I'm begging you to."

For a long moment, nothing was said. No one moved. The only thing filling the air was the increasing whine of the phaser moving toward an explosive discharge.

"Kill her," said Tusari Gyn. "Shoot her in the head, get the phaser, shut it down, and take the child."

They leveled their weapons. Robin glared directly into the barrels and spat in Tusari Gyn's direction.

The spittle fell well short, but at least she had made her feelings clear.

There was a thunderous explosion, and Robin jumped reflexively at it, thinking that the phaser had detonated prematurely, thinking that the soldiers had opened fire on her, thinking all manner of things that she belatedly realized made no sense because she was alive to think them. Then she realized the soldiers were looking around for the source of the explosions and there was another ship right there, right above them. It had shown up out of absolutely nowhere, with no warning, gotten impossibly close to them and was now firing on them with abandon.

The Boragi tried to fire upon the newcomer but it gave them no opportunity. Instead it continued to hammer down upon them, sending them flying in different directions. The Boragi had no trouble making a sneak attack with superior forces. Finding themselves assailed, however, they weren't exactly Klingons shouting defiance while battling to the last man. Instead they scrambled over one another to get out of the way of the onslaught.

The ambassador transport in which the Boragi had arrived was pummeled even as it fired up its engines and tried to lift off. It shuddered as the reverse thruster section blew off, sent spiraling and flaming through the air. The transport thudded back to the ground, helpless and crippled.

Unsure of what was happening, but willing to wait to see the outcome, Robin powered down the phaser. She scrambled to her feet and walked through the blasts around her as if she were a ghost and they could not possibly harm her. Sprawled on the ground was Tusari Gyn, grasping his right leg, screaming. A piece of metal, still quivering, was embedded in it. He looked up at her, his typically sallow skin now the color of curdled milk.

"You son of a bitch," she said, barely recognizing her strangled voice as her own. It sounded like someone had a hand on her throat. "I should kill you right now."

"Don't . . . please don't . . ." He was sniveling at her. The sound of it made her ill and she was tempted to squeeze the trigger if for no other reason than that she wouldn't have to listen to it anymore. "I . . . it was . . . I was just trying to . . ."

"I know what you were trying to—"

"Robin!"

It was a male voice, a wholly unexpected male voice. She turned, the phaser still locked onto its target, and she saw Xyon standing not ten feet away. He was cradling Kalinda in his arms with no apparent strain. Since he had his father's strength and Kalinda weighed about ninety pounds soaking wet, holding her thusly presented no problem. "Kill him or don't kill him, I really don't care one way or the other," he said, "but make a decision and let's go."

She looked back at Tusari Gyn. Then—and she had no idea why—she looked to the child that she clutched in her left arm. Cwansi gazed up at her with that same confident air that seemed wildly out of proportion to the size of the person he was.

She turned away from Tusari Gyn then and headed for Xyon's vessel. It was not a particularly large ship, but it would be enough to get her and Kalinda out of this hellhole.

"Thank you, Lady Cwan!" Tusari Gyn called after her. "Thank you for your mercy! Thank you for—"

Without bothering to look, she swung the phaser behind herself and fired off a shot. She heard Tusari Gyn let out a pained scream. She had no idea where she had struck him, nor did she care. As long as it was somewhere on his person, she was satisfied.

The *Lyla*

i.

"The *Lyla*?" Robin glanced around the small vessel, stepping carefully over scattered objects such as stray shirts or half-eaten food. Xyon obviously hadn't cleaned up after himself anytime recently. Xyon, for his part, kicked various obstacles in his path out of the way as he settled Kalinda into a chair near the helm. Kalinda looked up at him with a distantly puzzled gaze, as if she couldn't quite determine whether he was genuinely there or if she was just imagining it. "Why the *Lyla*?"

"Tell her why, Lyla," said Xyon.

A hologram appeared out of nowhere in the shape of an attractive blonde. "Hello. I'm Lyla," she said. There was a lyrical note to her voice.

"Um, hello," said Robin uncertainly.

"I am the artificial intelligence that runs this vessel. I serve Xyon in all of his needs."

Robin looked her up and down and there was a faint sound of derision in her tone as she said, "Oh, I bet you do."

"Hey!" Xyon said with annoyance. He had just finished strapping Kalinda into the chair. "If you're going to be snide, you can feel free to just hop out and take your chances here."

She was about to fire back a rebuttal but quickly appreciated her delicate position. "I'm sorry," she said contritely. "That was rude of me. To imply that you had . . . relations . . . with this hologram . . ."

"Oh, we have," said Lyla with a broad smile. "Oftentimes he asks me to make myself over so that I look like Kalinda."

Robin said nothing because she didn't trust herself. Xyon was an unpredictable individual. His interest in Kalinda was well-established, but he was perfectly capable of tossing Robin and Cwansi off the ship and departing without them. So instead of replying, she bit her lower lip and looked away, keeping her thoughts to herself.

"Smart move," said Xyon as if he had read her

mind. "Find someplace to grab hold of something. We're leaving."

He dropped into the pilot's chair and didn't bother to snap in the restraints as he had with Kalinda. Robin glanced around, looking for someplace to sit. Not seeing any, and having no desire to go into the rear quarters and flop down into Xyon's bed, she sat on the floor, curling up her legs and clutching Cwansi tightly to her breast.

The ship fired its thrusters and, seconds later, was hurtling toward space. The manor was illuminated on the ship's main screen, but in no time at all it had dwindled to an insignificant size. Shortly, the place where she had spent the last several years of her life was just part of a landmass on the surface of the planet.

"You have a cloaking device?"

He glanced toward her in surprise. Of all the things he had expected her to say, that obviously wasn't one of them. "Yes. I have to be careful in its use. It's an energy drain."

"Where did you get it?"

"Connections."

"And . . . why did you come to New Thallon? Just to visit?"

"I came because my father asked me to. He was worried about Kalinda. He said she was becoming disconnected or something like that and asked if I'd come and look in on her. It was blind luck that I happened to show up just when those bastards were attacking you. If I'd arrived only a few minutes later . . ." His voice trailed off and then he turned his attentions to Kalinda, reaching over and tentatively stroking her arm. "Kally? Do you know where you are? Do you know who I am?"

She had been staring off into air, but now she turned and looked straight at him with a faint air of incredulity. "Do you think I'm mentally impaired in some way, Xyon?"

He laughed in spite of the seriousness of the situation. "No. No, I don't. I was just . . . I wanted to make sure you were all right."

"Obviously I am," she said with great patience.

"All right. Now I know."

"And now that you know, are you planning to turn around and take me back home?"

She made it sound as if it was the most reasonable notion in the world. Xyon and Robin exchanged looks. For the first time that day, Cwansi whimpered slightly, as if he understood what Kalinda suggested and was appalled by the notion. It was Robin who said, "Kally . . . I don't think it would be the wisest option for us to go back right now. Do I need to explain why?"

"No," said Kalinda after a moment, and she sounded saddened but also resigned. "No . . . I saw what they did. They wanted to take Cwansi. We can't allow that. Si Cwan doesn't want that."

"No, he doesn't," said Xyon, obviously not the least bit thrown by Kalinda's referring to her dead brother in the present tense. He had evidently become accustomed to that particular quirk in her personality. "So that more or less leaves you women homeless at the moment."

"What should we do?" said Kalinda, sounding blessedly cognizant of the difficulties that lay before them. That was a relief to Robin, since Kalinda tended to be inconsistent in that regard.

"We contact my father," Xyon said. "He's the one who pulled me into the middle of this mess in the first place. I thought I was just coming to lend some aid and comfort to Kalinda. I didn't know I was going to wind up giving sanctuary to a couple of political refugees."

"A trio," Robin corrected him.

"What?"

"You forgot him," and she nodded toward her son. "Of the three of us, he's the one that matters the most."

"Sorry, kid," said Xyon, and then amended it to, "Sorry, your highness."

Cwansi made a *pbbthhh* noise and drool dripped from his mouth.

"I'm not sure if that means he accepts your apology or not," said Robin.

ii.

On the viewscreen of the *Lyla,* Mackenzie Calhoun listened to everything that Xyon and Robin told him about what had happened on New Thallon. Kalinda contributed nothing to the conversation, although she did smile gently every now and then whenever her name was mentioned.

"Well," Calhoun said finally once they had finished the tale. *"It appears we have a bit of a situation on our hands."*

"I'm sorry to have put you into it, Captain."

"Why in the gods' names are you apologizing to me, Robin? You haven't put me into anything. It's the people who

were willing to step over your dead body to get to your son who have created this situation."

"I'm not entirely sure Starfleet is going to see it that way."

"You let me worry about Starfleet."

"You never worry about Starfleet. You just do whatever the hell you want and leave Starfleet to like it or lump it."

"I see your time away from us hasn't diminished your memory of my command style," he said with what sounded like a touch of pride.

"You're unforgettable, Captain. So . . . what do we do?"

"Let me do some research and get back to you in about fifteen minutes."

Fourteen minutes and fifty-three seconds later, Calhoun was back on the screen, scratching his chin thoughtfully. *"To be honest, Robin, we have the makings of an interstellar incident here. The Council is the ruling authority of the New Thallonian Protectorate. The child is a citizen of the Protectorate. And you have no legal standing whatsoever."*

"That's ridiculous. I'm the Prime Minister."

"That's what they've been calling you, yes, but purely as a matter of form. Nor does it mean anything insofar as Thallo-

nian law goes. According to that law, if an off-worlder marries a Thallonian, she has limited legal status as a citizen for as long as the marriage continues. If the marriage ends, the status of citizen doesn't stay with the off-world partner."

"My marriage didn't 'end.' My husband was murdered!"

"Till death do you part. There's no distinction made based on the nature of a marriage's end; just the fact of it."

"Wait . . ." It was almost more than she could grasp. "Are you telling me that, according to Thallonian law, the Protectorate has more right to raise my child than I do?"

"Basically, yes."

"Who the hell wrote that stupid law?"

"Your late husband."

Robin felt as if she'd been hit in the face with a brick. "Oh," was all she managed to say.

"In his defense, he probably didn't write it; just signed off on it. Furthermore, I doubt he was thinking about any offspring of his own. It was clearly a politically motivated law designed to—"

"I don't give a damn what the motivation was!" she said angrily, and then reined herself in. "Sorry, Captain. I . . . had no business shouting . . ."

"It's all right," he assured her. *"It's an understatement*

to say that you have a lot on your mind. Xyon, are you clear of New Thallonian space?"

"Crossed over the border about twenty minutes ago. Doesn't mean they won't try to follow us," and he shrugged, "but if they do, I'll give them the slip. I'm good at that."

"Yes, I remember. All right: If we get involved, the Protectorate is going to sell it to Starfleet that you're kidnapping a Thallonian citizen of royal blood. If we provide aid and comfort, it's tantamount to an act of war."

"They're going to accuse me of kidnapping my own child?" Her head was whirling with the thought.

"That's exactly right. So if I take you in here on the Ex-calibur . . ."

"Captain, I fully understand where you're going with this. If you don't want to stick your head into the noose—"

"Are you joking, Robin? I've stuck my head into the noose so many times, I have rope burns on my throat."

She smiled at that despite the seriousness of the situation.

"I just wanted to warn you what we're likely up for, and up against. What I'm trying to say is that, if you thought you're going to be safe here, you may be disappointed."

"Maybe. But I have nothing to go back to on New

Thallon. I only really cared about three things there. One of them is dead, and the other two are on this ship. The only other place in my life where I've ever been happy was on the *Excalibur*. So if it's all the same to you, sir, I'd . . ." Her voice caught for a moment. She cleared her throat and continued, "I'd like to come home."

"I believe," he said solemnly, *"that that can be arranged."* He shifted his attention to Kalinda. *"What about you, Kally?"*

"What about me?"

Robin was pleased that Kalinda was responding. Maybe getting her off New Thallon was the best thing that could have happened to her.

"Do you wish to join Robin on the Excalibur? *We have plenty of room for you."*

"I could do that . . ."

"Or," Xyon suddenly said, "she could stay here with me." He had been addressing Calhoun, but now he turned to Kalinda and rested his hand on hers. "You could stay here with me," he said again.

Robin smiled to herself at that. Xyon's dedication to Kalinda had been nothing short of monumental. He had encountered her back when she literally had no idea who she was . . . eventually fell in love with her . . . then was dragged into the nightmarish circumstances surrounding Kalinda's engagement and short-lived marriage. In all that time, in all those situations—including when he had been unjustly tortured by Si Cwan himself for a crime that Xyon had no hand in—his love for Kalinda had remained unwavering. Now Si Cwan was gone, Kalinda's husband was gone, and it seemed the only thing standing between the two of them was the fragility of Kalinda's own sanity and awareness of the world around her.

Fortunately for Xyon's sanity, Kalinda seemed more than competent on that score. She put her hand atop his and said softly, "I would like that, yes. To stay here with you. I would like that very much."

It was one of the sweetest things Robin Lefler had ever seen. Xyon typically wore a bored, even cynical expression, but now that dour appearance seemed to light up in the face of Kalinda's gentle acceptance of his suggestion. Robin couldn't help thinking that Xyon might be taking on more of a challenge than he understood. The only thing predictable about Kalinda was her unpredictability. As calm and loving as her behavior seemed now, that did nothing to guarantee that she was going to remain that way.

Don't think like that. Perhaps it's all going to work out for

them. Not every relationship has to end tragically. Not every-
thing is like you and Cwan . . .

The stray thought, unwanted and unasked for, caused her eyes to sting. She blinked away the surge of wetness, bringing her forearm across her face to wipe away any tears. If Calhoun noticed—and she had every reason to assume he did, because the man missed nothing—he was at least generous enough not to comment upon it.

Cwansi touched her cheek, right where a tear had been that she had just wiped off. She knew it was purely coincidence. A child so young could not possibly respond to its mother's emotions in so direct a way. Yet she took solace from it, and even liked to entertain the notion that perhaps Kalinda could be believed, and the ghost of Si Cwan was hovering nearby, guiding his son's hand and providing comfort to his widow even from beyond the vale.

Starship Excalibur

S/he was out of danger. S/he was going to live. And yet Rulan 12 was still not coming out of hir coma, and Selar was running out of excuses.

Calhoun had praised her upon learning her prognosis that Rulan was not going to succumb. That, indeed, s/he was clearly healing. She was more than willing to accept the accolades for the achievement, but kept to herself the one detail that only she knew: Rulan's body would have healed itself even if she hadn't done a damn thing. Of that she was totally convinced.

Yet s/he wasn't coming out of hir coma, and she had no idea why.

And the captain was becoming increasingly frustrated with her apparent ignorance. Not that he blamed her for not being able to provide her answers. Calhoun fully respected her professionalism and knowledge, and was aware that she was no happier than he that she was unable to bring Rulan to consciousness, nor explain why s/he was still unresponsive. He was, however, reaching his limits regarding the patient's presence. "If you have done everything you can for hir," Calhoun had said to her, "then isn't it about time that we turned hir over to someone who might be able to do more?"

As much as she had hated to admit to it, Calhoun's argument was insufferably logical. If she truly had brought hir recovery along as far as she could, then there was no point to continuing hir stay in sickbay.

She had implored the captain to give her a final twenty-four hours with the patient before alerting Starfleet. Actually, "implore" might have been too strong a word, for she would never have been that demonstrative. But Calhoun had doubtless perceived the undercurrent of urgency in her "suggestion" that Rulan remain with them a time longer. He had scrutinized her when she had said it, those deep purple eyes examining her in such a way that she felt them peeling back her thoughts like the layers of an onion. She had never felt as uncomfortable as she did when Calhoun studied her as if he were capable of plucking the truth from her mind. "Twenty-four hours," he had finally said, "but no more."

Now, with three hours and thirty-seven minutes gone of that remaining time, Selar sat in the quarantine area that had become a second home to her. Technically there was no reason to keep hir there anymore, since all traces of radiation poisoning were gone from hir body. Nevertheless she continued to keep hir there, and none of the medtechs who worked with her had the nerve to ask her why.

The problem was that she knew she had not explored all avenues open to her. There was still one option, but she had no desire to pursue it.

Doctor Selar hated the process of the Vulcan mind meld. She simply hated it. She was perfectly capable of accomplishing it when the situation demanded it, and had done so in the past. Nevertheless, the process continued to hold extremely negative associations for her because of the traumatic experience she had years earlier. It had been her first night with her chosen mate and, deep in the throes of passion, their minds had merged as was typical for such encounters. There had been no barriers between them, physical or mental. It was at that point that her husband had suffered a massive heart attack and had died while their minds were still intertwined.

It had been as if she died along with him.

I wish I had.

It was the first time that she could recall thinking such a thing, and inwardly she recoiled at the thought. She was alive and he was dead, and it was illogical to wish that she had followed him into the abyss. Nothing would have been served by it. She would have had no opportunities to help others. Xy would never have been born . . .

And would that not have been a good thing? A preferable thing? To live as he is, racing through his existence in defiance of any sort of biological logic: What sort of life is that? Perhaps better that he had never lived at all . . .

With a force of will she shut down that line of thinking. Nothing was being accomplished, and frankly it was too painful for her.

She had forgotten the last time she had slept or had eaten. That was unusual for any Vulcan, much less Selar, since her kind had an awareness of the passage of time and of their own bodies in relation to it that other races felt bordered on the supernatural. She was starting to feel as if her mind were floating free of her head, going off and engaging in other pursuits without feeling the need to drag her body along.

You are not going to be of use to anyone this way. You should return to your quarters, lie down, get some sleep. It is illogical for you to continue in this manner.

But if you do that . . . if you go to sleep . . . it is entirely possible, given your current level of exhaustion, that you will not awaken for many hours. You have less than twenty-four hours remaining to solve the mystery of Rulan, and that may not happen if you are wasting time in slumber.

But if you do not sleep, then how much good can you do, realistically? You will encounter the law of diminishing returns, because you will be too fatigued to accomplish anything of any worth.

You are running out of time. You must overcome your antipathy and probe hir mind. It is the only chance you may have to discern where s/he was before we found hir, and perhaps understand what it is that made hir this way.

With her resolve came action. Selar rose from her chair and advanced, slowly but steadily, toward Rulan. She paused at the last moment, her fingers hovering just above Rulan's head, and then with determination she touched hir temples. Her eyes narrowed to slits. "Our minds are merging," she whispered, "merging . . ."

Her thoughts slid into hirs. She gazed into the abyss . . .

. . . and the abyss gazes back.

It is not remotely what she is expecting, for the abyss is doing more than gazing back; it is advancing upon her. And something is emerging from it, but it is not frightening, not at all, it seems quite pleasant, and patient, and even loving. It has an ethereal look to it, a translucent quality, the skin is so pale that she can practically see its musculature underneath. No, not practically. She can see its lungs expanding, or what passes for lungs, and its heart is not in the right place, which is a ridiculous thing for her to think because the heart is obviously wherever it needs to be; to some, her heart is not in the right place, either, and the creature is smiling at her, or grimacing, it is so hard to be certain. It is surrounded by a blue glow, some sort of aura, that seems to be in a constant state of flux.

Greetings, Doctor, *it says to her,* **we have been waiting for you for some time. We thought you would resort to this much sooner than now. We had not reckoned with your reluctance to employ the mental techniques so common to your kind.**

Who are you? What are you? *She does not speak it aloud, even though her impulse is to do so, because she is limited in her thoughts, so limited, she had not realized quite how limited she was until she confronted this being, this creature, this whatever-it-is . . .*

Do you not know who I am?

No. I have no idea. You act as if I should recognize you.

You should, for you have desired me ever so long. My dear Doctor: I am hope.

Hope?

I am the key to your salvation. To your son's salvation. I am the miracle that you have been praying for.

I do not pray. It is a passive and unscientific pursuit to express desires to an unseen presence that wishes will be fulfilled. I depend upon my own resourcefulness, thank you.

And how has your resourcefulness served your son thus far?

It is a cutting question, but not asked unkindly. She knows the answer, and worse, she knows that this being, this creature, this thing, also knows the answer.

Who are you and what are you? You have not told me.

Nor will we yet, except in a way that will be relevant to your immediate needs and to ours as well. Rulan was acting on our behalf.

On yours? In what capacity?

That is our concern, not yours. What you must concern yourself with is returning hir to us.

Returning hir . . . ?

Yes. You must bring hir to a world on the

outer rim. Hir and one other. Your star charts designate it as AF1963. An unremarkable world, insofar as your kind is concerned. Only there will your questions be answered.

This is absurd—

Life is absurd, my child. The monumental number of things that must happen to bring any single creature into existence can only be termed absurd. Against that consideration, is what I am suggesting any less absurd than the fact that your magnificent son will live a tragically short time . . . unless you do something about it? The means to save him lies before you, Selar. S/he is the key, and my brethren and I are the only ones who can unlock it for you.

And I am supposed to go to Captain Calhoun and ask him to divert the ship to the outer rim?

No. You must make the voyage on your own.

That is ridiculous. How am I supposed to find a vessel to take me all that distance?

You will find a way. If you value your son's life, you will find a way.

Is that a threat? Are you threatening me?

Telling you what will happen is no threat. It is simply a promise of what is to come.

She pauses. She considers what he is saying. She knows she should reject it. She should walk—run—to the captain and tell him what is happening. Tell him about the vision. The things this being is saying . . . it is illogical to listen to any of it. To believe it. He could be saying what he thinks she wants to hear in order to achieve his own ends.

This is a trap.

This is absurd.

But . . .

But her son is dying. His life is flashing before her eyes, and she has explored every other reasonable, practical, logical avenue. It may well be that the staggeringly illogical is the only thing left to her.

It makes no sense to embark on some mad adventure in the hopes of saving Xy. But the alternative is to stand by and do nothing. What sort of healer would that make her? What sort of mother?

The biology of the Hermat stretched out on the table before her has defied analysis. She has extracted cells from hir body, attempted to study the replication, and the cells shriveled and died the moment they were separated from the host body. She has tried and failed, and her son cannot live with her failure, cannot live, cannot live . . .

You know what you must do. You know.

Something clicks into place in her mind, like a switch being flipped. Considerations of right and wrong become secondary to logistics. Her worldview seems to shrink down until it is a narrow tunnel, with a desolate world on the outer rim at the other end.

You know.

Not everything. You said I must bring Rulan and one other. What one other? Xy?

No. The infant Cwan. The child whom you delivered into the world with your hands, you must now deliver to us.

How am I supposed to do that?

Events are transpiring to give you the opportunity. The rest is up to you.

But what if—

There is only one question remaining for you to ask, and it is not to be asked of us, but of yourself. And that question is simply this: How much do you love your son?

I . . .

How much?

She is trembling, out of control, and she—

"Doctor!"

Selar started awake so violently that she slammed her head against the back of the quarantine partition, which shuddered from the impact. The world swam around her for a moment and then she pulled herself together with her customary discipline and looked around. She was surprised to see that she was on the opposite side of the quarantine room, seated in her chair. She was nowhere near Rulan, which was damned strange considering she had thought she was standing over him, in the middle of a mind meld.

"Doctor Selar, are you okay?" It was a medtech, a middle-aged man named Janssen, looking down at her with concern.

"Why would you think I was not?" she said. She rubbed the back of her head. There was a slight ache from when she had struck it.

"Well . . . you had fallen asleep, which you hadn't done before. And then you were shaking your head back and forth . . . and then suddenly you started nodding your head. It was all kind of strange and—"

"And it seems to me," she said stiffly, "that you must have far too little to do around here if you have enough time to stand around and do nothing but watch me sleep for an extended period."

"I was just—"

"Go on about your business. I require neither your observation nor your ministrations."

He paused, looking as if he wanted to argue the

point some more. But he just shrugged and said, "Yes, Doctor." Janssen walked away, leaving Selar studying the motionless body of Rulan.

Slowly she rose from her seat, approaching Rulan tentatively, as if concerned that s/he would explode if Selar made any sudden movement. She raised her hand, brought it over Rulan's head, her fingers hovering inches from hir forehead.

You know what you must do.

She lowered her hand and closed her eyes. She took a deep, cleansing breath, let it out slowly, and when she opened her eyes once more, a universe that had seemed chaotic and random and brutally unfair now appeared to make sense once more.

No mind meld was necessary.

No doubt was necessary.

Only three things were necessary: Rulan, whom she had; a vessel, which she did not have; and the infant Cwan, whom she did not have.

Once she had all three, she would do what needed to be done. There was no question. Something deep within her mind endeavored to sound an alarm, but it was quickly and efficiently batted aside.

She would save the life of her son no matter what.

No mother could do any less.

Starfleet Headquarters

Edward Jellico rubbed the bridge of his nose and tried to fight down the beginnings of something that had become all too familiar when dealing with Mackenzie Calhoun: a pounding headache behind the eyeballs.

"You're killing me, Mac. You really are. You're taking years off my life."

"Come on, Ed," said Calhoun over the viewscreen.

"It's true. I can feel them withering away every time something new comes up with you."

"Yes but, to be fair, they probably weren't going to be terribly productive years. I'm likely doing you a favor."

Jellico would have started thudding his head against the walls of his office if he hadn't thought it would have been woefully inappropriate for a Starfleet Admiral to do so. Deciding to approach this budding debacle from a different direction, he said, "Where is she now?"

"She's just been brought aboard."

"Who brought her?"

"I'd rather not say."

That response indicated two possibilities to Jellico. Either it had been the work of Soleta, Calhoun's former science officer, who had defected to the Romulan Empire and was now working as an independent operator, or else it was Calhoun's son, Xyon. Jellico's instinct was that it was the latter, especially considering his history with Kalinda. The initial reports that he had received from the outraged New Thallonian Protectorate Council were vague and confused about who had removed Robin, Kalinda, and the infant from New Thallon. Reading between the lines, though, further verified Jellico's suspicions.

"All right. Fine. Don't tell me. I can take some educated guesses, but it doesn't matter. How . . ." He paused and then mentally shrugged. There was no reason he couldn't extend the simple courtesies. "How are mother and son doing? And aunt for that matter?"

"They're doing fine. Glad to be somewhere safe."

"New Thallon is safe."

"Not according to my s—" Calhoun caught himself and then said, *"—my sources."*

That pretty much verified for Jellico that it had been Xyon. "The Council indicates that there was no reason for Robin to leave the planet. That the attack was undertaken without the Council's permission or sanction."

"Yes, I just bet it was."

"They are willing to guarantee her safety from here on, but only if you return them to New Thallon immediately."

"Admiral, that's—"

The screen suddenly went blank.

If Calhoun had not been in mid-sentence, Jellico would have thought that he had severed the connection. It wouldn't have been Calhoun's style; he wasn't one to flee from confrontations. In fact, he tended to thrive on them. He tapped his combadge. "Lieutenant," he said, "raise me the *Excalibur* again." Nothing. He frowned. "Lieutenant?" Still no answer. "What the hell—?" he muttered and got up from behind his desk.

"Sit down," came a crisp female voice over his combadge.

Jellico stopped where he was, halfway up from

his chair, gripping the armrests. He looked at his combadge as if it were not the one he had placed onto his uniform tunic that morning. "Who is this?"

"You're not sitting."

"How do you—?" He looked at the viewscreen to see if someone was looking in at him, but the screen remained off.

"Asking questions isn't going to get you anywhere."

"All right," said Jellico cautiously. He sat, although his hands remained upon the armrests. He reasoned that a voice couldn't pose any real threat. "What do you want?"

The air in front of Jellico shimmered briefly and the familiar form of a black-haired woman materialized. She glanced at her hands appraisingly, then at the rest of her body. "Nice holoprojector, Admiral. When did you have it installed?"

His lips thinned. "Morgan Primus. I should have known."

"Yes. You should have," she said crisply. "You didn't answer my question."

"As it so happens, I don't believe I'm required to answer your questions, Morgan. . . . Miss Primus."

"Please. We're friends here. 'Morgan' will do."

"You were just barking orders at me," said Jellico. "What could possibly make you think that we're friends?"

"You bark orders at people. Are you saying you don't have any friends?"

"I have friends," he said in annoyance, and then was even more annoyed that he had let that emotion show.

"How about children?"

"You're a computer entity. You can access Federation personnel records easily enough. You tell me if I have children."

"One. A daughter. How nice for you. I have a daughter as well. Perhaps you remember her? Robin Lefler. The one that you are trying to execute a death sentence upon."

"I think you're overreacting."

"And I think I'm right, and since I'm her mother, and I'm also insinuated into the mainframe of the Starfleet computer core, I have to believe that what I think is going to carry some weight."

His gaze burrowed into her. "Is that supposed to be a threat?"

"No," she said. "A threat would be: Leave my daughter alone or with a passing thought I will bring the entire United Federation of Planets crashing down around your ears. I didn't say anything like that."

"You're bluffing. Even you're not that powerful."

She smiled. "So you say."

"I was in the middle of speaking to Captain Calhoun," Jellico said.

"Yes. And now you're in the middle of speaking to me."

"Are we speaking? I'm not certain that we are. Thus far all you've done is lecture me, treating me in a manner that is inappropriate to one of my rank—"

"What if it were your daughter?"

The question caught him unprepared. "What?"

"What if it were your daughter who was being threatened? Your grandson who was on the verge of being taken away by strangers? How would you feel then?"

"The Council has assured me—"

"The Council is full of it," she said tartly. "They will say whatever they think is necessary to get the son of Cwan back in their clutches. So the only question before us is whether Starfleet is going to aid and abet them."

"I believe there are a good many questions aside from that one—"

"None that matter. Not to Robin and not to me, and I really don't give a damn if they matter to you."

"Yes, you've made that abundantly clear." He started to stand and then paused and said sarcastically, "Is my standing acceptable to you?"

"I assume you feel the need because you're uncomfortable with my standing and looking down at you."

"Assume whatever you want." Jellico got to his feet. He went around the desk so that he was a short distance from her. "Just out of curiosity, Morgan, how do you see this ending?"

"With you allowing my daughter to go on her way unmolested, to raise her son in peace, rather than making her the pawn in a power struggle."

"Leaving us to clean up the mess. To tell the New Thallonian Council that yes, we have reason to believe that their runaway prime minister and the heir to a powerful family are fleeing aboard one of our starships, but that they should just leave her and her son the hell alone, because otherwise we're going to anger the baby's all-powerful grandmother?"

She seemed to be considering it. "It's you who said it."

He leaned against the desk. The pounding behind his eyeballs was becoming more pronounced.

"Look . . . Morgan . . . believe it or not, I'm sympathetic about the situation here."

"I'm leaning toward 'or not' but I'm willing to be convinced."

"Morgan," said Jellico slowly, "I'm not stupid. It's obvious that the New Thallonian Council will try to cast this in the best possible light for itself. Furthermore, I know Robin Lefler. She's not someone who runs from a challenge. So if she had to flee New Thallon, I'm thinking she had no choice and, furthermore, I figure that she did it to protect her son. And if she thinks there's something he needs to be protected *from,* well . . . let's just say that I would tend to trust her judgment on the matter."

"That's good to hear," said Morgan.

"However," he said, before she could get too relaxed, "the harsh truth is that there are politics involved here. We're walking a fine line."

"In other words, you have to act as if what the Council is saying may be true even though you know it to be false."

"Not 'other words.' Those are exactly the correct words."

"So . . . what do we do?"

He raised an eyebrow. "You're asking me? A computer entity that can access billions of bits of information in a second, and you're actually turning to a mere human being for answers?"

"I'm not seeking answers, Admiral. Believe it or not, having that degree of access to all that information simply makes clear to me a harsh fact: There are no answers. No definitive ones, at any rate. Just more questions. Furthermore, you keep referring to me as a 'computer entity.' I wasn't always. You know that. I was a living, breathing person before I wound up getting my engrams imprinted into the *Excalibur,* and I have all the same worries and concerns that I had before I arrived in this state."

"Meaning?"

"Meaning that when it comes to my daughter, I freely admit I may not always be thinking straight. And my not being able to think straight can be very dangerous for all concerned."

"And by 'all' . . ."

"I mean 'all.' Every sentient being in the Federation."

Jellico took a moment to consider that, and all its implications. "And here I thought Calhoun was a potent negotiator."

For a long moment, neither of them said anything.

"We don't need Earth in anyone's sights right now," Jellico said finally. "It's the base point of both Starfleet and Federation headquarters. If Robin returns now— at least for the immediate future—it's going to seem as if we're taking sides. And we need to remain neutral, at least for the time being."

"She's an Earth woman. Earth is her home."

"She hasn't set foot on Earth in years, and for that matter, neither have you. So don't start playing the nostalgia card for terra firma because that's not going to fly with me."

"Fair enough," she said after a brief pause. The response surprised Jellico a bit. He hadn't expected her to relent so readily, which led him to believe that she had already come to the same conclusion. "What about the *Excalibur*? Are you going to order her to return Robin to New Thallon?"

"Not at this point, if for no other reason than issuing orders to Mackenzie Calhoun is a dicey proposition at best. If he has decided to accommodate Robin Lefler and entourage . . ."

"Which he has."

"Then I don't seriously expect that he's going to turn around and return her to a situation he deems hazardous simply on my say-so." He shook his head.

"It's frustrating, though. Thallonian space remains a volatile, even incendiary area. Your daughter was exactly the right person in the right place to keep a lid on it."

"I agree. And if her dead husband hadn't left her pregnant, she'd be there now. But as they say, it is what it is, Admiral, and right now the best interests of her son would require her to be elsewhere."

"It would be better if I did not know where that elsewhere was."

"She's not planning to stay on the *Excalibur* indefinitely, if that's what you mean."

"That is what I mean. And when she does leave, it would be far better if neither I nor anyone in Starfleet knew where she had gone."

"Arranging for someone to live off the grid in this day and age isn't the easiest of missions."

"Perhaps. But since her mother, for all intents and purposes, *is* the grid, it might be easier for her than most."

"Yes," said Morgan with a smile. "I suppose it would be at that."

"Ironic, isn't it?"

"Isn't what?"

"When I first met Si Cwan, he was an exiled ruler.

A man who was seeking to reclaim the power that he felt was his by birthright. And now he leaves behind a son who is essentially going to be in the exact same predicament his father was."

"Yet his father eventually returned to his people and reclaimed that birthright."

"Yes, he did. And look how it turned out for him."

"Good point," she admitted. "So . . . we have an understanding then?"

"It appears we do. For what it's worth, however, I think you should know that I've agreed to nothing that I wasn't already prepared to do before you so rudely interrupted the conversation I was having with Captain Calhoun. You may not believe me—"

"I do, Admiral. I do believe you." She laughed softly. "I know you, Admiral. In your own way, you can be as damned stubborn as Mackenzie Calhoun ever was. That's probably why there was such antipathy between the two of you for so long. You were two sides of the same coin. There's no way that I could have simply come in here and strong-armed you into doing something that you weren't already prepared to do."

"If that's the case, then why did you do all this? Why the confrontation?"

"Because, Admiral, being a computer entity, I'm able to see many possibilities. And allowing for the possibility that I was wrong in my estimation of you, and that you might do something unanticipated—which humans tend to do on occasion—I simply thought it would be wise to make my case in person. Just to drive the point home."

"The point being?"

All the lights in Jellico's office promptly went out. His computer screen went blank, all power shut down. There were startled exclamations audible from adjacent rooms. His aide called his name and banged on the door, which was immobilized without power.

"I think it speaks for itself, actually," came Morgan's voice, sounding calm and detached and all the more threatening because of that.

Seconds later, the lights came up. Jellico's computer screen flared to life. Morgan Primus was gone.

The door to his office slid-open as if nothing had gone wrong, and his aide was standing there, looking concerned. "Admiral, are you all right?"

"Fine, Lieutenant. Just fine," Jellico said.

"Are you sure?"

"Yes, Lieutenant."

"Very well, sir. Oh . . . and Captain Calhoun is

calling in. He said your previous conversation was cut off?"

Jellico hesitated, and then said, "Inform the captain that nothing further needs to be discussed. That in this instance, the less I know about his actions, the better."

His aide frowned. He had never heard Jellico say anything remotely of that nature before. "Admiral—?"

"Just say it exactly that way, Lieutenant. Carry on."

"Yes, sir," his aide said.

"And inform Admiral Nechayev that I need to see her. We have a bit of a situation that I think she needs to be apprised of."

"Regarding Captain Calhoun, sir?"

"Actually, it's regarding his computer."

"I don't understand, sir."

"It's probably better that you don't, Lieutenant."

Starship Excalibur

"Nothing further needs to be *discussed*?" Burgoyne could do nothing to disguise the incredulity in hir voice. "Are you sure it was the admiral who said that?"

"Those were his aide's exact words," said Calhoun.

They were sitting in the conference lounge, digesting the specifics of Calhoun's aborted conversation with Admiral Jellico. Also grouped around the table were Doctor Selar, Kebron, and Robin Lefler, cradling her son in her arms. Calhoun could not recall seeing Robin lay the child down even for a moment in the entire time she had been aboard the *Excalibur*. He supposed he couldn't blame her. After everything she had gone through, she had probably developed a healthy degree of paranoia. Perhaps she felt that if she took her eyes off Cwansi for even a second, he would be seized by conspirators and carried away. How difficult it must be for her not to feel safe anywhere, even on the *Excalibur*.

"So . . . do I return to Earth?"

"You don't want to do that."

Robin jumped slightly because it had been her mother who had spoken up. Morgan had appeared out of nowhere, as she tended to do. Calhoun watched Morgan suspiciously, still uncertain what to expect of her.

Morgan gently reached over and stroked her daughter's hair. "How are you holding up, Robin?" The concern she expressed for her daughter made Morgan sound like her old self, giving Calhoun hope that the aberrant behavior he'd witnessed earlier was a thing of the past. Perhaps Robin's presence had served to reorient Morgan, or at least steady her.

"Doing fine, Mother."

Cwansi was sleeping. "My grandson," said Morgan lovingly, sounding just like any proud grandmother. "Isn't he beautiful, Captain?"

"He is," said Calhoun. "And we have to determine now where would be the best place for him."

"As long as he's with his mother, it can be anywhere and it doesn't matter."

"So then I can take him to Earth," said Robin.

"Anywhere except there," said Morgan.

"Mother!"

"No, she's probably right," said Calhoun.

"*Captain!*"

"The Federation is going to want to avoid being caught in the middle. That means trying to keep you as far from Earth as possible, at least for the time being," Calhoun replied.

"I—" She was about to respond, but then she clearly thought better of it. "No. You're right. That makes sense."

"So she should remain aboard the *Excalibur* then," said Kebron. "This has been her home."

"No. That was never an option," Robin said.

"It was always an option," Burgoyne said.

"Not for me. What purpose would I serve here?"

"We would find a place for you here, no matter what your status."

"Thank you, Burgy, but let's face facts: This is a Starfleet vessel, and I'm no longer a member of Starfleet. And if I return in an official capacity," she said quickly, before anyone else could suggest it, "then I'm just putting Starfleet into the same bind as my presence on Earth would. I can't stay here. For that matter, I shouldn't. Kalinda is at least trying to build herself a new life with Xyon. I think I should be following her lead. Find my own way."

"Bravo station," said Selar.

She had been so quiet for the entirety of the gathering that there was surprise on the faces of everyone else, save for Kebron, whose physiognomy wasn't exactly conducive to a variety of expressions.

"Bravo station?" Calhoun echoed her.

"Yes, Captain. Although Starfleet personnel run the day-to-day operations, that is simply a matter of convenience. Bravo station has no political allegiance and exists in neutral territory. Both Federation and nonaligned races use it as a port of call, and there are quite a few families in residence there, serving the main marketplace and various businesses that cater to those passing through. The Lady Cwan," she used Robin's formal title, "and her son would be able to blend in easily with the multiracial population. Furthermore, the bulk of the station is wired for holography, meaning that she would have continued access to her mother's presence. Your wife, Admiral Elizabeth Shelby, currently commands Bravo, so there would be that familiar face as well."

"It makes sense," Burgoyne said. S/he was smiling approvingly at Selar, and Calhoun couldn't blame hir. It was the first time in ages that Selar had spoken without a tinge of anger or bitterness in her voice. Granted, there was no trace of any emotion at all, but that wasn't all that startling for a Vulcan. Actually, she sounded less emotional than ever, almost as if she were speaking robotically. But Calhoun didn't give it any further thought, reasoning that at least she was putting forward worthwhile suggestions rather than stewing over her son's situation.

"It does make sense," said Calhoun. "You could stay there for as long as you needed to in order to get your footing. And if an opportunity presented itself— a job on a colony world, or someplace else where you could effectively blend in, disappear—you could depart Bravo station with no fuss. There are passenger vessels going in and out all the time."

"Yes. Sure. All right," said Robin. "It would be great to see the admiral again. I haven't seen her since . . ." Her voice trailed off.

"Si Cwan's death," said Kebron helpfully. When he realized that everyone was glaring at him, he said, "Don't give me that look. Refusing to talk about a difficult subject doesn't lessen the pain."

"Zak's right," Robin said, and she reached over and patted the top of Kebron's huge hand. "I haven't seen her since Si Cwan's death. So visiting her with a bundle of life seems exactly the best way to reintroduce myself."

"All right," said Calhoun with a smile. "Morgan, set course for Bravo station. Kebron, raise Admiral Shelby on subspace so I can tell her we're on the way. Everyone else, to your stations. Doctor," he said as everyone began to rise, "good thinking."

"Thank you, Captain."

"Oh, and while we're there, we can drop off Rulan 12. From my understanding, you've done everything you can for hir. Shelby can arrange for hir transport to a Starfleet medical facility." He paused and then said, "That is acceptable to you, I hope."

There was no hesitation as she said, "Of course, Captain. It is the only logical way in which to proceed."

There was something in her voice that abruptly twanged a chord of concern in Calhoun's mind, but he wasn't exactly sure what was prompting it. Since he had nothing concrete upon which to base his worries, he decided it would be preferable if, for the moment, he said nothing. He did, however, remain in the conference lounge until after everyone had left, at which point he called out, "Morgan!"

The ops officer promptly reappeared. "Yes, Captain? Are you checking to make sure we're on course for Bravo station? Because I can assure you—"

"Shut up."

Morgan looked surprised, even taken aback, but she did nothing except close her mouth with an audible *click*.

Calhoun got up from his chair and came around the table toward her. His voice was low and flat, a sure indicator that he was extremely angry. Calhoun was someone who became quieter in proportion to the ire he was feeling. In this instance he was speaking barely above a whisper. "Did you think I was stupid? That I wouldn't figure it out?"

"Captain, I have no idea what—"

"You went to the admiral. You went to the admiral behind my back and had a little conversation. Made some threats too, did you?"

"Captain, I don't know what Jellico told you . . ."

"I didn't say Jellico," Calhoun immediately pounced. "I just said 'the admiral.' Is Jellico the one you went to?"

"He's not who I went to."

"So you did go to someone."

"No, I—"

Then she scowled, her face becoming darker, like a storm rolling in across a roiling sea. "It's moments such as this," she said with visible annoyance, "that I regret having any human components left to me. I can think a million times faster than you. There is simply no way that you should be able to outthink me in these matters, and yet . . ."

"And yet," he said with no trace of amusement.

"How did you know?"

"Because it's my job to know. See the patterns that other people miss. You're the reason that I lost the signal to the admiral. That took me no time at all to figure out. Especially when, once we reestablished contact, he had changed his mind. Something happened during that interval, and my guess was that that something was you. Did you threaten him?"

"Not in so many words."

"How many, then?"

"Seventy. I emphasize again, though, there was nothing overt. Simply implied."

"You cannot do that, Morgan. It is inexcusable."

"I'm not looking for it to be excused. I had to protect my daughter."

"And she's my friend. Don't you think I would protect her as well?"

"Not the way I can."

His eyes glittered with barely controlled fury. "I will not have you circumventing my authority, Morgan. You are never to do something like this again."

"Or *what*?"

There was dead silence then, their gazes locked upon each other, and then Morgan looked down. "I apologize, Captain. Not for what I did. I will do anything I need to in order to protect Robin. But I regret the manner in which I did it. I should not have undermined your authority. There will be no recurrence." She paused. "May I leave now?"

"Dismissed," he said curtly.

She vanished once more. Yet long after she was gone, Calhoun stood there, as motionless as a statue. There was no question in his mind that he had a major situation on his hands, and he had to believe that—to some degree—he had brought it upon himself. Having Morgan as part of the ship's computer had been a tremendous advantage until now, combining the instincts of a human mind with the processing power of a computer. But, thanks to the trauma she had suffered from the incident months earlier, she had changed . . . and not for the better. The potential for abuse, for her to become something dangerous, had always been there. But he had turned a blind eye to it for as long as he was benefiting from her status. Now that blind eye had put them into an untenable position, and he had no answers for it.

That wasn't quite true. He had one answer for it.

He was going to have to find some way to eliminate Morgan.

She had lost her mortal existence once, and a bizarre series of events had granted her a second life.

Now he was going to have to undo that, exorcise the ghost from the machine.

He just didn't have the faintest idea how.

The *Spectre*

Soleta, the commander of the Romulan spy ship *Spectre,* had drifted to sleep, her hand resting on the chest of her lover and partner, Lucius. Typically at such times, after expending energy in carnal pursuits, Lucius would fall asleep as well.

This time, he did not.

He had no idea why that was, why he was just lying there staring at the ceiling. And he found it disturbing that he had no idea. Lucius prided himself on knowing his own mind at all times. He felt it was his responsibility, considering that Soleta so often appeared not to know hers. Initially he had found that disconcerting. If anything, he would have thought that Soleta would be far more logical and rational than the typical Romulan, thanks to her Vulcan blood and generally Vulcan upbringing. Then again, perhaps her unpredictability was related to that volatile mix. She had been raised a Vulcan, discovered her Romulan heritage, been rejected by Starfleet to which she had devoted her life, and then had watched the Romulan Empire crumble around her. All things considered, it was remarkable that she had held herself together as well as she had. Perhaps, Lucius thought, he should contemplate her shortcomings less, and should instead wonder why he remained so rock steady. Maybe she was the one who was more realistic in her outlook on things.

Lucius eased his feet out of the bed and stepped barefoot onto the floor, which felt unusually cold. He tossed on a robe. It was just he and Soleta on the ship, so what was the point in putting on his uniform? Nor did they have a rendezvous set up anytime soon; they were between assignments.

As he walked through the ship, he pondered the odd direction his life had taken. Never in a million years would he have expected that he and Soleta would become lovers, considering that he thought very little of her when she was given command of the *Spectre,* and even less of her when he had led a mutiny against her. On the other hand, because of that mutiny, the notion that they would wind up together must have seemed even stranger to Soleta than it was to him.

Lucius had never been a big believer in any sort of divine plan. Yet he found himself wondering about the unlikelihood of Soleta and him winding up together. Perhaps there was something to be said for an unseen hand manipulating them, drawing unlikely elements together. Certainly there seemed no rational explanation for it otherwise.

You would be amazed.

He jumped so high that he nearly struck his head on the low ceiling. The fleeting thought had not been his own, and it seemed so unreal that at first he thought he might in fact be asleep and still dreaming. When he landed he did so badly, thudding down on his right heel, sending a shiver of pain up his leg. It would cause no lasting damage, but it was enough to confirm for him that, yes indeed, he was in fact awake.

He looked around, trying to tell himself that it hadn't been in his head but instead someone speaking to him from close by. Who they were and how they could possibly have gained entrance into the ship were questions he would get to in short order. For now he just needed to determine what was happening.

You will not find us by looking out, but rather by looking inward, my child.

Lucius was in no mood to be patronized by a voice

in his own head. He briefly considered waking Soleta but discarded the notion. Awaken her and tell her what? That he was hearing voices?

He stopped at a wall panel and touched it with his thumb. It snapped open and there was a disruptor inside. He withdrew it, thumbed it to its highest setting, and kept going.

Within moments, he was on the bridge. That was the first thing he needed to secure. If there was indeed some sort of invader on the vessel, then he had to make sure the nerve center of the ship remained untouched. There was no one there, however. The ship's computer hummed along, calmly keeping the ship floating in space, with the cloaking device concealing them from passersby. The auto-nav was on standby so that, in the extremely unlikely event that another ship showed up out of nowhere and was on a collision course, the computer would guide the *Spectre* out of its way.

"Where are you?" demanded Lucius.

Right here.

Lucius jumped back as a glowing blue image of a translucent being appeared on the viewscreen. And then, as Lucius watched in slack-jawed astonishment, the being appeared to step right out of the screen and onto the bridge. Its arms were folded in a relaxed manner, and it smiled beatifically.

There is no need for you to be startled.

"With all deference to whoever you are or whatever you are supposed to be, I believe there is every need for me to be startled," he said. "People sending messages into my head or stepping off the viewscreen is hardly an everyday occurrence around here."

You will not need that. The being gestured toward the disruptor that Lucius held tightly.

"If it's all the same to you, I'll be the judge of that."

The being appeared to shrug. It was an oddly normal gesture for something so abnormal to make. **As you wish.**

"Who are you?"

Our name is unimportant.

"If that were the case, then you'd think nothing of telling it to me."

You make a valid enough point, but nothing will be gained by arguing it at present. Listen carefully, Lucius, because there is not much time. Soleta is stirring.

"You keep away from her . . ."

She is not relevant to the matter at hand, my child. You are. Your cooperation is required.

"For what? What are you talking about?"

You must take the *Spectre* to Bravo station.

"Bravo station?" Lucius slowly circled the translucent being, unable to tear his eyes from the sight of the creature's innermost workings. "The Federation space station, you mean? Why would I need to go there?"

You are going to pick up passengers. A woman and a child.

"Oh, am I now."

The decision is up to you, but it would be advisable that you comply, for they are a very special woman and child.

"Special in what sense?"

Special in terms of what they represent to you.

"I don't understand."

The creature's mouth was not moving: It continued to smile. **Words are so cumbersome. It will be simpler to show you.**

"Show me? What do you mean—?"

and images explode in his head, so many that at first it is impossible for him to sort them out. One overlays the next and he is convinced that his skull is going to explode, his brain is going to melt into liquid streams and come pouring out his ears and then suddenly the images begin to sort themselves out, become coherent and comprehensible, but they still fly past him, and there are people he does not recognize; he senses that they are important somehow but cannot discern their specific importance in the grand scheme, although one does stand out for him: a Vulcan woman, and she is holding a child with a curious skin tone; she is looking right at him, and then she is gone as the world continues to spin around him, and then he sees what he realizes he is meant to see . . .

It is he. He sits upon a throne with decorations that he recognizes immediately, the throne of the praetor of the Romulans. He is leaning on one elbow and smiling in a smug, satisfied manner that is so very typical for him.

He is the praetor. He has ascended to the throne, and he has taken the future of the Romulans in his hands and secured it; he does not know how he can be certain of it from only that quick image flashing through his consciousness, but he is . . .

Yes. What you see is what will happen if you bring the *Spectre* to Bravo station.

"You mean this is some sort of offer you're holding out? Am I supposed to believe—?"

Not an offer. Not any sort of reward. This is a vision of truth. Circumstances will be set into motion by your actions that will lead to this inevitable conclusion. Most men wish that they

had some control of their destiny. In this case, you do. You will be able to steer your fate toward an enviable conclusion.

"How do I know—?"

You do know. Look into yourself. You know that what I have shown you is the truth.

And he does. He does not know how he knows it, but part of his mind is shouting at him that he is allowing himself to be duped, that even his innermost beliefs are being influenced and controlled, but he does not care because he wants so much for it to be true that to think otherwise is simply not an option . . .

You believe.

"Yes. Yes, I believe."

Then do something about it.

He is trembling, out of control and . . .

"Lucius!"

He sat up abruptly and was astounded to discover that he was in bed next to Soleta. It was she who had spoken. She had one hand on his shoulder and had been shaking him, obviously concerned. "What's wrong?" she said. "You were trembling in your sleep. You never tremble."

"In my sleep?" He was utterly bewildered. "I was on the bridge."

"The bridge? No."

"It was not a dream, Soleta." He turned to look at her and, out of habit, brushed stray strands of hair from her face. "I had a vision."

"A *vision*?" Clearly she had no idea what to make of that. "Lucius, you have no history of psychic ability that I'm aware of. So it's asking quite a bit to accept that you're suddenly clairvoyant . . ."

"I am not claiming clairvoyance. I am saying that I had some sort of encounter."

"With whom?"

"I don't know."

"Lucius, this is ridiculous . . ."

He gripped her by both arms and said intently, "Soleta. You were a scientist. Surely you have to admit that anything is possible. And if an unknown intelligence chose to make contact with me in this manner, is that so impossible?"

"I do not, in fact, admit anything is possible. There are any number of things that are precluded by the laws of physics, for example."

"Don't pick apart my statements, Soleta."

Despite Lucius's best efforts, her hair had once again fallen in her face. She blew some of it out of the way. "I'm not trying to pick apart anything. I'm just trying to make sense out of it. Very well, if you cannot tell me who appeared to you in this so-called vision, can you provide me any details at all?"

"Yes. We need to go to Bravo station."

"Bravo station? Why?"

Because I will become praetor if we do.

"I do not know."

"Lucius! Of all the—"

"Soleta," he said with quiet urgency, "this is important. I cannot tell you how I know that it is. But it is. If you have any faith in me, any trust in me—"

"Don't frame it that way," she said, annoyance in her voice. She scratched the side of her nose. "Don't put me in that position." She leaned back and stared at him. "This is insane, what you're asking, you realize. I'm supposed to believe that a vivid dream was an alien encounter and, because of that, head to Bravo station for no particular reason."

"Not quite. There *is* a particular reason. The particular reason is that I am asking you to."

"All right. Fine."

"Truly?"

"Truly," she affirmed. "Let me get dressed and we'll get up to the bridge."

"I think," and he brought his arm across her chest,

brushing against her, "that acting on my vision can wait a little while longer."

She sighed at the contact. "I agree. Unless your alien visitor wishes to put in an appearance and say otherwise."

"Let him try," he said, and brought his lips down upon hers.

The *Lyla*

i.

Xyon brought his lips down upon Kalinda's mouth, kissing her with unreserved ferocity. Then he pulled her clothing from her and she uttered one word and one word only: "Yes."

All of this happened for the fifth time in the course of an hour, and all of it happened in Xyon's head. The reality was very different.

"Can I get you anything, Kalinda?" he said. Even as he asked, he mentally kicked himself. He'd lost track of the number of times he'd made that query since she'd come aboard, and he must have sounded like a complete idiot by now.

If she shared that opinion of him, Kalinda didn't indicate it. Instead, seated in the copilot's seat of the *Lyla,* she smiled in a manner that nearly melted Xyon's heart as she said, "I'm quite all right, Xyon. But I appreciate the offer. When do we rendezvous with the Ferengi smuggler?"

He was relieved that she had so promptly and deftly steered the conversation toward something practical. Normally he would have addressed the question to Lyla, who would have happily supplied the answer. But with Kalinda on the vessel, he was beginning to feel a bit self-conscious about Lyla's presence, especially considering the uses to which he had put her. Granted, it hadn't seemed to bother Kalinda, but still, it was . . .

"You could ask Lyla if you wanted. I don't mind."

The calmness in her tone was disconcerting. It was as if she had set up shop in his head. "That's okay," he said, and checked his chronometer. "I've got it at eighteen hours, twenty-seven minutes."

"And the cargo we're carrying?"

"The thousand bricks of gold-pressed latinum, you mean?"

"Yes." She glanced at her feet as if she could see into the cargo bay. "It all belongs to the Ferengi?"

"That's right."

"And you're returning it to him?"

"It was stolen from him. He's paying me a finder's fee for returning it."

"As opposed to your just keeping it all for yourself."

"That would be wrong."

"So it never occurred to you to just keep it?"

He smiled. "I never said that. And once upon a time, I might well have done exactly that. But as far as I'm concerned, it's a lot easier to take things from thieves than be a thief yourself. Besides, that would then make me a target for this particular Ferengi, and that's not trouble that I need."

"Can you trust the Ferengi to give you your share?"

"No. But I've taken the liberty of already stashing my share."

"Where?"

"Sorry, my love. Need-to-know basis."

"All right, Xyon," she said calmly. She was always calm. It was almost unnatural; she might have been part Vulcan. Then, coyly, she said, "Can I see one? I've never seen a brick of gold-pressed latinum. Bars, yes, but—"

"Sure. I suppose so. Wait here."

He disappeared into the cargo bay for a few minutes and when he emerged he was carrying a brick. Her eyes widened when she saw it. "Is it heavy?"

"It's not light, but it's not terrible. Here." He handed it over to her. Standing, she lifted it experimentally.

"You're right, it's not too bad. It's very pretty."

She placed it carefully on the floor, then put her feet up on it as if it were a footrest. Xyon laughed and then settled back down into his chair.

They said nothing for a time, and then he was surprised to hear her say, "I'm sorry."

"Sorry? About what?"

"That I have not been more . . . how to put it? Demonstrative. Physically demonstrative." She rested a hand on his and said, "I know that's what you would like. What you were assuming was going to happen once I chose to come with you."

"I wasn't assuming anything—"

"Don't lie, Xyon. You're not terribly good at it, and I can see through it, so it's a little bit insulting for you even to try."

"I didn't mean to insult you."

"I know you didn't," and she squeezed his hand affectionately.

"You've been through a hell of a lot," Xyon said. "I had no intention of pushing you on anything. After all this time, I'm just happy for the pleasure of your company."

"That is so sweet. Not much more convincing than what you were saying before, but still—"

"Kalinda, for the love of—"

She brought his hand to her lips and kissed his knuckles. He sighed when she did so, enjoying the contact. Then her kisses trailed up his arm to his throat, and then to his lips. She pulled away and smiled, caressing his cheek. "Soon," she whispered. "I promise. I just need to get settled in, to feel comfortable."

"Take all the time you need. I'll be waiting. Because nothing is going to—"

Her head snapped forward so violently that it broke his nose.

"Kalinda! Grozit! What the hell—!?"

He leaped up from his seat, clutching at his nose, blood pouring from it. While applying pressure, he grabbed at the med kit that was under the control panel, yanking it out so violently that its contents spilled onto the floor. He was about to reach for the sonic cauterizer to stop the bleeding, but then he forgot about it as he saw Kalinda pressed against the wall, her body shaking, her eyes wide.

She had been so calm, so reasonable, so very much the Kalinda of old, that he had managed to forget, or at least ignore, the reason that his father had summoned him to New Thallon in the first place. Now, though, he was being presented with irrefutable proof of her delicate state of mind, because she was clearly having some sort of fit and he was helpless to do anything about it.

"Kalinda," he said even as he applied the cauterizer to the side of his nose and activated it. Immediately the bleeding stopped, although the lower half of his face was still a mess and his nose wasn't going to heal anytime soon. "Kalinda, what's wrong? Tell me what's wrong. Everything is going to be okay—"

"The baby." She sounded as if she were speaking from the next star system over. "The baby is in trouble."

"Baby? What baby? You mean Robin's baby?"

"Yes."

He wasn't about to ask her how she could possibly know this. He couldn't help but think it was better to simply take it as a given and go from there. "What sort of trouble?"

"I don't know. Something. He's very agitated."

"The baby is agitated?"

"Si Cwan is."

"You mean Cwansi."

"No, Si Cwan. My brother. We have to go, right now."

"Go where?"

"I'm not sure. He will guide us."

"Okay, Kally, you have to listen to me," and he knelt down and gripped her firmly by the shoulders. "We can't just go gallivanting across the galaxy because you say a dead man is whispering in your ear."

"We have to—"

"*We can't!* For one thing, my customer is waiting for this delivery. I'm on a timetable. If I fail to meet it, he's going to assume that I'm doing exactly what you thought he might accuse me of, namely, trying to make off with his latinum. Trust me, that would be bad for both of us. It is in our best interest to get my cargo where it's supposed to go—"

"We can't. The baby—"

"Look," he said patiently, "if you think there's some sort of problem, then the easiest thing is for me to send a subspace message to the *Excalibur*. They can handle this . . ."

"Si Cwan says they won't believe it. He says we have to go there ourselves."

"Si Cwan says," he repeated with growing disbelief. *Son of a bitch made my life a living hell when he was alive. Now he torments me from beyond the grave.* "Kalinda, this is insanity."

"You have to believe me."

"I believe that you believe it, but that's as far as it goes. I am not going to change our route and risk winding up with an irate Ferengi bringing down all his angry relatives on my head. I haven't survived in my dubious profession for as long as I have by making enemies unnecessarily. Do you understand what I'm saying, Kally? Do you?"

She didn't appear to see him. Her mouth moved but no words emerged, and then suddenly she slid sideways and hit the floor heavily. Surprisingly heavily, considering how little she weighed.

"Oh, wonderful," he said with a growl.

He reached down and pulled her upward. She'd gone limp in his hands. He moved her over to the chair and sat her upright. "Unbelievable," he muttered as he stared at her insensate form.

Xyon dropped into his own chair and put his face in his hands. "What the hell have you gotten yourself into?" he said aloud, and he had no ready answer. It had seemed like such a good idea at the time, but now he was hip-deep in problems. He had once again allowed his impulses, rather than what would be best for him, be his guide. Life was much simpler when it was just he and Lyla and open space.

The thing was, he was becoming bored with "much simpler." He felt as if he had been ready to share his life with someone, and there was no one he wanted to share it with more than Kalinda. There was no point being irritated with Kally, even though that was his first impulse. He had gone into this with both eyes wide open and had no one but himself to blame for his current predicament.

The best way to go, as much as he hated to do so, was contact his father and tell him everything that had happened. Xyon wasn't sure just how seriously to take all this business about Kalinda getting her marching orders from the ghost of Si Cwan. After all this time, Xyon was prepared to allow for the possibility that Kalinda had some sort of connection to the other side. He preferred to believe that, since the alternative was that she was simply delusional, perhaps even insane, and he didn't find that particularly appealing.

He had instructed Lyla not to materialize unless explicitly summoned or if he were incapacitated. Obviously now was the time to summon her, if for no other reason than that he felt the need to talk to someone who wasn't seeing things. "Lyla," he said.

"Behind you!" came Lyla's voice even as her holographic body flared into existence.

Xyon started to rise from his chair, turning to see what could have possibly alarmed her. It didn't make sense; the only thing behind him was—

Something slammed into his head, something large and heavy, and even as his mind processed the fact that it was a brick of gold-pressed latinum, the floor suddenly leaped up at him. He slammed into it. He tasted something in his mouth, a familiar coppery taste. It was his own blood. Xyon tried to stand but his body was disinclined to cooperate. Kalinda stood over him, wielding the brick, and there was a look on her face that he had never seen there before. It did, however, seem familiar, that look of disdain and unconcealed contempt. He had just never seen it in her face.

"Stay down," said a rough voice that was hers, but not hers, and it only served to motivate Xyon to double his efforts. Unfortunately, since his efforts were coming to naught, doubling them was simply doubly unsuccessful.

"It's . . . it's not . . . you can't be . . ." Then Xyon's thoughts lost coherency as the world went black around him.

ii.

Kalinda glanced down at Xyon's motionless form and then tossed aside the latinum brick. It thudded to the floor, and she stepped over Xyon toward the controls. Lyla simply watched, making no effort to interfere. Kalinda quickly discovered why. The systems were frozen.

"Release command of the ship to me."

"No."

Kalinda rounded on Lyla and snarled in her face, "You are simply a machine. You do not have the option of refusing a direct order."

"That's true—"

"Then release comm—"

"—if the order comes from Xyon. Whoever you are, or whoever you think you are, you are not Xyon, and I am under no requirement to do as you command."

"Fine." Kalinda stepped back over to the brick of gold-pressed latinum and held it over Xyon's head. "If you do not do as I command, he dies."

Lyla was more than calm. She was actually sweet about it. "If you do that, then you will leave me no choice but to blow the hatches and vent all the air from the ship. You will be hurled out into the void—"

"I understand."

"—where you will die from exposure in approx—"

"I said I understand. We're at an impasse."

"So it would appear."

Kalinda drummed her fingers on her forearm thoughtfully. "Look, Lyla . . . a child's life depends upon what we do next."

"As does yours. Because I assure you that if Xyon does not wake up, you will not long survive him." Lyla crouched next to Xyon, gently moving his head from one side to the other to check the damage. Then she reached over to the medkit and began ministering to his wounds.

Kalinda, meantime, watched the proceedings with a scowl. She focused her seething anger upon Xyon, ignoring the fact that he would not be unconscious had it not been for Kalinda bashing his head.

"Know this, hologram," Kalinda said in a voice that was not hers. "If anything happens to my son, then your master there is going to live to regret it. But not for very long."

Bravo Station

"So you've rigged your ship to guarantee that no one can take it over if you are incapacitated?"

"That's right. Got the idea from Xyon. Since he's been on his own for so long, he's had plenty of time to think about nothing except all the things that can go wrong."

Admiral Elizabeth Shelby sat back at her desk, nursing a glass of Romulan ale. She did not even bother to make any comments about the ale's illegality. It would have been a waste of time considering who her guest was, that her guest had brought it, and that her guest was—well—Romulan.

Soleta had removed her jacket and was sitting with her feet up on the desk. She threw back a glass of Romulan ale as if she were drinking water and poured herself another. "Have you heard from Xyon recently?"

"No. But things happen unexpectedly around here. I wasn't anticipating hearing from you anytime soon either, Soleta."

"Yes, well—"

"Well, what?" said Shelby, and when Soleta did not respond immediately, Shelby continued, "Look, Soleta, don't get me wrong. I am thrilled to see you—"

"Are you?" said Soleta, and there was a coldness to her tone that Shelby was surprised to hear. "How thrilled can you be to see someone who was drummed out of the organization that gave you your high rank and command?"

"Come on, Soleta. You know that's not fair. I would be dead if it weren't for you."

"And the injuries I sustained while saving your life were the reason that Starfleet medical discovered I was part Romulan. A Romulan/Vulcan mixed breed was simply unacceptable to the purity of Starfleet."

The admiral scowled at that. "What flushed your career away wasn't just that you were half Romulan. It was that you covered it up. If you had been forthcoming with Starfleet—"

"They would have kicked me out even faster."

"You don't know that."

"Yes, I do."

"No, you—" Shelby caught herself and closed her eyes, taking a deep breath through her nose and letting it out slowly between her lips, making a faint hissing sound as she did so. "Soleta," she said, controlling herself, "we've had similar conversations before. I know my saying that I'm sorry about what happened doesn't make a damned bit of difference. I fought to try and salvage your career. I did not succeed. What do you want me to do? Resign my commission?"

"Yes."

Shelby blinked at that. "What do you mean, yes?"

"I mean yes. If you resign your commission, abandon Starfleet, then I will know that you sincerely regret what happened and are totally dedicated to evening the balance between us."

"Let me see if I get this straight: If I resign Starfleet right here, right now, then you and I will be friends again."

"Yes."

"I am willing to accept that."

It was Soleta's turn to be caught unawares. "You . . . you are?"

"Yes, I am. I am willing to accept that we will never be friends again, because if you think I'm giving up my rank and command, then you're nuts."

A flush of green appeared in Soleta's cheeks, and then—much to Shelby's surprise—Soleta actually laughed. She had an almost musical laugh, reminding Shelby of just how much Soleta had changed over the years. When she had been aboard the *Excalibur,* she had been no different from any typical Vulcan. She had been humorless, serious, unflappable. Shelby hated to admit it, but Soleta's discovery of her true nature had made her a lot more fun to be around. It was as if she had been liberated from years of stultifying discipline. It made Shelby wonder briefly if all Vulcans would prefer a simple life of exhibiting emotion over an intense dedication to the art of smothering one's feelings.

"I suppose," Soleta said once she had regained control, "that little would be accomplished if you took that action. Nor," she added quickly, "would I truly desire that you do such a thing. I did not save your life so that you could throw away your career."

"I appreciate that. And I have missed you, Soleta. I truly have. With that said—" and her voice trailed off.

"What am I doing here?"

"It is a reasonable question. Bravo station is not a typical port of call for the *Spectre.* You're a freelance spy vessel."

"Leading you to wonder if someone hired us to spy on you?"

"The thought did cross my mind."

Soleta poured herself yet another glass of the ale. It didn't appear to be affecting her. Shelby was starting to wonder if Soleta had a wooden leg, or two wooden legs, or perhaps she was simply wooden from the neck down. That would actually have explained a great deal.

"Believe me, Elizabeth, if the *Spectre* had been hired to spy upon you, I would not be here chatting with you in your office. You would never know we were here. Besides—and please do not take offense at this—you're simply not all that interesting. Bravo station is not exactly a hot spot of Starfleet activity. There really isn't all that much reason to spy on you at all."

"That's good to know," and then she added hesitantly, "I suppose. But if that's the case, then—"

"Why am I here?" Shelby nodded. Soleta leaned forward and crooked her finger, indicating that Shelby should draw closer. Shelby did so and Soleta whispered, "I haven't the faintest idea."

"What?"

"Lucius, my second in command, said we should come here."

"Why did he say that?"

"He didn't give specifics."

"You're not serious."

"I'm not?" Soleta appeared to be considering the charge, scratching the underside of her chin thoughtfully before finally proclaiming, "No. No, upon reflection, I have decided that I am indeed serious."

It certainly appeared as if the ale was beginning to work its magic on her. It had taken its own sweet time doing so. She was a far sight from drunk, but she was certainly relaxed.

"What did he say, if he didn't give specifics?"

"He said that he had a vision that we should come to Bravo station."

Now it was Shelby who reflexively laughed, but she quickly gained hold of herself when she saw that Soleta wasn't the slightest bit amused. "Seriously. A vision?"

"Yes."

"Is he prone to such foresighted pronouncements?"

"Never. He has never had one like it before."

"And you trust that he's being truthful with you? That he's not just fabricating this for some unknown reason?"

"Of course I don't trust him," said Soleta as if the suggestion that she might was the most absurd thing she had ever heard. "Why do you think I made certain that he can't take over command of the ship? He led a mutiny against me, for God's sake. How am I supposed to trust a man like that?"

"So why do you tolerate his presence on your vessel?"

"Because it pleases me to do so. And at this point in my life, I am satisfied for that to be the case."

"He has you come to Bravo station with no indication as to why he wants to come here and that satisfies you?"

"No, that does not," she said. It was a reluctant admission. "But I am sure that even you will have to admit that one cannot have everything."

"And what if you find, while you're content to indulge Lucius in his desires, that you take issue with whatever the hell it is he wants to do here."

"I will deal with that if and when the time comes."

"Don't give me that, Soleta," she said, stabbing a finger at her. "You haven't managed to survive for as long as you have without thinking ahead. I do not believe for one moment you haven't determined exactly what you're going to do if Lucius pulls some sort of double cross. Arranging it so that your ship goes dead in space isn't enough. You know that as well as I. There's going to be an aftermath, consequences. If he tries to betray you, you can't just pick up as if it's business as usual. Which brings us right back to the question of what you're going to do if faced with that situation."

"I won't be faced with that situation. It will not happen," said Soleta, but she did not sound either convincing or convinced.

The *Lyla*

The first thing that Xyon became aware of was that his head was throbbing. The second thing he realized was that he was on the floor. *Why in the world would I go to sleep on the floor?* Xyon wondered, and it was only belatedly that he started to remember—piecing the shards of memory together, reconstructing it as if it were a shattered mirror—precisely what had happened. He had a vision of Kalinda standing over him, an unlikely expression on her face and strange words on her lips.

He started to sit up and almost fell back.

"I would take my time, were I you," came Kalinda's voice, except it sounded different. Contemptuous, bordering on derisive. "You were hit rather hard."

"And you're the one who hit me . . ."

"That is true. You got off lightly. I could have crushed your skull once and for all."

"Lightly? Of all the—" Xyon forced himself to

sitting again and this time he grabbed onto the edge of his pilot's chair and pulled as hard as he could. Despite the fact that his surroundings were swimming around him and he wanted to do nothing else save lie back down, or vomit, or both, Xyon kept himself upright. He took a few deep breaths and let them out slowly, and then pulled himself to a standing position. He needed to lean on the back of the chair to steady himself, but at least he was on his feet. He reached up and touched where the latinum brick had slammed him on the head. It was covered with dried blood, and his hair felt sticky and stiff.

Kalinda was leaning against the wall, her arms folded across her breasts.

"Kalinda . . . why? Why did you . . . I mean, I don't understand."

"You understand. You just refuse to acknowledge it. Look at me. Look into yourself. Admit what is happening."

As insane as it sounded, even to himself, he was looking at Kalinda's features, but the expression was distinctly that of . . . of . . .

"Lyla!" he called abruptly. "Lyla, get out here—!"

The holographic entity flared into existence before him. She had the same gentle smile she always did. "Hello, Xyon. I hope you're feeling better after your enforced rest."

" 'Enforced rest'? Lyla, she knocked me out!"

"I am very aware of that, Xyon."

"Did you immobilize the ship?"

"Of course I did, just as you programmed me to do." She indicated Kalinda with a slight inclination of her head. "He seemed most put out about it."

"Watch your pronouns, Lyla. That's a she, not a he. A she who is in desperate need for the kind of help that I cannot provide for—"

"You are mistaken, Xyon. That is not a 'she.' That is a 'he.' He has told me his name is Si Cwan."

Si Cwan. That's it. That's the end of it. Except . . . damn, she looks so much like . . .

No. She's lost her mind. That explanation is the simplest and most straightforward and is the only one that is remotely acceptable.

"She may have told you that," said Xyon with forced patience, "but all that means is that she is not well."

"I cannot agree, Xyon. I have scanned him quite thoroughly and he seems perfectly health—"

"Would you stop calling him—I mean her—him!" He clutched at the sides of his head in frustration and then moaned loudly because any physical contact made his skull throb all the more. *"She's not Si Cwan!"*

"You are an idiot, and we are wasting time," Kalinda said.

Xyon shook his head forcefully, clearing the last of the muzzy-headedness from his brain. "Listen—"

"No. There is nothing that you can say other than that you are offering your cooperation that could possibly be of any interest to me."

"What am I supposed to believe, Kalinda? That you assaulted me because the ghost of your brother took over your body?"

"That is exactly correct. You surprise me, boy. You have been so single-minded in your pursuit of my sister that I was of the opinion there was room for nothing else in your mind save your obsession with her. Apparently you can actually grasp other concepts as well."

"Oh, I grasp it. I simply don't accept it."

"Your acceptance is of no relevance to me," said Kalinda. As ludicrous as it was, Xyon had to admit to himself that she certainly had Si Cwan's walk down, and body language, and that staggeringly imperious air he radiated. Xyon could never have guessed the depth of Kalinda's madness until this moment. "All that is relevant is to take this vessel immediately to Bravo station. That is where the threat presents itself."

"Fine. If you think there's such a threat, I can call it in."

"And say what?" said Kalinda derisively. "That the ghost of Si Cwan has issued warnings through the body of Kalinda?"

"You see? Even you admit it's ridiculous. So how am I supposed to believe it?"

"I do not care if you believe it. I simply require you to act upon it. This annoying vessel of yours," and she glanced around in unfettered contempt, "refused to cooperate. So I have waited a very long time for you to regain consciousness—"

"Because you knocked me out!"

"—and now that you have," said Kalinda, ignoring Xyon's interjection, "I require you to do as I instruct."

"How?"

"Order your vessel to—"

"No, I mean how do you know that the baby is in danger?"

"I simply do."

"Not good enough. Not good enough by half, Kally."

"You would not understand," said Kalinda. "It involves an awareness of the flow of events. We may be in space, but nothing happens in a vacuum. There are some who possess this ability on a rudimentary level, including your own father."

"What are you talking about?"

"His awareness of when there is danger in the air. He perceives it even when no ordinary method of detection does. Some would call it a sixth sense, a self-preservation instinct. Perhaps he possesses it because he has nearly died so many times that he has become keyed into that which I can sense routinely, being already dead."

"Yes, so you say."

"Save your sarcasm, Xyon. Take us to Bravo station."

Xyon straightened his back, folded his arms and simply glared. "Forget it. I don't take orders on my ship. Especially from a crazy slip of a girl who ambushes me when my back is turned."

"And you believe that was the only reason I was able to defeat you?"

"Coldcocking me with a brick is hardly defeating me."

"Very well. I offer you a bargain. You have precisely one minute to touch my face."

He stared at her. "What do you mean?"

"Which word did you not comprehend? I offer you a challenge. Your back is not turned; I hold no brick. You must know that Kalinda has little, if any, skill at self-defense. I challenge you to lay one finger upon my face within the count of sixty seconds. If you are able to do so, I shall remove myself from Kalinda's form and leave you to your miserable little life. If you are unable to do so, you will immediately do as I instruct and take us to Bravo station. Are we agreed?"

"That's ridiculous," said Xyon, and he laughed, but it was an uncertain laugh.

"Afraid? Afraid that what you see as a mere girl can best you at a simple challenge? Or afraid that there may well exist concepts beyond your ability to comprehend?"

Xyon had had more than enough. "Lyla," he said, and he squared his shoulders. "Inform me when one minute has passed, beginning . . . *now.*"

He came straight at Kalinda even as he said it and reached out, her face directly in front of him.

And then it wasn't.

It took him a moment to register that she had side-stepped him and then she was behind him and delivering a swift kick to his backside. Xyon stumbled forward and banged his head against the bulkhead. He spun, momentarily confused, and he saw Kalinda's mocking expression just a few feet away. He came at her again, his hand spearing forward, expecting her to try and dodge. She did not. Instead she brushed his hand aside with a sweep of her arm that seemed slow but was somehow much faster than he could possibly have expected. He tried again, and again she deflected it. He feinted with his left, came in fast with his right. She caught his wrist, swung it down and around, and suddenly he was facing away from her with his arm twisted behind his back.

Xyon's father, Mackenzie Calhoun, was one of the most formidable hand-to-hand combatants in the history of his homeworld of Xenex. Xyon was not on his father's level, but he was not exactly inept. Yet that was how he was being made to feel now as Kalinda immobilized him just long enough to bring her foot up, plant it in the small of his back, and shove him forward. Xyon hit the ground, rolled, and bounded back to his feet.

"Care to give up?" said Kalinda.

With a roar of fury, Xyon barreled toward her.

Kalinda drove her foot forward and, with perfect timing, nailed Xyon in the crotch.

He went down, gasping and grasping. He lay there moaning, his eyes wide with pain, as Kalinda stepped around in front of him and looked down. "I felt I had nothing more to prove to you in terms of hand-to-hand," she said by way of explanation, "and, frankly, you left yourself open for that."

Lyla appeared on the other side of him and said pleasantly, "That was one minute, Xyon. Do you require me to time another minute for you?"

"Actually," Kalinda said, since Xyon was hardly in a position to draw sufficient breath for speech, "I believe all Xyon requires you to do at this time is set us on a course for Bravo station."

"Is that true, Xyon?"

Xyon was barely able to manage a nod.

"Very well," she said. "Course laid in. Best possible speed?"

Xyon nodded again.

"As you wish." She vanished again.

"By the way," said Kalinda, "I would prefer it if, for the duration of our stay together, you addressed me as Lord Cwan."

Xyon was still unable to gather sufficient breath to respond.

Kalinda dropped to the floor, crisscrossed her legs, and closed her eyes. Xyon stared at her. "And do not," Kalinda said as if reading his mind, "even think about trying to touch me. If you do, I will stop going easy on you."

Bravo Station

i.

She moves through the corridors of the station but is only aware of her own presence in a distant manner. People nod to her or greet her as she passes. She responds, acknowledging them, only because some small part of her brain informs her that that is the proper response. She may draw attention to herself if she ignores them, so she goes through the motions. But it means nothing. Only one thing means anything to her.

She has never felt this way before. In some small part of her, she knows what she is experiencing. It is a word that is not commonly spoken, a state of mind that some refuse to believe exists. She now knows herself that it does, in fact, exist. But she does not care. She welcomes it, for it is the only means by which she will be able to accomplish her aim.

She moves with a sense of purpose and destiny that she had never thought possible. There is no doubt in her mind that everything will fall into place. She cannot be stopped. She must not be stopped.

A man sees her. She does not notice him. He notices her. His eyes widen in shock, and then he turns and follows her at a safe distance, waiting to see what happens next.

ii.

"I hope these quarters will be sufficient, Lady Cwan."

Robin Lefler looked with amused suspicion at Admiral Shelby, who was affecting a formal manner. Shelby even bowed slightly in deference. "Yeah, okay, Admiral, you really need to stop that now. 'Lady Cwan'? Since when do you call me that?"

"Why are you still calling me 'Admiral'?"

"Because that's your rank."

"And that was relevant when you were in Starfleet. You haven't been for quite some time now, and I think that by this point 'Elizabeth' will do nicely.

"Very well, *Elizabeth,*" she said with a smile. "Yes, this room is quite sufficient."

"I'm sorry it's not yet rigged with a holoprojector. I have a technician coming in first thing tomorrow and he'll outfit it so that your mother will be able to visit with you."

"Just make sure I can turn it off if I feel like it."

"I totally understand," Shelby assured her.

Robin was seated, suckling her son. Shelby watched with a broad smile and Robin looked up at her curiously. "Ever given any thought to having one of your own? Mac and you must have talked about it at some point or other . . ."

"You know . . . actually . . . we haven't," said Shelby thoughtfully.

"You're joking."

"No, I'm not. Mac already has a grown son—"

"Who he didn't even know existed until Xyon was already grown."

"And an adopted son. And I just—well, I never really gave much thought to it. I figure we have time for that."

"That's what you always think," Robin said with a tinge of sadness to her voice. "You think you have all the time in the world. And the next thing you know . . . you don't."

"Are we talking about me? Or you?"

Robin glanced toward her and Shelby looked immediately regretful that she had said it. Before she could apologize, Robin said, "A little of both, I guess."

"Robin, I—"

"No, it's okay. It was a fair question. I thought Cwan and I would be together for years and years. *I* was wrong. We were wrong. But I got off lucky. My lack of foresight didn't prevent our having a child. Honestly, we weren't even sure we could. Genetic tests were inconclusive, and there was no known case of a Thallonian breeding with a human." She laughed bitterly. " 'Breeding with a human.' God, that sounds awful."

"It sounds scientific."

"Well, that's kind of the point, I guess. Having children isn't about science. It isn't about making a carefully considered decision, because frankly I think that in any given circumstance, there are always going to be more reasons not to have children than to have them. It's not a decision you make with your mind so much as with your heart."

"And lower down, in some instances."

Robin laughed at that, and Shelby allowed herself a soft chuckle. "I don't know," Shelby said after a few more moments. "I guess I just don't feel it in my heart, then. I don't know that Mac feels it at all either. Plus there's the little matter that I'm here and he's running around on the *Excalibur*."

"You wouldn't be the first woman who raised a child with her husband not around a good deal of the time."

"But why would it be incumbent on me to raise him or her? Why couldn't Mac have the baby with him on the *Excal*?"

Robin stared at her. "Do you really want to see Mackenzie Calhoun trying to manage a baby?"

"You're thinking disaster, huh?"

"At a bare minimum."

"I suppose."

"Still—" Shelby paused, thoughtful, and then continued, "there was that time when I thought that Mac was dead. And after that happened, I was just . . . I was consumed by thoughts of missed opportunities. Of what might have been. I think that's one of the reasons I was so ready to marry him when it turned out he had survived. I felt that I had been given a reprieve, and I wanted to take advantage of it. So now you've got me wondering what it's going to take to prompt me to have a child. What new disaster am I going to survive so narrowly, or is going to affect my worldview so drastically, that I'm motivated to have a baby?"

Before Robin could respond, there was a chime at the door. "Come," called Robin.

The door slid open and Doctor Selar was standing there with her medical kit.

"Selar! I was hoping to have a chance to say hello." Shelby stood and extended her hand. Selar stared down blankly at it and Shelby wiped it on the side of her uniform trousers. "So . . . did you get your patient settled into our medlab?"

"Yes. Your facility seems adequate."

"Please, my head will turn with such flattery."

"It was not intended as flattery."

Shelby didn't bother to try to explain that she was being ironic. Irony died on Vulcans the way that humans died on worlds with no oxygen. "Then you succeeded," she said.

"Good."

"Anyway, s/he won't be here long. A medical transport should be along in a—"

"Yes." She spoke flatly, mechanically. Robin was accustomed to Selar's total lack of bedside manner, but this was a bit much even for her. Apparently having lost interest in Shelby, assuming she had any in the first place, Selar turned to Robin and said, "I felt it would be wise if I examined both you and your son once more before I depart."

Well, that explained it. She was simply being

thoroughly professional in her demeanor. What some might see as mechanical was probably, as far as Selar was concerned, focused. "Yes, of course." Robin noticed that Cwansi was no longer nursing, but instead lying in her arms with his eyes mostly closed and a bit of milk dribbling down his chin. "He's in a milk stupor," she said in amusement.

"Then now would be a good time. Admiral, if you would excuse us . . ."

"Yes, of course," said Shelby, rising. "Actually, I have a date."

"A date—? Oh. Of course," Robin said as she fastened her tunic. "With the captain in town . . ."

"Exactly. Ladies, if you'll excuse me," and with a grin she turned and walked out of Lefler's quarters with what certainly seemed some additional spring in her step.

Selar turned to Robin and said calmly, "Lay the baby down and let us begin the examination."

iii.

Shelby entered her quarters and Calhoun was already there.

Within moments their uniforms were scattered all over the floor, over furniture, every which way. As they flopped down onto the bed, a tangle of limbs, kissing each other with fierce urgency, Shelby came up for air and said, "I have to ask you . . ."

"Anything."

"Have you ever thought about us having a baby?"

"No," said Calhoun.

She paused only the briefest of moments, said, "Yeah, me neither," and returned to what she had been doing.

iv.

Selar consulted her medical tricorder and slowly shook her head. "This is not satisfactory."

"What isn't?" said Robin. She was suddenly nervous. Was there something wrong with her? Was her body breaking down? *My God, what's going to happen to my baby if he's an orphan? Oh my God oh my God . . .*

"You appear to have a vitamin deficiency."

Robin breathed a sigh of relief. "That's not generally fatal, is it?"

Selar gave her an odd look. "Not generally, no."

She removed a hypo from her medical kit. "A simple shot should correct it."

"Okay, good." She extended her arm as Selar applied the hypo. The contents hissed into her system. "Doctor, I just want to thank you again for coming to New Thallon and delivering Cwansi."

"I was simply doing my job."

"No, you were doing far more than that. This was above and beyond. This was . . ." She yawned. "This was more than . . ." She yawned a second time, then a third, and unaccountably her eyes were getting heavy. She didn't understand why she was suddenly so tired. Cwansi was, unlike Earth children, already sleeping through the night even though he was only several weeks old. So it wasn't as if he was keeping her awake. She couldn't fathom any reason for such overwhelming fatigue—

Then she made the connection between the hypo and her sudden exhaustion.

Robin looked up uncomprehendingly, tried to stand, tried to speak and call out for help, tried to do something, anything. Instead her legs gave out and she collapsed. She hit the floor hard and she heard Selar say, "Do not try to keep standing. You will accomplish nothing and may injure yourself in the process."

Her throat was tightening. Summoning aid was out of the question; Robin couldn't even muster enough energy to utilize the voice-activated comm system. Instead all she managed to produce was a single whispered word: *"Why?"*

"The Vulcan nerve pinch can actually be rather painful for the victim. I sought to spare you that pain. If you cause yourself injury, I will have failed in that endeavor. If you mean 'why am I taking this step,' then I will simply tell you that it is because I have no choice."

Selar reached over to the small, makeshift bed and picked up the sleeping Cwansi, still basking in his milk-induced haze. Robin attempted to get to her feet, but all she managed to do was move forward a few inches. Selar barely gave her a glance, but she was clearly aware of her attempts to get to her. "I must save my son," said Selar. "I am certain that you can sympathize with my situation. If your son is required to accomplish the goal of saving mine, then so be it. Besides, if you will recall: My son was here first."

She headed for the door, darkness drawing a curtain over Robin's eyes. But just before she slipped into oblivion, she heard the bell chime outside her room.

And then she was gone.

V.

She is heading for the door, Cwansi sleeping in her arms, and then freezes as the chime sounds. Robin is lying unconscious on the floor. The room is too small to hide her, nor is there time to do so. Certainly the inevitable noise made by dragging her body around would alert anyone out there.

"Robin? Robin, are you there? It's Soleta."

Selar realizes that the best course of action is to do absolutely nothing. There is no reason for her to respond. She can simply stand there without moving.

That is precisely what she does. She remains bolt still. A statue could take immobility lessons from her.

Time seems to crawl by, even though Selar knows precisely how much time has, in fact, passed. The baby whimpers slightly. She looks down in surprise; his eyes are open. He has come out of his stupor and, as impossible as it seems, appears to regard her with some measure of suspicion.

He whimpers again.

She brings her fingers to his shoulder delicately, as if she were picking up a piece of shattered glass from the floor, and squeezes as gently as she can. Cwansi's eyes roll up into his head and he lapses into unconsciousness that will last for several hours. Then she returns her attention to the door, waiting to see if there is anything further from the other side. Nothing. Soleta must have departed.

She steps toward the door and disengages the lock. It slides open.

Soleta is standing on the other side, her eyes narrowed, her manner suspicious. In the split second it takes for Selar to react, Soleta sees the motionless form of Robin Lefler. Selar takes that instant of reaction to reach out with her free hand as if driving a spear forward, to clamp it onto Soleta's shoulder.

vi.

Soleta was about to depart, deciding that Robin was somewhere else on the station, or perhaps taking a nap. There was no urgency to her visit; she was just stopping by to touch base.

Then she heard a small, whimpering cry.

To a human it would have been inaudible, but to one with Soleta's ears, it was unmistakable, and positively plaintive.

Just as quickly as it began, it ceased.

She had no idea what to make of that. Perhaps Robin and her son indeed were asleep inside, and the baby had simply fallen back into slumber after voicing protest over some tiny nightmare it was having. Yet something still seemed wrong to her.

Soleta remained where she was, unsure of what to do. She could have summoned help, but for what purpose? What if there was nothing more ominous than a mother and child napping within? She was supposed to sound an alarm over that?

And then, as she remained frozen with uncertainty, the door slid open and she saw Selar standing there with an unconscious baby in her arms. Just behind her, on the floor, was Robin Lefler, lying still and no more conscious than her son.

They stared at each other for a second, and then Selar tried to apply a Vulcan nerve pinch.

But Soleta was not caught unawares so easily. She blocked the thrust, and Selar was hampered in her movements by the fact that she was holding an insensate child. Soleta knocked her hand aside and, rather than attempting her own nerve pinch, rammed her clenched fist into Selar's upraised chin. There was nothing elegant in the move, but it was effective nonetheless. Selar staggered back and Soleta entered quickly, pressing the attack.

Selar had no choice. She dropped Cwansi and launched herself at Soleta. It was a mark of Soleta's insular nature that it never occurred to her to call for help, not for a moment. The door slid shut behind

them, although it did not lock, since Selar had removed the seal.

Soleta grabbed Selar's arms by the wrists. She had
no idea what was happening, or why Selar was doing
this. All she knew for sure was that Selar was coming
at her with a fierceness and implacability that made
her feel as if she were seeing the Vulcan doctor for the
first time instead of having known her for years and
considered her a friend.

Selar's expression never wavered, so immobile
that she might as well have been a machine. She
shoved against Soleta, trying to bear down on her,
and Soleta pushed back. They stood in the center of
the room, strength against strength, and slowly Soleta
found herself giving ground. Selar was bending her
back, back, and Soleta did the only thing she could
think of.

She used the mind meld as a weapon.

Soleta was aware that Selar had serious trepidation
about employing the Vulcan telepathic technique. Soleta, on the other hand, had no hesitation about it at
all. Whether using it to obtain information or enhance
her pleasure with Lucius, she had become remarkably
skilled in the technique. She had not, however, made
a practice of utilizing it in an offensive capacity.

She did so now, sending her mind into Selar's like a javelin of light. Selar staggered, and not all her Vulcan training, not all her vaunted restraint or lack of emotion, could stop a look of sheer astonishment from spreading across her face.

Sensing an impending triumph, sensing her advantage, Soleta pressed further, hoping to render her opponent unconscious through sheer force of will . . .

. . . and a word leaps out at her, and it is not just a word, but a sensation, a feeling, a knell of doom that reverberates in her skull, and Soleta would not have thought it possible that she could be as stunned by a single word or concept as she is by this one, whispered in academic circles, spoken of as a mere myth or as something that had long been left behind by the race that furnished half her genetic makeup, but there it is, right in front of her, not at all mythic, but real and alive and totally horrifying, like walking into your quarters and discovering that Medusa is standing there waiting to paralyze you with her stare, and in just that way Soleta is paralyzed now, by that one damned word, and she speaks the word aloud, this word that no one of her heritage ever speaks because it runs contrary to everything they are or at least everything they fancy themselves to be . . .

"Shal'tiar . . ." *she whispers aloud, or in her head, or both, or neither, it is impossible to say.*

Selar recoils, and mentally she snarls like a caged animal in a most un-Vulcan-like way, violently reacting to the word. She knows the truth of the word but has no desire to acknowledge it, for she fears the notion in the same deep, primal way that Soleta does.

Soleta presses her advantage, fighting down her terror over the prospect of Shal'tiar, *knowing that whatever has led Selar to this state, Soleta may well be the only person on the station—indeed, in the entire quadrant—who is capable of not only understanding what is at stake, but stopping her before—*

And suddenly the blow comes from behind; she is completely unprepared for it because her attention has been entirely upon Selar. Soleta tries to turn, to fend off whoever is assaulting her, but she is fighting a two-front war and she is just distracted enough that Selar clamps an iron hand upon her shoulder. She tries to shove Selar away, but it is too late as the nerve pinch shuts down the flow of neurons from her brain to the rest of her body. She goes down, and the last thing she sees is not, in fact, anything actual, but rather the word etched in blackness by her mind, burning like a wildfire in the night . . .

Shal'tiar . . .

vii.

It took Selar a few moments to clear her head and realize that she was no longer struggling against Soleta. Granted, she had ultimately taken Soleta down, but she had been operating entirely on instinct. So even though the fight was done, she hadn't fully grasped that it was finished.

She looked up and saw a male Romulan standing there. He was studying her with a mixture of disbelief and amazement.

"Who are you?" she said, even as she reached down and picked up the sleeping form of Cwansi.

"Lucius. Late of the Romulan Empire, now in allegiance to no one. And you are . . . ?"

"Selar," and then she paused and said for the first time a truth that she knew was a harsh one to face, but a necessary one. "Late of the *Starship Excalibur*. What are you doing here?"

"I saw you in the corridor and followed and waited. I would have come in earlier, but I saw my commander enter here."

"Your commander?" and then she looked down at Soleta's body. "You betrayed your commander?"

"As, I suspect, have you."

"A valid point. What is your purpose here?"

"I am here to help you. That is, for the moment, all that you need to know."

"Do you have a vessel?"

"Yes."

"Then you *can* be of help to me. Take me to your ship. Once there, we have one other matter to attend to, and then we can depart."

"To where?"

"To planet designated AF1963."

"Why?"

"That," she said, "is all *you* need to know."

He considered that for about a second and then nodded. "I find that acceptable."

They left as quickly as they could, leaving the motionless bodies of Soleta and Robin Lefler lying on the floor.

viii.

"Bridge to Captain Calhoun."

Shelby moaned and sat up in bed, Calhoun rolling off her. It was not the *Excalibur* bridge that was summoning him. His combadge was still on his jacket, which lay on the floor. It was instead the command center of the space station. "I guess the entire 'do not disturb' business was more of a guideline than an order, eh?" he said dryly.

"I told them to leave me alone unless it was an emergency. I forgot to mention you."

"There's always a loophole." In a louder voice, activating the comm system, he said, "Calhoun here, go ahead."

"This is Lieutenant De Paulo. Sorry if I, um, interrupted anything, sir—"

"Don't worry about it, Lieutenant. I was just going over fuel consumption reports in my head." Ignoring the fact that his wife was sticking her tongue out at him, he continued, "What's up?"

"It's about that patient you brought into the medlab, sir. The Hermat."

"What about hir?"

"S/he's gone."

Calhoun stepped out of bed, already yanking on his clothing as he said, "When? How?"

"Less than a minute ago, sir. One minute s/he was lying there, then there was the sound of transporter beams, and then s/he was gone."

"I'll handle it."

"But—"

"I said I'll handle it, Lieutenant. Calhoun out." He picked up his uniform jacket. Shelby started to ask him what was going on but he was already tapping his combadge and saying, "Calhoun to *Excalibur.*"

"Excalibur, Burgoyne here."

"Burgy, have you had any unauthorized transporter activity over there?"

"Unauthorized?"

"Anything other than the normal flow of people coming and going for shore leave."

"Nothing that I know of, Captain."

"I want you to send a security team to sickbay. Find Selar. If she's not there, find her wherever she is on the ship and hold her for questioning."

"What?" Clearly Burgy wanted to find out what the hell was going on, but then s/he caught hirself and instead simply said, *"Aye, Captain. We'll get right on it."*

"Mac, what the hell is going on?" said Shelby as Calhoun pulled on his boots. "Why do you think Selar—?"

"Because she's been obsessed with holding on to that patient."

"But that still doesn't . . ."

She didn't have the opportunity to complete

the sentence because Burgoyne was back on the combadge with Calhoun. *"Sir,"* and there was unmistakable worry in Burgoyne's voice, *"Doctor Selar isn't on the ship."*

"Find out who was the last person to see her—"

Now Shelby was yanking on her uniform even faster than Calhoun was his, and she said quickly, "Shelby to security."

"Security, Grant here."

"Grant, get a squad to the Lady Cwan's quarters right away. If a female Vulcan is there, apprehend her immediately. And alert the docking bays and perimeter patrol. No ships in or out. Lock down the entire sector."

"Yes, Admiral."

She replied to the unspoken question on Calhoun's face, "I may be the last one to have seen her. She was in Robin's quarters. She said she was following up on the birth of Robin's baby."

"I don't like the sound of that at all. Something's wrong with Selar, and I think we're about to reach the tipping point."

Calhoun sprinted out of Shelby's quarters and she was right behind him. Even though there had been no way she could possibly have suspected that something was wrong with Selar, Shelby blamed herself for not spotting it. She prayed that whatever was going on, they were in time to head it off. But the fact that Rulan had not been beamed back aboard the *Excalibur* was particularly worrisome. It suggested to her that there was someone else involved, and that placed a serious wild card into the deck.

ix.

A normal human would have been incapacitated by the Vulcan nerve pinch for several hours. Even a normal Vulcan would have been out cold for at least an hour or more.

The fact that Soleta was a Vulcan/Romulan halfbreed already served to make her unique in terms of her biology. Furthermore, she had impressive control over just about every muscle of her body. Therefore, when Selar had applied the nerve pinch, Soleta had just enough time to tense the muscles in her shoulder, rendering them just short of rock-hard. Even though she lost consciousness, it was for a far briefer time than if she had experienced the full brunt of the attack. So it was that not really all that long after Doctor Selar had departed with Lucius, Soleta had fought her way back to wakefulness.

She felt a slight stiffness in her neck, but she knew what the cause was. As quickly as she could, she got to her feet and shook off any lingering dizziness.

"Robin," she said as she saw her friend still lying unconscious on the floor. She went to her quickly, knelt next to her, and checked her over. Uttering a quiet prayer of thanks that Robin was not dead, she stood up. Unsure of how to activate the voice responsive comm unit in the small quarters, she called out, "Security team. I need a security team to—"

The door slid open and a security team charged in.

"That was fast. Well done. I—*oooof*!" The foremost security man slammed straight into her and knocked her to the ground.

"Don't move!"

"I can't very well do so. You're lying on top of me."

"Bridge, this is security," one of the guards said as Soleta was hauled to her feet and her hands secured.

"De Paulo here. Go ahead."

"Tell the admiral we have the Vulcan."

"You can tell her yourself—she should be there any moment."

Sure enough, Shelby arrived seconds later, preceded

by Calhoun. He took one look at Soleta and visibly deflated. "No, no, no. You've got the wrong Vulcan."

"With all due respect, Captain, you didn't specify which Vulcan. And we found her crouched over Lady Cwan."

One of the security men had picked up Robin, who was still unconscious. "I'll get her to sickbay, Admiral."

"Yes, do it," said Shelby, but she was looking suspiciously at Soleta. "Bring her to the brig. We'll question her there."

"You can question me here if you want. I've got nothing to hide. Don't you trust me, Admiral?"

"Right now I don't trust anybody."

Least of all a former member of Starfleet who went over to the Romulan Empire. She didn't say it aloud, but the sentiment remained unspoken between them.

X.

Robin Lefler heard something before seeing anything, and what she heard was extremely familiar: the voice of her mother.

"I'm reading a jump in brain activity. She's coming around."

It was at that point that Robin heard the steady beeping of various monitoring instruments she knew to be typical for a sickbay. Her eyes were still closed, and it required a conscious effort on her part to force them open.

Morgan was looking down at her, smiling gently. She reached down and touched her face. Her hand didn't feel the way it had when she was truly alive, another reminder of the fact her mother existed only as part of a technological miracle. Still, it was better than nothing.

"They have holotech here in the sickbay in case they need to activate the emergency medical program. I'll be here with you the entire time."

Robin fought to recall the details of how she had come to be there. Everything was confused, fragmented. She reconstructed it, piece by piece, recalling that Selar had come to her . . . examined her . . . and she had . . .

Understanding rushed back to her, and suddenly she sat up much faster than she should have. Everything swirled around her and she gripped the sides of the medical table. "Doctor!" called Morgan, and a medtech immediately approached Robin. "Robin, you need to lie down—"

"Where's Cwansi?!"

"Selar pumped something into you to knock you out. She—"

"I don't give a damn about Selar! Where's my son?" When Morgan hesitated, she grabbed the holographic representation of her mother by the arm and practically shouted in her face, *"Where is he?"*

"Robin," said the medtech, "please calm yourself before—"

"Shut up! Where's my son?!"

"She took him," Morgan said in a flat tone. "Selar took him."

"Where? Where did she take him?"

"We don't know. She's vanished from Bravo station."

"She couldn't have just vanished! She has to be somewhere, and wherever she is, she has Cwansi with her! We have to find him!" Robin was trembling and was so agitated she could barely string words together. "We have to! We—"

"The captain and admiral are working on it . . ."

"I don't want them to *work* on it! I want them to find him! Before she's done God-knows-what to him! I need you to—*what the hell are you doing*?"

Her voice had risen to a scream as the medtech

shoved a hypo into her arm. She tried to knock it away but it was too late: The contents were injected into her with a hiss. Robin lunged toward the doctor, who stepped back to avoid her fingers that were curved like claws. She started to tumble off the table but Morgan caught her before she could. "What . . . what did you . . . ?"

"Just something to calm you a bit, take the edge off. It won't knock you out, but—"

"Kill her. I'm going to kill Selar . . . and then," she said and looked balefully at the medtech, "I'm going to kill you."

Then she slumped back onto the table, Morgan easing her down. Robin continued to stare up at the ceiling, and she kept muttering, "Kill her. Kill her . . ."

"It's going to be all right," she said soothingly. "The captain is going to take care of everything. Why, I'll wager that right now he knows exactly where Cwansi is and he's on his way to get him back safe and sound."

xi.

It was everything Mackenzie Calhoun could do not to punch the wall. He did consider it for a moment, the alternative being to punch Soleta who was seated in a chair looking up at him blandly. "You have to have some idea of what's going on."

"I wish I did," she said. "I'm just an innocent, in the wrong place at the wrong time."

Shelby was standing at the opposite side of the room, leaning against the wall. "You're telling me you just happened to show up at precisely the moment when Selar just so happened to launch a kidnapping attack?"

"Coincidence does happen in real life, Admiral. Look," she said tiredly, "I have no reason to steal the child."

"No reason that we know of."

"What is that supposed to mean?"

"I mean that you're freelance now, Soleta, and that I know you've done work for the New Thallonian Protectorate," said Shelby.

"Not for the Protectorate. For *Robin Lefler.* If she needs some espionage performed, yes, I am the one she comes to. Who else would you seek for such endeavors except someone you trust? Are you saying her trust was misplaced?"

"I'm saying her baby was misplaced, and your ship is gone."

Shelby's words rocked Soleta with the effectiveness of a blow to the face with a granite glove. It was all she could do not to go slack-jawed from the news. "Are you sure?"

It was Calhoun who replied. "We've locked down the sector, but it wasn't fast enough. The *Spectre* vanished before we realized anything was wrong. And that ship of yours is undetectable when it needs to be, thanks to the combination of your cloaking device and ion glide drive. Even we can't find something propelled by starlight."

"Strains coincidence beyond the point of credulity, wouldn't you say?"

"Yes, it surely would," replied Soleta slowly. "It would seem, Admiral, that the concerns you expressed regarding Lucius were well taken."

"Except Lucius has no prior relationship with Doctor Selar; at least none that we know of," said Shelby. "You, on the other hand, do."

"So what are you saying? That I acted as an intermediary between Selar and Lucius, and then was double-crossed by Lucius?"

"It certainly seems like a viable chain of events."

"If that were the case," said Soleta, "then I would be as betrayed as you, and thus as much in the dark."

"Except you would know the reasons behind the kidnapping," said Calhoun. He leaned in toward her, placing one hand on the back of her chair. "Was the Protectorate Council behind it? Has the baby been brought back to Thallonian space?"

"I do not know."

"To New Thallon itself?"

"I do not know."

"To another safe location?"

"I do not know."

"Dammit, Soleta!" yelled Calhoun with such ferocity that she jumped slightly. "You were the last person to see Selar! She must have said something to you, done something!"

"Yes. She rendered me unconscious. So it wasn't as if we had a chance to catch up on old times." She forced her voice to remain level and steady. "And she was aided by someone whom I didn't see. I was assaulted from behind, giving Selar the opportunity to finish the job."

"Who was it?"

"My apologies, Captain, when I said 'someone whom I didn't see,' what I really meant to say was that it was someone whom I can identify."

"Who do you think it was?"

"If I had to guess, I would say it was Lucius. With my vessel gone, he would seem the most likely perpetrator."

"Except," said Shelby, "you said you rigged your ship so that it would not depart without you, that it would shut down if someone else attempted to take it over."

"Yes, well," Soleta said slowly, "that wasn't quite accurate."

"What do you mean?"

"I mean that the design of the *Spectre*'s computer was such that I couldn't arrange for the programming to be as user specific as I had hoped because I didn't have enough time, so I simply reversed a genetic coding subroutine that was designed to prevent other races from assuming control."

Understanding dawned on Shelby. "You rigged it so that only someone with Vulcan DNA could command it."

"That is correct."

"And since Selar is Vulcan . . ."

"I effectively handed her the keys to the kingdom on a genetic level."

"Which still brings us back to the *why* of it all," said Calhoun. "None of this makes any sense."

"I am quite confident in saying that to Selar it makes nothing but *logical* sense."

"And what do you know about it?"

"You're going around in circles, Captain," said Soleta. "I don't know any more than I've already told you."

"And you've no clue as to Selar's state of mind? She shared nothing with you?"

Soleta hesitated, but the hesitation could well have been seen as weariness over the protracted questioning. "No. Nothing."

"She's lying."

No one in the brig had spoken. Shelby, Calhoun, and Selar looked around automatically; they recognized the voice instantly. "Morgan?" said Shelby. "Is that you?"

"Of course it's me." There was cold, implacable fury in her tone. "And I can tell she's lying. I'm employing the brig scanners used to monitor and maintain the health of prisoners. I can use them to detect any change in heartbeat. For all I know, Soleta could regulate her bodily processes sufficiently to deceive any normal lie detector, but she can't fool me. Did you hear that, Soleta? You can't fool me."

"Yes, I heard you," Soleta said hollowly. "Since you are the only one talking—"

"Come down to sickbay and we'll be done with talking," came Morgan's voice. "My daughter is sedated because she was going out of her mind with worry."

"Did she say what happened?" Shelby asked.

"She said, Admiral, that Selar knocked her out. That's all she knows."

"How gratifying that you're willing to take *her* at her word," said Soleta.

"Bring her down to sickbay, Captain," Morgan urged Calhoun. "I have ways to force the information out of her."

"That would take you quite some time," said Soleta.

"I have nothing but time. I'm dead, and I never tire. I can have you begging for death, and I'll feel as fresh at the end as I am at the beginning."

"That won't be necessary, Morgan," said Shelby. She walked over to Soleta and fixed her gaze upon her eyes. "Because Soleta is going to tell us what she is lying about. She's going to tell us absolutely everything she knows. And she's not going to do it because she's forced into it. Hell, that would probably just make her more intransigent. She's going to cooperate because she's someone who nearly got herself killed trying to save me."

"An action that resulted in my being thrown out of Starfleet."

"I'm all too aware of that. And I owe you."

"I see. And how, precisely, do you intend to repay that debt?"

"By offering you this: If you tell me right here, right now, what you're holding back from us . . . then I'll still be your friend."

Soleta stared at her. "And you think that's going to sway me?"

"I'm hoping it does."

Slowly nodding thoughtfully, Soleta lowered her gaze and studied the floor. Calhoun looked as if he were about to speak, but one cautioning look from Shelby brought him up short, and he waited instead. To a man of action like Calhoun, it seemed interminable.

"We don't speak of it," Soleta said finally.

"Who's 'we'?"

"Vulcans. Vulcans do not speak of it."

"Well, you're not exactly a pure Vulcan, are you," said Calhoun.

"Yes, Captain," she said, ice dripping from her words. "I am all too painfully aware of that."

"All I'm saying is that perhaps since you are part Romulan it gives you some leeway in that regard."

"You don't understand. You cannot understand. It's . . . I don't know that telling you would be of much help. It wouldn't give you anything concrete in terms of her whereabouts or her plans. All it would do is address her state of mind."

"And that could be of use," Calhoun said. "Because, frankly, her behavior has been incomprehensible. She's been a good and loyal member of Starfleet, despite her personal trauma. To see what she's doing now . . . Soleta, if you can help us understand what's going on in her head, it could be invaluable. If—"

"All right," she said, putting up her hands as if in surrender. "But I need you to comprehend that I'm still dealing with this knowledge myself. What she is experiencing . . . it's not like the Vulcan mating ritual, *Pon farr. Pon farr* is meant to lend at least some semblance of dignity to a biological drive. The thing I believe has seized hold of Selar has no ritual associated with it. There is scarcely even an acknowledgment of its existence."

"What is it?"

She had trouble forming the word on her lips, and even when she finally spoke it, neither Shelby nor Calhoun could quite make out what she had said. They glanced at each other and when they both realized that neither had heard her properly, Shelby said, "We didn't catch that."

"*Shal'tiar,*" Soleta said again, with visible effort. Once she had managed to repeat it, she let out a breath as if she had just managed to clamber to the crest of a steep hill. "It is called *Shal'tiar*. It is not written of in any texts. What knowledge of it there is exists purely in oral tradition and rumor."

"But what is it exactly?"

"It is a sort of 'logic madness,' for want of a better term." She shook her head. "People think we Vulcans are emotionless. We are not. We restrain emotions, bury them as deeply as we can, but they are always there. Every single minute of every single day, we make a conscious effort to suppress them. *Shal'tiar* is the opposite. It is said, or believed, that if a Vulcan is faced with a severe enough crisis, one that cuts to the core of his or her soul, then she can enter the state of *Shal'tiar*. Understand, Captain, that one of the underpinnings of our belief system is that any problem can be solved with the proper application of logic. *Shal'tiar* can occur when there is a massively traumatic problem to be solved, and no logical means of doing so. But when no logical option exists, a Vulcan can make a conscious decision to jettison logic out the nearest airlock. In such an instance, the affected Vulcan can become dangerously obsessive. Nothing matters except solving the problem."

"I'm not sure I understand," said Shelby.

Soleta paused, trying to figure out the best way to explain it. "In my Academy days," she said slowly, "the logs of James T. Kirk were required reading. I was particularly interested, for obvious reasons, in anything he recorded about Lieutenant Commander Spock. There was one instance involving a life-or-death situation with a shuttlecraft—the *Galileo,* I believe it was—in which Lieutenant Commander Spock faced a problem that could not be solved through logical means. The shuttle was trapped in orbit around a planet, and Mister Spock had no means of summoning the *Enterprise*. Spock jettisoned and ignited the fuel, transforming the hours of survival to mere minutes."

"A signal flare," said Calhoun immediately.

"Very good, Captain. A signal flare."

"Clever."

"Illogical. Totally illogical. Yet against all odds, the *Enterprise* detected the flare and rescued the crew. When pressed by Captain Kirk on his reasoning for such a suicidal ploy, Spock said—and this is Kirk's paraphrasing, I must emphasize—that he reasoned it was time for an emotional outburst."

"Are you saying that Spock was seized with this . . ." Shelby hesitated. *"Shal . . . ?"*

"Shal'tiar. Perhaps he was. The thought process is similar to what my understanding of *Shal'tiar* is. But since he solved the problem very quickly, it was transient at best. Selar, however, has been faced with the insolvable problem far longer, and I believe it is straining her to the breaking point."

"The problem," Calhoun said, "being her son's condition."

"Exactly."

"But . . . wait," said Shelby. "What does Cwansi have to do with her son's condition? For that matter, how do you know any of this?"

"As to the former, I have no answer. To the latter: I struggled with Selar when I came upon her in Robin's quarters, and my mind brushed against hers. I perceived the concept of *Shal'tiar* in her thoughts, her very being. The human equivalent of it would be an untameable rage. When in the throes of *Shal'tiar,* a Vulcan will proceed on a path to solve a problem, and it doesn't matter who is standing in the way or who may get hurt. Think of it as a form of temporary insanity, except since a Vulcan is involved, the insanity is painstakingly methodical. Selar has come up with a plan to save her son, Xy, and she is not going to let anyone or anything—especially a thing as trivial as morality—stand in her way."

In the ensuing, thoughtful silence, Calhoun said, "Morgan?"

Needing no further prompting, Morgan's voice said, "Every word is true, Captain. Or at least she believes every word is true."

"And how long does it last? This *Shal'tiar?*"

"Until she accomplishes her goal. Or comes to her senses on her own. Or until she dies. There's no way to tell. I'm sorry, Captain. I truly am. But that woman out there with Cwansi is not the Selar you've known all this time. She is, for all intents and purposes, an enemy, and if you do not treat her as such, under the influence of *Shal'tiar,* she will not hesitate to kill you if you get in her way."

"Selar would never do that."

"Aren't you listening? *She is not Selar*. Not for the time being. Not in any way you understand."

"This is insane," said Shelby. "Cwansi kidnapped. Selar seized with logic madness. I don't know how this day could possibly become any stranger."

Calhoun's combadge beeped. He tapped it and said, "Calhoun, go."

"Captain, this is Burgoyne." S/he sounded frustrated, concerned. That was understandable considering hir attachment to Selar and her apparent complicity in Cwansi's kidnapping. "We've been patrolling the perimeter, enforcing the shutdown, and just made contact with your son's ship, the *Lyla*."

"Xyon's here?" That was coincidence that didn't sit well with Calhoun. "Did he say why?"

"Yes, sir. He said—" Burgoyne hesitated. "He said that Kalinda insisted he come here, and that the rest is too insane to say except in person."

Calhoun stared at Shelby, who closed her eyes in pain. "I had to open my big mouth," she said.

Starship Excalibur

i.

The moment Calhoun strode into the conference lounge where Xyon and Kalinda were waiting for him, he knew something was off. Kalinda typically sat in a very relaxed manner, looking with interest at the world around her as if she were seeing things that no one else was able to perceive. This was, as Calhoun knew, quite likely the case.

This time, though, when he saw her, Kalinda was sitting stiffly with her shoulders squared, gazing fixedly at the doorway so that she was looking straight at Calhoun when he entered. Upon the captain's doing so, Kalinda got to her feet, her spine perfectly straight, her chin held high. She acted as if she were looking down on Calhoun from a much higher posture even though she was a head shorter. "Greetings, Captain," she said. "I regret the unusual circumstances of this latest encounter."

Xyon was seated with his feet up on the conference lounge table, as was his custom. As was *his* custom, Calhoun swatted Xyon's feet off the table. "What the hell have you gotten me into?" said Xyon.

"I thought I had left matters in a satisfactory manner to all concerned. Why don't you tell me what happened?"

"Well, to begin with, Kalinda has been possessed by the ghost of Si Cwan."

Calhoun looked from Xyon to Kalinda and back again. *"Excuse me?"*

"I don't know that I would have put it in that manner," Kalinda said calmly. "It is a little more complicated than that. Unfortunately, it's not anything I can readily explain."

Calhoun stared at her, at a loss, for one of the few times in his life, as to how to proceed. "How inconvenient for both of us."

"Inconvenient but nonetheless true. I am indeed Si Cwan. And I am here to save my son . . . except," she added, "I perceive that I am too late. And it is your fault."

"My fault?" Calhoun was more amused than annoyed at the charge. "How is it my fault?"

"Your vessel intercepted ours. Had I been allowed to pass unmolested, I might well have headed off the ship that took Cwansi. Instead your first officer insisted on escorting us here, when here is the last place I need to be."

"And the first place is—?"

"With my son, of course," she said matter-of-factly. Kalinda paused and then regarded Calhoun with what appeared to be sympathy. "Captain, I know this is a great deal to ask you to accept . . ."

"Oh, you think so?"

"But you of all people know that there are aspects of this universe that are beyond our comprehension."

"Yes, I know. I know that there are new frontiers beyond those dreamed of even by Starfleet. On the other hand," he said, circling the table, "I'm reminded of Occam's razor, which states that the simplest explanation tends to be the correct one. So I ask you, which is more likely? That you are the spirit of a dead leader inhabiting the body of his sibling to warn us of danger? Or that you're a troubled young girl who has simply gone over the edge?"

"It's obviously the latter. But you, Mackenzie

Calhoun, have not always been so quick to embrace the obvious."

Calhoun turned to Xyon, about to ask him to explain what had happened when he noticed something. "Is that a lump on your head?" When Xyon nodded, Calhoun asked, "How did that happen?"

"Kalinda Cwan ambushed me with a latinum brick."

"What?"

"I required his ship," Kalinda said imperiously.

"And you expect me to cooperate after you—?"

"I couldn't lay a hand on her," said Xyon.

"What do you mean?"

"I mean after I came to, to prove she's who she says she is, Kalinda invited me to try to touch her face. I tried. I tried a lot."

"So what? Even Moke could beat you in a fight. What does that prove?"

"Thanks, Father," Xyon said with an annoyed expression. "I'd like to see you take a shot at her."

"I'm not going to—"

"Try," said Kalinda, coming around the table to face Calhoun. "Try to lay a hand on me."

With no hesitation at all, Calhoun thrust his hand forward. To his mild surprise, she deflected it. To

his greater surprise, she blocked the next several attempts.

Calhoun stepped back, assessed the situation,
and then lashed out with a snapkick. Kalinda bent
backward, avoiding it, and slammed upward with a
double-handed block, knocking Calhoun off his feet.
Calhoun rolled and came up quickly as Kalinda advanced on him, and then suddenly dropped to the
ground and brought his legs around in a scissor hold
that caught Kalinda across the knees. She went down,
narrowly missing striking her head on the table as she
did so. Instantly Calhoun was atop her, one knee on
her chest holding her down, his fist cocked.

"Yes, well, you always did get lucky when you
fought me," Kalinda said with a growl.

"Cwan, you pompous ass, you—" And then Calhoun heard what he was saying and his eyes widened.
His fist remained frozen where it was.

"Still embracing the simplest answer?" said Kalinda.

ii.

Robin Lefler had never wished more to be Vulcan
than she did now as she walked through the corri-

dors of the *Excalibur*. She was grateful for the fact that Elizabeth Shelby was alongside her, but her emotions were still running riot within her.

The ship had once been her home, the ship's population her crewmates. On the one hand she felt as if she had returned to where she belonged; on the other, she felt like a complete outsider. It had been rough enough when she had boarded the ship to be brought to Bravo station. Fortunately she had had Cwansi to focus her attention on, which had helped the sense of disorientation. Now Cwansi was gone and she felt adrift, a rudderless ship.

Crewmen didn't know how to look at her. Whereas with Cwansi in her arms there had been smiles and coos and compliments for the baby, now everyone seemed uncomfortable because of the tragedy that had befallen her. Moreover, it was general knowledge that one of their own was in some way mixed up in it. There were guilty feelings in the mix, even though there was no reason for any of them to feel this way. It wasn't as if Selar had confided her plans to any of them.

There were murmured words of sympathy and plenty of downturned looks. Were the gods out to get her? If so, why didn't they just cause her to spontaneously combust and be done with it? Why did everyone she loved have to suffer? Her husband dead; her child gone; her own mother dying horribly and being transformed into a bizarre computer entity. Was she such a terrible person, done such awful things, that she had so much negative karma to bring this much tragedy to those around her?

Shelby's hand rested on her shoulder and gave it an affectionate squeeze. "It's going to be okay."

"How is it?" she said in a low voice, even as she forced a smile toward a passing crewman who greeted her by name.

"Because Mac is on it, and he never fails. Ever. You can trust him."

"I trust him with my life. But asking me to trust him with my son's life . . . that's a different story, you know?"

Shelby nodded. She understood, and Robin took some comfort in it.

They entered the deck five conference lounge, as Burgoyne had instructed them to do upon arrival. Burgoyne had not met them at the transporter room; instead s/he'd issued the orders to the transporter chief who, in turn, conveyed them to Shelby. Robin was reasonably sure she understood why. Burgoyne probably didn't feel as if s/he could face Robin. S/he had been Selar's companion, after all. There was probably no one on the ship who felt more guilty over what had happened than Burgy, a shame since it really wasn't hir fault, yet s/he was doubtless blaming hirself.

Shelby entered, Robin right behind her. She recognized Xyon immediately and recognized Kalinda even though Kally's back was to her. Calhoun was studying a star chart on the wall screen.

"Okay, we're here," said Shelby. "What have you got?"

Kalinda turned, took one look at Robin Lefler, and then, to Robin's utter shock, threw her arms around her and kissed her passionately.

For a heartbeat, Robin almost melted into it, because there was something astonishingly familiar about it. Then realization slapped her in the face and she peeled Kalinda off her. "Kally! What the hell—?"

"I'm sorry, I . . ." Kalinda was clearly trying to compose herself. "I should have warned you. Or restrained myself. Or—"

"I don't understand," said Robin, wiping her lips clean and giving Kalinda a very puzzled look. "Could someone explain what's happening here? I mean, I only just came off medication; I'm not sure how much excitement I can reasonably handle now."

"Yes, well, I don't know that explaining is going to help much," said Calhoun.

Kalinda stepped forward and took Robin's hands tentatively. "Robin . . . it's me. It's Cwan."

She stared at Kally.

"I know that look," said Calhoun. "I had a very similar one on my face not too long ago."

"What does she mean? Kally, what are you talking about?"

"I know this is a lot to grasp, Robin, but I'm Si Cwan."

She released her hold on Kalinda's hands and backed up against the wall, a look of revulsion on her face. "That is . . . this is sick. This is a sick joke."

"It is not a joke."

"Kalinda, for the love of God—"

"Your favorite color is purple," said Kalinda. "You enjoy standing outside in light rain because you like the way it feels on your face."

"Stop it."

"When you were a child you had recurring dreams about the ocean," Kalinda was speaking faster and faster. "Your favorite quote is by Voltaire, that God is a comedian playing to an audience too afraid to laugh. Your favorite joke includes the line, 'Hark, I hear the cannons roar.' You hate the Terran foods tomatoes and cinnamon."

"*Shut up!*" Robin screeched. Her eyes were wide, as she punched Kalinda in the face. Kalinda staggered but did not go down.

"Oh, right, *she* gets to hit you," said Xyon.

Refusing to rub her face even though it was already beginning to swell, Kalinda said as patiently as she could, "Robin, if you'd only—"

Robin clapped her hands over her ears and sank into a chair. She wasn't looking at Kalinda. She wasn't looking at anyone.

"Mac," said Shelby, feeling as if she had wandered into the final act of a mystery play. "What the hell is going on?"

"Kalinda," said Calhoun, "has a connection to Robin's son. She believes Si Cwan possessed her. At first, I thought Kalinda was insane, but at this point I don't know what to think. Here's what I know for a fact: Kalinda insisted on Xyon coming here with her because she was sure that Cwansi was in danger. And she was right. Whatever else Kalinda may think about what's going on here, she was right. Which means that even if I reserve judgment over her more *dubious* claims, she's earned the benefit of the doubt. And she's now telling me"—he paused while indicating a point on the star chart—"that the *Spectre,* the ship carrying Cwansi, is heading toward the outer rim of the galaxy. Whether that's really his destination, I obviously couldn't say."

"You mean you believe her?" Shelby looked incredulous. "This young, disturbed girl claims to have some sort of psychic knowledge of the baby's whereabouts and, oh, by the way, she's actually possessed by the baby's father, and you're just going to accept this? Mac, have you gone as crazy as she is?" she said to Mac, then turned to Kalinda and said, "No offense."

"None taken," said Kalinda.

"We've alerted Starfleet to the baby's kidnapping, Eppy, but the fact is that the *Spectre* can elude most normal means of pursuit. Without any sort of edge, any sort of inside information, finding it is going to be problematic. If Kalinda, Cwan, or whoever this is, claims to have a means of tracking him, then I for one don't see the downside."

"The downside is that you're taking a starship on what is probably a wild-goose chase," Shelby said. "You can't really be considering this, Mac; it's absurd!"

Despite the gravity of the situation, Calhoun smiled. "I've missed this," he said. "This thing between you and me, back when you were my second in command, and we'd have a disagreement and you'd explain all the reasons why what I wanted to do was wrong on every level; then I would go ahead and do it anyway and it would all turn out all right."

"Yes, except that now I outrank you," Shelby reminded him. "So I get to have a little more say than when I was your first officer."

"That's true," he said. "However, you have a post on Bravo station, which means that, sooner or later, probably sooner, you're going to have to return to it. At which point, I leave, and I don't think you'll have much luck stopping me from pursuing the course I feel is right once I'm out of your immediate piece of space."

"Thanks for your continuing respect for the chain of command," she snapped, and then stared at Kalinda, hoping that if she did so for long enough Kalinda would return to normal and this whole demented interlude could be put behind them. "Mac, what could possibly make you think she's Cwan?"

"I beat her in a fight."

"You did *not* beat me," Kalinda said, annoyed.

"You momentarily gained the upper hand while I was coping with a body that is still not wholly familiar to me."

"Mac, for God's sake—"

"Eppy, listen to me," Calhoun said firmly, no trace of humor in his voice. "I have already freely admitted I don't know what to believe. But what I never forget is the way someone moves in a fight, especially when it's someone who knows what he's doing, as Cwan did. I fought Kalinda, and, yes, I know it sounds ridiculous, but Kalinda moved just like Cwan. It wasn't a perfect imitation of him. I mean *it was him.*"

"Do you hear what you're saying, Mac?"

"Yes, but I don't think you're hearing what I'm saying. So I'll make it clear." He tapped the star chart. "Kalinda says the baby is roughly here, heading"—he paused to indicate the outer rim—"here. I know it lacks common sense. And at this moment I think the situation calls for uncommon sense. I'm not asking for your permission or endorsement. I'm telling you that I'm going. I don't need you abandoning your post to accompany us, but I think the Lady Cwan deserves the opportunity to join us if she's so inclined." He looked at Robin. "Robin? Care to join us?"

Robin felt as if she were sinking into a black hole

while Calhoun tossed her a rope covered with grease. Then, to her surprise as much as everyone else's, she laughed. "Sure," she said. "Sure, why not? What have I got to lose?"

"Robin," Shelby said gently, "perhaps this isn't the best time to—"

"That wasn't a rhetorical question, Admiral," said Robin. "Tell me, what have I got to lose?"

Shelby tried to come up with a response but nothing presented itself.

With that silent affirmation, Robin turned to Calhoun and said, "I'm in, on one condition."

"Name it."

"I'm back at ops. I'm not going to sit around being a passenger. I have to be part of something, think about something other than Cwansi or I'm going to wind up crazier than . . . than . . ."

"Me?" suggested Kalinda.

"I wasn't going to say it, but . . . yes. Look . . . Kally . . ." Robin tried to keep her gaze fixed on Kally, but it was impossible because those eyes, *his* eyes, were looking back at her. She knew that if she kept staring too long she'd end up pulled into her insanity. "I know what you want me to say, what you want me to believe. But I'm coping with a lot right now, and that's just too much for me to handle. Understood?"

"Yes. Of course."

"I'll have a uniform brought to the guest quarters where you'll be staying," said Calhoun. "Welcome aboard."

Within moments, the conference lounge was empty save for Calhoun and Shelby. "Admiral," he said in a formal tone, "I would like to make one further request of you."

"Soleta."

He nodded. "You're ahead of me."

"No one on this ship knows the *Spectre* better than she does, not to mention the state of mind of Vulcans," said Shelby. "She would be a valuable asset to you. She'd certainly do you far more good than she would me by sitting in the brig. I'll attend to the transfer immediately. A pleasure doing business with you, Admiral."

"And you, Captain. I just wish that . . ."

"We could have made more pleasure during our business?"

"Now you," she said with a sad smile, "are ahead of me."

iii.

Xyon walked across the hangar deck toward his vessel, which was parked, prepped, and ready for him. He felt like he was more than ready for it. This whole thing had been one big, ghastly mistake.

"Xyon . . ."

He turned and saw Kalinda running across the deck toward him. She wasn't running the way she normally did. Instead she ran with precision, arms scissoring, legs moving smoothly, rather than the almost balletic movements she utilized. She stopped a short distance from him, looking a little out of breath. "I . . ."

"What?"

"I wish to apologize for the manner in which I dispatched you on your ship. I should have at least given you the opportunity to make an informed decision. When you're dead, you tend to become disconnected from reality."

"Maybe I'm dead, then, because I've felt that way for years."

"I want you to understand . . . I've never liked you."

"Yeah, I figured that out the time you subjected me

to an extended torture session. Right between the moment when I lost all feeling in both my arms and the moment I passed out from blood loss, I thought, You know what? This man really doesn't like me."

"You said *you*."

"What?"

"You said *you*, acknowledging, however unwillingly, that I am who I say I am."

"I'm just tired of arguing. I'm tired of a lot of things and, frankly, Thallonians are at the top of the list." He turned to head into the *Lyla*.

"She does love you, you know. She never stopped," said Kalinda. "Her heart and mind are there for me to see. When this is over—"

"It's never going to be over. Because I have the feeling you're always going to be lurking in the background, in her conscious or unconscious mind. And I'm not really interested in having a three-way relationship, especially with someone who never liked me." He bowed mockingly and said, "Farewell, Kalinda, Cwan, or whoever you are. I wish you the best of luck. Do let me know how it all turns out."

The hatch of his ship opened and he clambered into it without a backward glance. Minutes later, the *Lyla* was heading into deep space.

"Xyon?" Lyla said, appearing next to him. "Is there anything I can do? Would you like me to make myself appear as Kalinda—?" Her image shifted and she was a perfect replica of Kalinda.

"Actually," he said, "I want you to delete that image from your memory. Do it now."

"Xyon, are your eyes wet—?"

"Do it now!"

As he drew an arm across his eyes, Lyla did as she was instructed, assuming her normal appearance as an attractive blonde. "How is this, Xyon?"

"Fine, Lyla. Just fine. Let's get out of here. We still have a cargo to deliver to a potentially cranky customer."

The *Lyla* angled off and away, yet Xyon kept the monitor screen view on the *Excalibur* the entire time, until the great starship was long out of range.

iv.

Calhoun stared at the four walls of the conference lounge long after Shelby had left, and finally said, "You can come out now. I know that you're listening. You're always listening."

Morgan appeared, facing the captain. There was a

doubtful look on her face. "Would you like to know why I didn't make my presence known sooner?"

"Not especially."

"I'll tell you anyway."

"I suspected you would."

"It's because I didn't feel it would be my place to contradict the captain openly in front of his superior officer and son."

"Plus you didn't want to risk having your daughter objecting if you attempted to do so."

She made a face. "That barely factored into my consideration."

"Glad to hear it."

"Captain, these claims that Kalinda is making—"

He put up a hand. "I very much suspect there's nothing you could possibly say that hasn't already occurred to me, Morgan. Nevertheless, I've decided this is the best course of action, and I intend to pursue it no matter how unlikely the source. I cannot justify ignoring a possible means of tracking down Robin's child, even if it appears that our guide is a young woman who has lost her mind."

"And then there's the matter of putting Robin in charge of ops."

"It's her old station. She was there before you

were. I would hardly think that you, of all people, would present a strenuous objection. You're still the heart and soul of this vessel, Morgan. It's not as if you won't have anything else to do with your time."

"That's good to hear you say, Captain. I had thought—"

"You thought what?"

"I had thought that after our previous contretemps, you were anxious to replace me on ops at the first opportunity."

"Well, you are wrong."

"Am I?"

"Yes."

She stayed quiet.

"Morgan," he said slowly, "are you monitoring my heart rate to see if there's any variation?"

"Yes," she said with no hint of shame.

"Then you know that I am being honest. Just as I'm being honest now in saying I consider such actions to be intrusive, and I am instructing you to refrain from doing so in the future."

"Of course, Captain. It will not happen again."

"Good. As for Robin, let's face it: I think nothing short of Kebron blocking the door would prevent her from staying on the bridge to find out what's going on. We might as well put her to use in a way that will benefit both her and us."

"Yes, of course. Your point is well taken, Captain."

"I'm pleased that you agree. Now I have a question for you, Morgan. Why haven't you been able to track the *Spectre*? You've told me that you're able to transfer your personality, at any point, into any vessel where you've been before. You've been in the *Spectre*. Why can't you just place yourself into her computer core and take charge of her?"

"Because when I had my *accident* some months ago and crashed, it wiped my presence out of every place I'd previously been. I can still interface at will with any Starfleet computers, but I need to rebuild from scratch everywhere else. If you manage to transmit a message to the *Spectre*, I can project myself along the subspace band and get in that way. Until such time, I have no more means of finding the *Spectre* than you do."

"All right. With any luck, we'll find a way to do just that. You'll get into the *Spectre*, and we can shut this entire thing down."

"Anything I can do to help, Captain. It is, after all, my grandson we're talking about."

"I know. Now why don't you spend some time with your daughter?"

"I am, Captain, even as we speak. I *am* capable of doing more than one thing at a time. I know a good deal more than I'm letting on at any given moment."

"Yes, of course. Carry on, then."

Morgan vanished, leaving Calhoun with a smile that was rapidly fading. The fact was that he knew a good deal more than he was letting on as well. For instance, he knew that Xenexians were even more capable of controlling their bodily functions than Vulcans. It aided a warrior race to be able to keep their hearts beating at slow, steady paces even in the midst of combat, since it lessened the chances of getting overly aggressive and sloppy.

The upshot was that Mackenzie Calhoun was perfectly capable of brazenly lying without betraying the slightest spike in his heartbeat or pulse rate.

It was a bit of knowledge that he had every intention of keeping to himself.

The *Spectre*

i.

She gazes at the sleeping child. It has taken a while to settle him down, for he has been desirous of his mother's breast and naturally she is unable to provide him that. She is prepared now, however, having used the replicators on the Excalibur *to synthesize liquid nourishment for the child before departing. She has enough to supply them for the journey, and she took Robin's supply of diapers with her when she left Bravo station. She has accounted for everything.*

Except . . .

Except . . . What happens when they arrive at their destination? The unknown beings to whom she is bringing the baby, the ones who offered to help Selar cure her own child. Have they made preparations? Certainly they must have. They must have food ready for him. Except . . . where would they have obtained it? Synthesized it, perhaps, as she did. But do they have the capability to do so? They must. They must if they are advanced enough to help her cure Xy. But . . .

But what if they don't?

Surely, that is not her problem. Her mission, her purpose, her job is to bring the baby. To exchange it for a cure.

Except . . .

Except there will be no one to care for it. Not the way a mother is supposed to. Not the way she did for Xy during the all-too-brief period that he was an infant. He will be in the hands of beings who are not human. They will smell and sound different from his mother. Perhaps they will not even be able to touch him. Perhaps he will never know the loving touch of a mother again.

Perhaps . . .

Except . . .

Why is she dwelling on these things? She cannot fathom it. None of it mattered before. All that mattered was Xy, her son, not Robin Lefler's . . .

Yet how is that remotely fair, remotely just? How can she bemoan the inequity of a world where her child is saddled with a condition that expedites the aging process, robs him of his youth, speeds him toward the grave, while she acts in just such an unfair manner? Is it that perhaps the world itself is not unjust, but rather the people in it?

Everything had been so clear to her before, so pure, so

direct. There had been no doubt in her mind of any of it, and now doubt was creeping in, long shadowy fingers caressing her mind and stirring her uncertainty. It is as if she were beginning to shake off the remnants of a dream. Or a state of mind. Or . . .

Shal'tiar.

The word echoes in her head and she recoils from it. The cursed word, the ultimate betrayal of all she has learned and studied and believed in. If to be a Vulcan is to embrace a state of mind, then to embrace Shal'tiar is to commit a crime against that state. A crime. A betrayal. Treason. Nothing less than treason against all governing thought of Vulcan civilization.

She cannot have done that. She cannot grasp the thought; she rejects it, or at least endeavors to. But try as she might, she cannot. It sticks to her like barnacles to a sea vessel.

Yet how else to explain where she is, what she is doing? She looks at the baby again, and his eyes are open to slits. He sees her. He smiles. Impossible. Infants cannot smile in response to an individual. Yet he seems to be doing just that, and he gazes upon her in semi-slumber with trust so achingly pure that it's like a spear to the heart, a spear of flame to a heart of ice.

His eyes close. He is peaceful.

The ice melts.

ii.

On the bridge, Lucius checked the heading for what seemed like the hundredth time. Once he was satisfied that the vessel was on course and remained locked in, he ran a long-range sensor scan to see if anyone else was near them or in their path. He picked up a small freighter, a passenger line, and a science exploration vessel. Hard to believe just how crowded space was getting, especially when one considered its infinite size. None of those ships presented a problem, though, and he was satisfied that the *Spectre* would remain undetected.

He nodded in satisfaction, certain that he had taken into account all possible aspects of the endeavor.

He knew he was staking everything on what was little more than gut instinct. But that instinct had typically served him well before. Besides, he had to admit he had been getting bored with the status quo. Lucius was someone who was always seeking to advance himself in some manner, and the existence he was leading with Soleta was simply a dead end. As matters stood, he would never be anything more than a freelance spy, doing someone else's dirty work. It was a waste of resources.

Yes, the circumstances here were questionable, but certainly the possible outcome was worth the risk.

And he found that, when he tried to picture Soleta, he was already finding it hard to remember her face or the sound of her voice.

Small loss.

The door to the bridge hissed when it opened and Selar entered. He was pleased to see she did not have the baby in her arms. Lucius wasn't exactly fond of children. He was willing to accept that the infant was instrumental in his mission, but it didn't mean he had to spend a lot of time near the brat.

"We need to go back," she said without preamble.

"Do we?"

"Yes. You see—"

He had no need to hear another word. His disruptor was already in his hand, and in one smooth motion he targeted Selar and fired. He derived a certain amount of smug satisfaction from the startled look on her face.

The blast lifted Selar off her feet and slammed her into the wall. She was unconscious even before she slid to the ground, her head lolling to one side. He went to her and checked her pulse, which was slow but steady.

Lucius picked Selar up, slung her over his shoulder, and brought her down to the brig. The unconscious Hermat was already there because Lucius had no desire to leave hir unattended in sickbay. At least in the brig, a force field could keep hir out of trouble. For convenience, Lucius went to the quarters he'd given Selar, picked up the baby, and brought it to Selar. He held it delicately, uncertainly, as if he were carrying something potentially explosive. Lying the child next to Selar, he backed up, never taking his eyes or his weapon away from her.

It would have been easier to kill the woman and be done with it. But he could not be sure that he wouldn't require a Vulcan to regain control of the *Spectre* should there be some sort of problem with the ship's computer. Damn Soleta for rigging the controls to respond only to someone of, or with, Vulcan DNA. It was a tragic sign of the times that there was so little trust in the universe.

For the time being, Selar would live. If nothing else, it meant he would have someone around to take care of the infant, which was not a duty Lucius craved. He would just as soon have thrown the brat out the airlock, but obviously the child was of interest to the species who had contacted him. So he didn't really have any choice in the matter.

There was a shackle against the wall with a length of titanium chain extending from it. Old-fashioned to be sure, but sometimes the old ways were the best. To play it safe, Lucius attached the shackle to Selar's ankle. This way if he had to enter the brig for some reason, she would remain on a very short leash, so to speak. He placed the infant's nourishment closer to her so she would be able to attend to him as needed.

"Do not even think about causing trouble," he said to the two unconscious adults and the sleeping baby, not really expecting anyone to answer. "You do not want to cause me any aggravation, because I assure you that it will pale in comparison with the aggravation I cause you." With that admonishment he activated the force field, turned, and walked away, leaving them to their slumber.

He had no idea why Selar had abruptly changed her mind. Fortunately, he didn't care all that much. The whys and wherefores were incidental and of no consequence.

Lucius had greater things to worry about.

Starship Excalibur

Robin Lefler had been amazed by how easily she had slid back into her old duties.

Perhaps they had been cued by Calhoun; perhaps not. Ultimately the bridge crew had acted as if it were not at all unusual to see Robin back at her old ops post. At most there had been slight nods, gentle greetings, and that was all. No one addressed her by rank since technically she had resigned her commission and thus had none. The fact that a non-Starfleet officer was stationed at ops didn't faze anyone. Certainly the crew of the *Excalibur* had experienced more unusual circumstances.

Not for one minute during her time on the bridge did she cease thinking of her son. But, just as expected, it gave her something additional to think about.

The one person—if the term *person* could apply to her—to acknowledge that Robin's presence was a little odd, naturally, was her mother. Morgan would appear from time to time, looking over Robin's shoulder, asking if there was anything she could do to make Robin's stay more pleasant. It seemed a little odd to Robin. On the one hand, her mother was coming across as solicitous; on the other, it seemed like she was being territorial, trying to ensure that Robin didn't get too comfortable at the ops station. Robin reasoned she might have well been imagining it.

Several hours later, Robin started to feel fatigue setting in, dropping over her mind like a fuzzy blanket. She realized she hadn't slept properly in more than twenty-four hours. She was running on fear and adrenaline, and it was starting to take its toll, but she was unwilling to ask for any special treatment. It didn't matter because Calhoun noticed her movements seemed slower. He ordered her to go to her quarters and get some sleep. "You'll be of no use to me if you're passing out at your station," he said, and she knew he was right.

When she got to her quarters, she flopped down onto her bed fully dressed. Her eyes had just started closing when she heard the door chime. "Come," she said, forcing herself to sit up and rubbing the sleep from her eyes.

The door opened. It was Kalinda.

Robin moaned softly and flopped back onto the bed.

Kalinda stepped in, the door sliding shut behind her. "If that's intended to interest me, you're succeeding."

"Oh, God. I don't need this."

"I know. It's unfortunate—"

"It's unnatural!" Robin nearly exploded with frustration. "Dead is dead!"

"In the universe as you experience it, yes," said Kalinda. "But there are aspects *beyond* your experience—"

"Don't start."

Kalinda smiled sadly. "With all the things you and the crew have experienced, is this truly so beyond the pale? How could I have known the things of which I spoke to you—"

Robin shrugged. "Cwan confided in you. Or you overheard. Or you were listening in. Or you read my mind."

"You would readily believe in psychic abilities? Such phenomena are scarcely more unusual than that which I'm claiming."

"At least they're measurable!" Robin said in frustration. "At least they're scientifically established! Not superstition or magic!"

"I tend to think that your ancestors would have

been more comfortable with the notion of ghosts than vessels flying through the stars."

"That's not the point."

"You're right," said Kalinda, sounding very much as if she understood everything Robin was going through, which inexplicably annoyed Robin all the more. "That's not why I came here anyway. I just wanted to find out what was happening. I've been supplying the heading . . ."

"You mean your best guess as to the heading." Robin shook her head in disgust. "Part of me still can't believe the captain is taking you at your word."

"Intellectually he finds it just as difficult to accept what I've been telling him as you do. But the captain also tends to trust his instincts. Besides, as has been pointed out, you really don't have anything better to go on."

Robin remained on the edge of the bed, staring into space. Kalinda walked over, sat down next to her, took her hand, and squeezed it tightly. "Whether you believe I'm who I say I am, or whether I'm just a woman who's lost her mind . . . either way, we're stronger together than we are apart. We should be united in our concern for Cwansi, be he my son or nephew."

Robin nodded reluctantly, allowing Kalinda to continue to hold her hand. Despite the unusual aspects of the situation, she found it oddly comforting.

"Do we know anything more of Cwansi's whereabouts?" Kalinda said.

"You mean," said Robin, "other than the direction we're heading on your say-so?"

"Yes."

"Well, if you're correct, and if the *Spectre* maintains a consistent heading, then it's going to make planetfall on a rim world designated AF1963. The captain has alerted Kat Mueller's ship, the *Trident*. They happened to be in that general area on a star charting run. So they're heading to AF1963, hoping to head them off. I'm not sure how Mueller is going to have any more luck detecting them than we do."

"And this planet. What's even there?" asked Kalinda.

"Nothing. Nothing that I know of. Nothing that anyone knows of. It's an inhospitable ball of rock. Why would Selar be heading there?"

Kalinda shrugged. "I don't know. My connection is only to Cwansi, not to the people surrounding him."

"Do you have any idea how insane that sounds?"

"I have every idea," said Kalinda. "If the situation were reversed, I would be as doubtful as you. I don't know what to tell you, Robin, except that my love for you and our son is so great that—"

"Stop it," Robin said, standing up and turning away. "Just stop it. I'm begging you."

Kalinda remained seated, but there was sadness in her voice. "Are you so unwilling to accept a miracle when it's being presented you?"

"How am I supposed to accept it?"

"You can just—"

"*How* am I supposed to *accept* it," she repeated, her voice rising, "knowing that, sooner or later, you'll go right back to whatever spirit world spat you up? I'm right, aren't I? If you're who you say you are, this . . ." She gestured helplessly. ". . . this situation isn't going to last indefinitely! At some point I would lose you again! How many times am I supposed to lose the same person I love? *How many?*"

She sagged against a wall, and when Kalinda tried to walk over to her, comfort her, embrace her, Robin's arms whirled about, driving her back. Robin covered her head with her arms and sank to the floor, sobbing uncontrollably.

"I'm sorry," whispered Kalinda helplessly. She backed up until she reached the doors, which slid open behind her, and retreated from the cabin.

Robin continued to sob, slumping over onto the floor, and she remained there until she fell asleep.

The *Spectre*

i.

What have I done? What have I done?

A feeling of hopelessness seized Selar, but she knew that indulging it was not an option.

A haze had been removed from her mind, like fog dissipating. She could not even dwell upon what she had done; it was too much for her to contemplate. It was all she could do not to be overwhelmed by the consequences of her actions.

The word that summarized her state of mind in the past few days echoed in her head, but she refused to acknowledge it. It was considered the bottom rung in the ladder of Vulcan development, a state of mind shunned by every right-thinking Vulcan in the galaxy. How was it possible for her to have allowed herself to descend to such a level? She could not have allowed it, and therefore she had not done so.

No. It is not demonstrated. That is a logical fallacy, circular reasoning. What is wrong with you, embracing logical fallacies to avoid taking responsibility for your behavior?

She put her face in her hands and slowed her breathing, straining to pull herself together. Then she looked down at the shackle around her ankle and the length of chain that attached it to the wall. She pulled on it experimentally. The chain did not display the slightest interest in breaking, which was not very accommodating of it.

She checked the child. Cwansi was still asleep. She had no idea how long he had been sleeping. When she was awake, she was perfectly able to keep track of time, down to the second. However, since she had been rendered unconscious, she wasn't certain about how much time had passed.

How could you not have anticipated that Lucius would do such a thing? He was willing to betray his own companion. What could possibly have made you think he would hesitate to turn on you the moment you ran contrary to his wishes? Especially when he's been so vague about his motivations. Nothing beyond "For the good of the Empire."

Selar tried to tell herself that there was no point in dwelling on the past. She could not correct her mistakes; her only choice was to try to create a future that was more to her liking. The problem was that, given her current state of affairs, contemplating her mistakes was the only pastime available. It wasn't as if she could accomplish much of anything else.

Except that is not entirely true, is it.

She looked once more to the unconscious form of Rulan. There was still the possibility that she could discern from hir information that would be helpful to Xy. Perhaps it might even provide her insight into the predicament that she currently found herself in. She had been reluctant to probe hir mind earlier. And thanks to the dreamlike events that had terminated her previous attempt to do so, she was uncertain now whether there was even any point in trying.

Why not? You have already lost your ship, your son, your good standing in Starfleet. There is simply no way you are ever going to be able to recover from this. You have nothing left to lose.

She was across the room from Rulan. That was going to make effecting a mind meld with hir more challenging, but not impossible. Selar closed her eyes, slowing down her heart rate. She envisioned hir thoughts, hir essence, pictured them as a pure glowing ball of energy. Then she reached out with the tendrils of her mind, merging her thoughts with hirs, *and she is searching, carefully, meticulously, and there is a towering wall in front of her, and she cannot quite believe it, because there it is, an actual wall that seems to go on forever in all directions, and she is floating in front of it, trying to go above it or around it and there is no way, she is blocked every which way, and then she tries to see if there is a way to get under the wall, some crack overlooked, some hole that will provide access, and she goes to the bottom and envisions herself starting to dig away at the foundation so that her essence can get through, and she believes she is beginning to make headway when there is a rumbling around her that seems impossible, yet there it is, and it is becoming louder, and it's everywhere, and suddenly she looks up and realizes that the impossibly high wall is beginning to crumble right over her, and she throws her arms up over her head to try to shield herself, but she fails and down it comes, all of it, collapsing on her, burying her, and she hears screaming coming from outside and she thinks it may be the baby or it may be Lucius but she cannot be sure, and she is looking in too many directions at once, and then she is completely entombed by the collapsing wall, and darkness claims her once more . . .*

ii.

Even in the bridge, Lucius could hear the reedy, plaintive wails of the infant. He cursed the ears that enabled him to detect noises others would have been unable to perceive. He waited for Selar to attend to the child, but apparently she was not doing so. Was she still unconscious from the disruptor blast? How could that possibly be? That had been hours ago.

A ploy. That was it. It had to be a ploy to bring him down to the brig, possibly in the hopes of ambushing him. Well, there was simply no way he would be foolish enough to fall for something that obvious. He was going to stay right where he was.

The cries escalated in volume and intensity and finally Lucius could not stand it any longer. With a furious growl he bolted from the bridge, down to the brig, and stood outside the force field. Selar was lying there, unmoving, still chained to the wall. The Hermat had not budged from where s/he'd been before. And sure enough, there was the baby, hands balled into tiny fists, face scrunched, crying. The child had been screaming so long and so intensely that his face was nearly as red as the natural skin color of his father's race.

"Shut up!" shouted Lucius at the child, which he knew was a waste of time. The child ignored him. If anything, his screams seemed to become louder. "Selar! Attend to him! Don't think you can lie there pretending to be unconscious! Attend to the child, or I'll kill him myself! My future be damned; I'll not tolerate his howling for another minute!"

Selar didn't move. Looking closer, he realized that her eyes were open, but they were darting about furiously as if she were dreaming while awake. Her breathing was shallow, almost impossible to perceive. It was as if she were in some sort of self-induced trance. If this was a stunt on her part, then it was well-conceived and amazingly pulled off.

There was nothing he could do on the other side of the force field. Lucius reached over and touched the control panel that was just to the right of the doorframe. As he did so, he pulled out his disruptor so that he would be ready for anything. The force field arcs withdrew into the sides of the wall, leaving the doorway unobstructed. Lucius entered, keeping his disruptor leveled on Selar. He stopped several feet away from her, beyond the reach the chain would have allowed her to attain if she suddenly came to—presuming she was faking. He afforded the Hermat one more look. There was no movement there, but Lucius had extremely good peripheral vision. If the Hermat made any move, Lucius would see it. Then he turned his attention to the baby, who was continuing to howl.

He switched his target from Selar to the baby and said warningly, "Last chance, Selar. Attend to the child or I swear by all the gods, I will attend to him myself, and it will be permanent." It was a bluff, or at least he thought it was. The baby was the whole point of the mission. Still, the damned thing was getting on his nerves in a terminal manner.

She didn't move. The baby continued to cry.

"Fine. On your head, then."

He swung the disruptor toward the child, threatening to pull the trigger.

That was when his peripheral vision alerted him.

The Hermat was coming right at him.

Lucius swung the disruptor back around, bringing it to bear on the Hermat, and there was no way the Hermat should have been able to cross the distance of the room before Lucius pulled the trigger. The Hermat was moving faster than Lucius would have thought possible. Lucius fired, but the Hermat had darted inside Lucius's reach and slapped his arm to the side. The shot went wide, and Luicus tried to bring his arm back around again. But it was as if he were moving in slow motion compared to the Hermat.

The Hermat's hand swung, and hir fingers were thrust outward, flat, like the head of a spear. It swung across Lucius's throat and Lucius grabbed at it reflexively. His eyes widened as something warm and wet began to soak his hand. He looked at it and saw that his hand was covered with greenish blood, and he realized with a sort of distant surprise that it was his own.

The Hermat was now standing several feet away, hir hand up in front of hir face. Lucius saw, to his surprise, that claws were extending from the tips of hir fingers. He hadn't seen those before. *Must be retractable,* he thought. *Interesting. Once I've attended to this minor wound, I shall have to find a way to remove them, preferably from the wrist up.*

That was when he realized the bleeding wasn't ceasing, despite the pressure he applied to it. If anything, it seemed to be flowing faster. It was pouring down the front of his clothing, a huge green stain that was spreading quickly.

The Hermat appeared to be looking right through him, and then the Hermat collapsed once more.

Lucius tried to bring up his disruptor, but it slipped from his suddenly nerveless fingers and clattered on the floor.

He was losing strength in his legs. He stumbled backward, barely making it to the door, and then he hit the force field control panel. The force field flared to life, once again imprisoning Selar, the baby, and the Hermat within.

Lucius turned on his heel, certain that all he had to do was get to sickbay to attend to this minor, if profusely bleeding, wound.

The gravity of his situation finally began to dawn on him when the floor tilted wildly beneath him, yet he heard nothing attacking the ship that might have caused the vessel to skew in such a manner. By process of elimination, he came to the realization that his legs were giving way. By that point, he was already hitting the floor.

He lay there, trying to command his body to move but getting nowhere. Instead his legs made feeble motions that produced no forward movement, and he couldn't get his arms to move at all. He lay in front of the brig, staring in.

At least the damned baby has stopped crying, he thought, and then realized the baby was lying on the floor, staring at him. At. Him. There was no smile on the baby's face, no frown. Instead it seemed to be fascinated by him, as if someone who was so young found the prospect of witnessing death to be utterly intriguing.

Death . . . ?

No . . . this cannot be how I die. I am a warrior. I am a soldier. I am destined to be the ruler of the Romulan Empire. I saw it.

Help me . . .

Soleta . . . she will help me . . . she will . . .

Soleta . . . I am so sor—

Lucius's blood continued to flow out of his severed jugular vein until most of it was on the floor. Some of it rolled up against the force field and made crackling noises as it fizzled against the energy grid. The rest stained the floor dark green.

In the meantime the *Spectre*, with no one at the helm, continued on its way to AF1963, and there was no means available to anyone in the brig to alter its course.

Starship Excalibur

Tania Tobias, conn officer of the *Excalibur,* had just come off shift and was entering the Team Room for some relaxation when she saw Kalinda seated on the far side, all by herself. It was obvious to Tobias that Kalinda was the subject of conversation by many of the crew, who were giving her sidelong glances and speaking to one another in hushed voices.

She supposed it was to be expected. After all, she was not only walking around claiming to be a dead Thallonian lord, but also, in defiance of all logic, the captain was following her lead to pursue Robin Lefler's missing baby. It seemed a ludicrous concept on the surface, but the crew of the *Excalibur* had long come to trust their commanding officer. That did not mean, however, they were necessarily going to trust Kalinda or welcome her in the same manner they had welcomed her when she was merely

Si Cwan's sister, rather than a young woman claiming to be the vessel for her late brother's return.

Still, she looked rather lonely. Tobias could sympathize. She certainly had had her share of bumps and bruises as a Starfleet officer. She was, as one Starfleet officer had commented, "damaged goods." Calhoun had taken a chance on her and put her at the conn of his ship. She would be eternally grateful for that, and if that man believed in Kalinda enough to take her at her word, then that was sufficient for Tobias to invest some time and energy in Kalinda.

Deciding to make a move before she thought better of it, she made her way over to Kalinda, who looked up at her curiously. Kalinda frowned. "Do I know you?"

"Tania Tobias. Lieutenant. Conn officer."

"Oh, right. Right. You replaced McHenry." Kalinda shook her head, a pensive look on her face. "I never knew what to make of McHenry. Very curious fellow, he was. He wasn't quite of this world." Then Kalinda studied Tobias, as if finding her suddenly interesting. "Give me your hand."

"What?"

"Your hand. Give it to me."

"Can it remain attached to my wrist?" She said it

with what she intended to be humor, but the look on Kalinda's face remained solemn. Not understanding, but feeling the need to cooperate, she extended her hand and Kalinda placed it between the two of hers. She closed her eyes, as if she were reaching deep into herself, and then she opened them and gazed at Tobias. There seemed to be some sort of new understanding reflected in them.

"I see," said Kalinda softly, "that you have a touch of other worldliness about you, do you not? A spark within you. It was not there when you were born. Whence did it come?"

Tobias yanked her hand away. Part of her wanted to bounce up from the chair, turn, and bolt from the Team Room as quickly as her feet would take her. Instead she remained where she was, staring in fascination at Kalinda. "How were you able to tell?" she whispered.

"I keep saying, but no one quite believes, once you have been on the other side, things become clearer. Your own Shakespeare said it best: There is more in heaven and earth than is dreamt of in your philosophy."

"I don't know about that. My dreams are pretty far-reaching."

"And they've tormented you. Dreams are the worst. Especially when you have them while you're awake."

Tobias nodded slowly. "You understand."

"Yes."

"I've been . . ." Her eyes began to tear up and she fought them back with effort. "I've been wishing I could find someone who understood." Her voice was so soft that Kalinda leaned forward to hear her better. "How could I? I have to pretend that everything's all right, and I've gotten so good at it. If I said what was really going through my mind, they'd all think I was insane. A lot of them already think that. Starfleet thought that. If it weren't for Captain Calhoun—"

"Yes. Exactly. And he accorded me the same latitude. There is no one else in Starfleet quite like him. The things he has done and experienced grant him a unique perspective. Just as you find it difficult to believe in me, others would find it difficult to believe in you. Yet Captain Calhoun is, at the very least, open to possibilities. You see, Tania Tobias, how much we have in common?"

"I . . . I guess . . ."

"No, you don't guess. You know," said Kalinda with a smile. "It's just a matter of admitting it to yourself."

It was at that point that Tobias realized Kalinda was still holding her hand. Then she realized a number of people in the Team Room were looking in her direction with expressions ranging from mild interest to outright bewilderment.

Tobias withdrew her hand quickly, feeling her cheeks flush. She had no idea what she had to be embarrassed about, and yet she was. She put her hands down flat on her legs.

"It's all right. I understand," Kalinda said again. "More than you can believe. More than perhaps you're even comfortable admitting."

"I have to go."

"No, you don't."

"Yes, I do," she said and got up so quickly that she banged her leg on the underside of the table. She bit her lower lip to prevent herself from crying out and managed to say, "It's been nice talking to you."

"We shall do so again and soon. I have no doubt."

She headed quickly out of the Team Room, trying to ignore the eyes upon her. Just as she got to the door, she glanced back at Kalinda, to see if she was looking her way. She was not. Instead she was staring in front of her, and Tania Tobias would have given anything if she could have seen things from Kalinda's point of view. Then the doors hissed shut, closing her out from sight.

The *Spectre*

A field of blackness slowly began to dissipate as Selar started to come around. It was the child's cries that summoned her back from unconsciousness. Slowly she opened her eyes and, as illogical as it may have been, she briefly hoped that she would discover herself waking up in sickbay, just as she had when she first had the dreamlike connection with the alien entity. No such luck this time. Reality had overtaken her dreaming mind and, yes, she was still lying on the floor in the brig.

Cwansi was wailing piteously. She shook off the lethargy that begged her to just close her eyes and surrender yet again to the darkness, and forced herself to her feet.

She made her way to the bottles of nourishment she had brought along, prepared one quickly, and moments later was feeding the grateful infant. Liquid bubbled out of the edges of his mouth and he almost choked a couple of times, because he was fighting down the remains of his sobs so that he could focus his attention on consuming sustenance.

As she fed him, she tried to assess her situation. She glanced toward Rulan and saw that s/he was as s/he had been before: unmoving. The fact that her attempt to meld with Rulan had yet again met with failure prompted her to conclude that there was more going on than just inadequacy on her part. Something was actively blocking her attempts. The first time she had been interrupted by the vision that had spurred her onto this course of madness. The second had been far more direct, the mental equivalent of a slap in the face.

Even more daunting was the suspicion—well founded, she suspected—that her most recent mishap had been a warning. It could have been far more cataclysmic. Instead of dumping a psychic wall upon her, she could have been—what? Impaled? Beheaded? Experienced some vast psychic trauma from which she would not have recovered?

If she had to, she would try again. But it was the last thing she wanted to do, because she might well not survive the experience.

Although, really, would that be so terrible, if you did not survive? What do you have to return to?

Then her nostrils wrinkled. She smelled something.

She realized what it was instantly. It was the stench of death. As a doctor, she had experienced it enough times, particularly on occasions when she had strode through a battlefield, shaking her head as she looked at the remains of those who had annihilated one another for no damned reason.

The scent wafted to her, and she quickly discerned the origin. She didn't have to move from where she was, nor did she have to disturb the infant's feeding. She could see from where she was sitting the pool of green blood on the floor. It was copious, coating the floor, and she was forced to conclude that Lucius was the source.

Her eagerness to determine what had happened ate at her, but she didn't want to do anything to disrupt the child since he had finally calmed down sufficiently to eat. So she remained where she was, minutes passing like hours, until Cwansi had had his fill. He did not drift off to sleep as she had thought he might. Instead he looked up at her with interest. She found herself staring down at him. "What is going through your mind?" she asked. She remembered how she had considered embarking on a mind meld with Xy when he was an infant, just to get an idea of what the world looked like from his point of view, but she had never been able to bring herself to do it. Infants were little balls of pure emotion and need, and she had been daunted by the prospect of experiencing that firsthand.

She got to her feet and, still cradling the child in her arms, moved toward the door. She stopped just short of the door, though, and tentatively extended a finger. Energy crackled where the tip of her finger touched it.

"Perfect," she said, coming as close to annoyance as she ever allowed herself. She moved to the right, trying to get a better angle, and she was rewarded with a clearer view of Lucius's unmoving body. Her eyes narrowed as she tried to make out the cause of death, aside from the obvious: all his blood being on the outside of his body.

Then she spotted it. There was a slash across his throat. As near as she could tell, his jugular had been severed.

"That would do it," she murmured. "But how—?"

Then she realized.

There were only three possibilities.

The first was that Lucius had taken his own life. That seemed unlikely. He had no reason to do so, and furthermore there was no sign of a knife nearby. Granted, he might be lying on top of it, but it didn't make a good deal of sense.

The second was that an unknown intruder had gotten aboard the ship, killed Lucius, and then departed leaving Selar, the baby, and Rulan unmolested. Possible.

There remained a third and far likelier option.

Rulan had killed him.

Selar, better than anyone, knew what Hermats were capable of and of the formidable claws they possessed.

She turned away quickly and went over to Rulan. Instantly she saw telltale flecks of green on the tips of hir fingers on hir right hand. The claws had retracted, as they typically did when no threat presented itself. But the evidence of the damage they had inflicted was clear for her to see. Rulan had come to long enough to kill Lucius with one swipe of hir hand and then collapsed again.

Selar had no idea what had brought hir out of it and it frustrated her. Moreover, she had to consider the possibility that Rulan could, at any given moment, come out of hir coma and turn against Selar. Should that happen, Selar would be the only thing that stood between Cwansi and death.

Selar's mind raced, trying to conceive of some plan of attack, some means of getting out of the brig. Lucius, in a final display of perversity, had apparently made his dying act to reactivate the force field. Surely they were still on a direct course to AF1963, presuming they weren't already there. She had, as before, lost all track of time.

There would be no point in repeatedly slamming into the field in hopes of overloading it. Her shackles allowed her to reach the door, but she couldn't go beyond. Perhaps she could find some means of tapping into the ship's computer and ordering it to shut down the force field. But she had no idea how to go about it. Soleta might well have been able to, but Soleta wasn't there. Thanks to Selar, she had been rendered unconscious back on Bravo station. A squad of firefighters could not begin to extinguish all the bridges she had burned in the past few days. And besides, there was still the matter of the shackles.

How could you have done this to yourself? How could you have—?

She forced herself to stop dwelling on such things, because there was no point. She had to focus on making things better, rather than contemplating how she had made them so much worse.

And then, as she continued to try to devise a way out of her predicament, something caused the ship to shudder. Had they hit something? As far as she knew, the ship was moving on autopilot. Ordinarily if there was something in the ship's path, the computer would know to avoid it, but what if that was not the case? What if they had just wandered into a meteoroid field and were about to be repeatedly pummeled? She had no way of raising the shields, no way of controlling anything.

Then there was a loud noise, and it sounded metallic, as if something were banging up against the ship. Cwansi stirred in her arms, and as she looked around confused, she held the child closer to her. "Everything will be fine," she said to the baby, issuing assurances that she herself did not remotely feel.

For a time, she heard nothing. And then, footsteps in the distance. They were moving smoothly, rhythmically, as if they were marching in unison. For a moment she had hoped, prayed, that they had been intercepted by a Federation vessel, perhaps even the *Excalibur.* She dreaded the prospect of having to look into the hurt, betrayed eyes of Burgoyne and Calhoun, and even Xy for whom she had done all this. That, though, would certainly be preferable to the prospect now facing her: some militaristic, extremely advanced race that had taken possession of the ship and would be doing who knows what to her and the baby. There was simply no way that the steady cadences she was hearing would be indicative of Calhoun or any Starfleet crew. And they had to be advanced, because they had been able to detect the undetectable *Spectre*.

She was worried the infant would sense the jeopardy of the situation, and perhaps even start crying. Selar stepped back against the wall, flattening against it, hoping that perhaps whoever it was would walk past the brig hastily without spotting her. It seemed unlikely, but it was the only thing she could think of under the circumstances. Her heart was pounding furiously against her chest and she willed it to slow. There would never be a better time to exercise all her discipline and Vulcan training.

The marching came closer, and then stopped right outside the brig.

Not good, she thought.

Selar did the only thing she could think of. She

put the baby down behind her and then turned to face whoever or whatever was about to enter the brig.

A massive humanoid figure appeared, clad in plated blue body armor, from head to toe.

She had no means of defense, no . . .

Then she spied something protruding from under Rulan's body. Her eyes widened. It was the butt of a disruptor.

He must have dropped it. Lucius must have dropped it.

Her action matched her thoughts as she lunged forward and yanked Rulan's body back without caring whether s/he suddenly came to life and tried slashing at her. Fortunately, Rulan remained insensate. She pulled the disruptor out, turned, and aimed it at the armored figure, which still hadn't moved.

There was no point in firing because the force field was still activated. At least she now had some firepower when it shut down the field, as it inevitably would.

The armored figure paused and then walked forward, not deigning to bother with the force field controls. The field crackled furiously around it and blew out.

Even as her heart sank, Selar opened fire. As she suspected, the disruptor did not slow down the armored figure in the slightest.

It ignored her and went straight for Cwansi.

"Keep away from him!" shouted Selar, violating her own resolve not to waste her breath in such endeavors. She kept up a steady blast, disruptor waves cascading along the back of the creature's armor. It didn't cast a glance in her direction.

A second one and then a third walked through the archway that had previously been protected by the field. The one in the forefront went straight toward Selar. She whipped the disruptor back around. The advancing entity swung its armored hand as if it had nothing but time, and it struck Selar on the side of her skull. Selar went down, her head spinning.

Something slammed her in the small of her back. It was another one of the armored beings, kicking her savagely. She tried to roll away from it, but now its associate had stepped in on the other side and kicked her back in the other direction. There was nowhere for her to go, nothing for her to do. Now it was just about survival, as she curled herself into a ball and brought her arms up over her head.

The two figures converged, continuing their assault. She kept her teeth clenched, her lips tight, determined to do the one thing that was still within her abilities: Selar would not cry out. And she did not, even as she felt bones breaking beneath the impact.

The pounding continued for, by her reckoning, fifty-three seconds. Then they withdrew. She peered out from between her arms and saw that Rulan was still on the floor, but the baby was gone.

Although there was technically no way she had of knowing for sure, she was nevertheless positive that these . . . these monsters . . . were connected with the alien who had appeared to her. The alien whose blandishments had preyed upon her obsession, had tipped her over into a forbidden state of mind.

One of their kicks had caught her across the face. Now, with her lip swelling and her mouth filling with blood, she managed to say, sounding as if she had marbles in her mouth, "What about my son? You said you would help him! I gave up everything for him! What did the Hermat have to do with any of this?" And it all surged within her, the frustration, the anger, the despair, and not all the training in the world could prevent it from bursting and pouring out of her as she howled, "What about my son, you bastards?! I've given up everything!"

Not yet, you haven't.

The words were in her head as a soft glow filled the air in front of her. It seemed to be humming with power, crackling into existence, except it wasn't via a transporter. Or if it was, it was some sort of technology that she had never seen before.

The general outlines of the being she was perceiving were instantly familiar to her. It was the alien whom she had seen in her vision on the *Excalibur*. She was almost relieved to see him, for at least it was the final proof that she had not simply been hallucinating back in sickbay, embarking on this disastrous course because her mind had completely cracked and sent her sprinting down the road to damnation.

But then its body began to shift as it became more substantial. The outlines filled out, the face filled in, smiling at her, and Selar felt as if her sanity were slipping away.

Her son, Xy, was standing before her, apparently genuinely happy to see her. He was brimming with understanding and compassion, and this time his lips were moving as he said again, "Not yet, you haven't. But do not worry, brave Selar. There will be time enough for that. There will be time enough for everything . . . and understanding of it all."

Starship Trident

i.

Planet AF1963 seemed like nothing special, and Lieutenant Mick Gold, conn officer of the *Trident,* didn't hesitate to say so.

"Why would Selar be heading here?" said Gold with obvious disdain in his voice. "It's just a big rock."

"If the woman's gone out of her mind," drawled Romeo Takahashi from ops, "then she don't rightly need a reason, do she."

"Even insanity has a reason, Hash," said Captain Kat Mueller. She had risen from her chair and was studying the planet, indulging in the no doubt fruitless task of trying to see the world through the eyes of a demented Vulcan. Mueller had witnessed many things in her time as the *Trident*'s captain, and as the executive officer of the *Excalibur* before that. But the notion of an insane Vulcan was almost beyond her comprehension. What must have been the stress upon her that would have driven someone as calm and unflappable as Selar to do such a thing?

Part of her still hoped that this was an outsized misunderstanding. After all, it hadn't been all that long ago when Admiral Edward Jellico was believed to have turned traitor, grabbing a prototype time vessel and making off with it, presumably to turn it over to enemies of the Federation. In that instance, though, not everything had turned out to be as it appeared. Perhaps that was the case here.

She feared, though, that it was not.

"Any readings, M'Ress?" she said.

The science officer slowly shook her head, her huge mane sweeping back and forth. "Nothing out of the ordinary, Captain. If there's some sort of presence there, it's masking itself. My sensors aren't picking up a thing."

"Captain, shall I assemble an exploratory landing party?" said Arex from the security station.

Mueller pursed her lips, considering it. "Inform Squad A that they may be needed. Put them on post at the transporter room. But we'll hold off on sending them down until we get a better idea of the situation. Our job here is to intercept the *Spectre,* not to explore the planet. Along those lines, M'Ress, how are we coming along with attempts to spot her? Between the cloak and that damnable ion glide, it's like trying to pick a single breeze out of a whirlwind."

"True enough, Captain. And if we were simply cruising the area and trying to pick her up randomly, then we wouldn't have a prayer," said M'Ress. "The one hope we've got—and I think it's a reasonable one—is that they're approaching via warp drive. The ion glide is fine for slow approaches, but it won't be nearly sufficient enough to travel the sort of distances they'll need to cover."

"If it did," Hash said, "then by the time they get here, the baby would be old enough to slap them around and make his own escape."

"Okay, so, granted, they'll need warp to get here," said Mueller. "And we can detect a vessel coming out of warp."

"Exactly. What they'll probably do is cut out of warp space and allow the ion glide to take them in."

"They could even cut the engines entirely and just let momentum carry them," said Hash.

"Yes, they could," said Gold with a trace of sarcasm, "but they'll have to use *something* to control themselves or, best case scenario, they shoot right past the planet."

"The problem is," said Mueller, "if we know they're here but they're running silent, we're still unable to find them."

Commander Desma, the Andorian second in command, spoke up for the first time. "That's not actually a problem."

"How do you figure that?"

"Easy," she said with a shrug. "The moment we detect their approach, we bracket the area that they've projected to drop out of warp space. With any luck we disrupt their power flow and they'll have to come out of cloak."

"And without any luck," said Mueller, "we blow them out of space. We won't be doing much of a job saving the baby if we wind up killing him, will we."

"The odds are slim of our destroying the ship outright, Captain. It is much more likely that we would simply knock them out of commission."

"Are you willing to make that call, Commander?"

Desma stared at her and then said, "It is not the prerogative of the executive officer to do that, Captain. The responsibility rests with you. But I would be derelict in my duty if I did not offer to you all the options that present themselves."

Nodding slightly, Mueller said, "Fair enough." Standing next to her command chair, she drummed the armrest thoughtfully for a moment. "Arex. Set phasers to half strength. Same with the photon torpedoes. I have no desire to risk destroying them, but perhaps we can scare them into showing themselves."

"If a Romulan is operating that vessel," said Gold, "they don't scare. Trust me, I know."

"As do I, Lieutenant," said Mueller, "but I still have no desire to risk—"

"Captain!" M'Ress said suddenly. "I'm detecting an energy surge on the planet's surface!"

"What sort?"

"I'm not sure. I—" She looked up from her station, concern on her face. "It has some common elements with our own transporter beams, but far more powerful."

"Shields up," Mueller said immediately. "Go to red alert. If there's something down there, we don't need them beaming a bomb on board."

The shields immediately flared into existence around the *Trident* as the red alert klaxon sounded through the ship. "Trace the origin of that energy spike. See if you can—"

ii.

The armored figures began appearing throughout the ship. They simply popped into existence, without any warning, as if the shields were nonexistent. Engineering, sickbay, every corridor throughout the vessel. They did not appear to have weapons on them, but it was clear they had not simply shown up to introduce themselves.

Security teams charged in from all directions, phasers drawn. Everywhere throughout the ship, the same scene was repeated. Security teams would inform the armored beings that they were trespassing, that their unauthorized presence would be regarded as a hostile act unless they surrendered immediately. If they did not, then they, the security teams, were prepared to use force.

Each of the groups of armored beings had arrived in threes, standing in a perfect triangle, back-to-back with one another. They raised their hands, outstretched, in a "Y" formation. Interestingly, in every single instance, the security guards breathed silent sighs of relief. These creatures looked formidable, and no one was looking forward to engaging in combat against them.

That was when the blistering force beams ripped from the palms of the armored figures' hands.

The foremost security guards were blown back, blown apart. The troops farther back opened fire, and they watched in shock and frustration as the phaser beams ricocheted off them.

"Shoot to kill!" security guards were shouting all over the ship, and power levels of phaser beams were thumbed upward. Again they opened fire, with power intensities that should rightly have vaporized the armored figures.

Nothing. The armor absorbed impact without any visible effects.

The newcomers did not fire again. Instead they waded into the security forces, smashing into them with their fists. The intruders moved far more quickly than one would have thought possible considering the apparent heaviness of their armor. They weren't lumbering. Instead they were catlike, pouncing upon anyone standing in their path.

They tore through anyone and anything standing

in their way. The crew of the *Trident* was too seasoned to permit anything such as fear pervade the air, but scarcely controlled panic? Yes.

They tore through sickbay, medtechs scrambling to get out of their way, for they were healers, not fighters. But the attackers did not make the distinction, crushing all beneath their gloved hands or booted feet. Doctor Villers, the veteran CMO of the *Trident,* who made it a practice to always go armed no matter what because one never knew when a combat situation would arise, yanked out her phaser and opened fire. She experienced for herself the sight of the phaser ricocheting off the armor. Then one of the armored figures advanced on her, grabbed her by the head, and twisted. She was surprised to hear a cracking sound, her own neck snapping. It was the last diagnosis she ever made.

Crew members ran, but blood ran faster.

iii.

Frantic reports were coming in from all over the ship to the bridge. Mueller shouted orders, trying to boost the power to the shields, to block the beam that was apparently penetrating it at will and flooding her vessel with enemies.

And then three of them were on the bridge. They did not enter through any door, nor did the humming of a transporter beam signal their arrival.

Arex immediately pulled out his phaser and fired. The blast ricocheted and struck Desma, who went down clutching at her chest, moaning. One of them raised his palm and unleashed a blast straight at Arex, but his three legs made him extremely mobile and he dodged the blast even as he fired again.

The emergency weapon array slid out of the side panel in the command chair. Mueller went for it, and one of the armored figures moved faster than she would have thought possible, smashing its foot down and crushing the tray of phasers beneath its boot. It swung a fist that backhanded Mueller, sending her flying. She landed near Mick Gold, who was on his feet and came between the advancing figure and the captain.

Arex fired again and tried to dodge once more, but this time wasn't fast enough. The blast of energy caught him on the shoulder and he screamed as one of his three arms was blown clean off. It flopped to the ground, still spasming, as pinkish blood poured down the side of his body. The armored figure swung its hand around, prepared to fire again.

With an ear-splitting scream that was not a sound of panic but rather a roar of challenge, M'Ress hurtled through the air, claws bared, as she landed on the back of Arex's attacker. Her fingers sought desperately to find some breech in the armor, something she could reach into and attack. Instead she let out a screech and lost her grip, falling backward. Smoke wafted from her. Part of her uniform and some of her fur had been burned away, for the armor had been scalding to the touch.

The intruder that had assaulted Mueller advanced on her, and Mick Gold, even though he must have known it was hopeless, drew back his fist and punched the creature as hard as he could in the head. It did not so much as stagger the thing, although Gold cried out and clutched at his fist.

The armored figure grabbed Gold by the shoulder, put its palm flat against Gold's chest, and ignited the weaponry that was in its palm. Gold's body practically lit up, energy blasting out from his ears, his mouth, his very pores. Mueller cried out his name as Gold hung there for a moment, as if the energy were suspending him in the air, and then he collapsed next to Mueller.

She saw that his eyes were gone, burned away in the sockets, his skin blackened and crispened. *Gold,* she thought bleakly, *those sons of bitches . . .*

She looked up at Gold's killer, at this monster that had shown up out of nowhere and started slaughtering her crew. She looked up at where the helmet joined the armor, and there was a vent, a tiny vent barely the width of a fingernail from which steam was rippling.

They're superheated, they're superheated from within and the armor regulates it somehow and that's how they vent, maybe they have to vent when they're in battle because their metabolism speeds up . . .

In the next second, as the armored being started to reach for her, Mueller reached into the top of her boot and yanked out the slender stiletto that she always kept secreted there. The one that she had always carried, without exception, ever since attending the University of Heidelberg. The stiletto was in her hand and she dodged under its arm and to its side and rammed it with precision into the vent.

The armored figure spun; if something clad head-to-toe in armor could look surprised, then this creature certainly managed it. Something liquid poured from where she had stabbed it. It looked like thin streams of lava trickling down the armor, leaving steaming channels behind it as it went. Mueller smiled grimly, and if this were to be the last action of her life, at least it would provide her some satisfaction. "The man you just killed was Mick Gold. Remember his name," she said with a snarl. "Let it be the last thought as you die, you son of a bitch." She lashed out and drove her booted foot into its chest, and it stumbled back, crashing into the command chair, bouncing off it and hitting the floor. It thrashed about, the two beings accompanying it looking down with what Mueller fancied to be stupid expressions.

"Attention all hands, this is the captain!" shouted Mueller, and her voice boomed all over the beleaguered vessel. "They have a narrow steam-release vent on the right of their helmets! They're vulnerable at that—"

An armored hand swept in and caught Mueller on the side of the head. She went down as the remaining two intruders converged on her and brought their hands up. She stared straight into the weaponry in their palms that was charging up, preparing to unleash its lethal contents.

"Go to hell," she said.

And suddenly their bodies began to shimmer.

They looked around in confusion and then the hum of the transporter beams overwhelmed them and they vanished.

"Hold on," said Romeo Takahashi. There was cold fury on his face. He was manipulating the controls of his ops station. "And . . . there!"

On the viewscreen there was a brief shimmering and then thousands, perhaps millions of bits of particles materialized and floated off in as many directions.

"Took control of the transporter. Locked onto those bastards from here, beamed them out, and set it for widest possible dispersal," he said.

"Can you lock onto all of them? All these creatures running around on the ship?"

"It'll take a while," said Hash, "but for you, Captain?" and he looked grimly at Gold's corpse on the floor, "and for Mick? Sure. I'm on—"

Even as he reached toward the ops station, it exploded in a burst of sparks. Hash jumped back, crying out, his hands convulsing in pain.

Mueller started toward him, and then the air was suddenly filled with a glowing blue light. She pivoted and watched in amazement as something new materialized on the bridge, taking form before her eyes.

"What the hell?" she whispered.

Moments earlier it had looked like something else entirely, something bizarre and translucent and she'd barely been able to make it out. But as the glow subsided, she was stunned to see Mackenzie Calhoun smiling at her. Those familiar purple eyes were tinged with quiet patience and seemed far older than they normally were. Calhoun's eyes, but someone else's soul peering through them.

He looked at Hash, who had crisscrossed his chest and shoved his hurt hands under his arms. "Are you all right?" he said solicitously. Then, without waiting for him to reply, he looked to M'Ress who was still writhing in pain from being so severely burned. "And you?" Again without waiting for response, he turned his attention to Arex. He frowned. "Oh, dear. That's rather catastrophic, isn't it."

"Who the hell are you?" said Mueller. She was still holding the stiletto. "And I'd answer quickly, because if you think that impersonating Mackenzie Calhoun is going to make me hesitate to bury this in your chest, then you are sadly mistaken."

"As are you, if you believe you have the slightest degree of power in this situation," said the fake Calhoun. He sounded almost sympathetic. "Although,"

he said as he glanced toward the fallen armored figure, "that showed extreme resourcefulness on your
part. We were not anticipating any casualties on our
side."

"There's going to be a lot more if you don't have
your soldiers stand down."

"Soldiers?" He seemed amused by the notion. "Is
that what you think they are? No, no, Captain. They
are our *helpers*. Our brothers in spirit, if not in genetic
makeup."

"I don't care what they are. They're killing my
people and you will order them to stand down, or—"

"May I offer a counterproposal?" he asked, as if a
random thought had just occurred to him. "Why do
you not tell *your* crew to surrender? If you do, their
lives will be spared. As will yours. I am sparing your
life even as we speak, because I am certain you realize
how simple it would be to take it from you."

And suddenly three more of the armored attackers appeared on the bridge with as much ease as the
others had. She moaned inwardly even as she gave
visible response with a slight uptick of the corner of
her mouth.

"You are a leader, you see. My people respect leaders, since we are fundamentally leaders ourselves,"

said the fake Calhoun. "Now . . . order your people to surrender. Order them to stand down before we kill them all."

She stepped toward him. Two of the armored beings stepped in, preventing her from drawing closer. "You will find," she said in a low, taut voice, "that my people are extremely resourceful. You're the ones who have committed an act of war. *You* surrender."

"It appears we are at a stalemate," said the fake Calhoun sadly. "Let us consider, I have lost one of our people, as you say. And you have lost . . . well, quite a few more. So let us see, then, who runs out of people first. Are we agreed?"

Starship Excalibur

i.

Burgoyne stood at the doorway to the captain's ready room. Calhoun was seated behind his desk, his fingers steepled.

"I think we need to talk, Burgy," he said.

"I was afraid you'd say that," said Burgoyne and walked in as the door closed behind hir.

ii.

Robin Lefler stepped into the turbolift and said, "Deck Seven." As the doors started to slide shut, a pair of slender hands reached in to stop them. The doors automatically opened once more. Robin looked up curiously and then her heart sank when she saw who it was.

"Can we speak for a few minutes, Robin?" said Kalinda, and insinuated herself into the turbolift before Robin could respond. The turbolift began to move to the requested destination.

"I'm not entirely certain what there is to talk ab—"

Kalinda started to reach toward her, moving in to kiss her as she had before, and Robin pulled back, putting her hand up to keep her away. "Lift, halt." The turbolift obediently came to a stop.

Glancing around, Kalinda said, "Hoping to ensure privacy?" There was a faint teasing in her voice that sounded so familiar, so damned familiar . . .

"I cannot deal with this," said Robin. "I just . . . I cannot. Deal. With it."

"Do you find it so difficult to conceive—?"

"This isn't about conceiving!" Robin said, her voice rising. "This isn't about trying to figure out if you're him, or whether you only think you're him! Either you're a disturbed young woman or a creature that's neither alive or dead. But either way, you're not my husband, and even if you were—"

"Even if I were? Even if—"

She drew back a hand and slapped Kalinda as hard as she could and all the fear, all the frustration, all the terror that she had been trying to deal with exploded out of her as she screamed, *"How could you have let them kill you?!"*

"Wh-what?" Kalinda stammered uncomprehendingly. "Let them? I didn't let them! I—"

"You got outmaneuvered and outwitted by people who had a fraction of your cunning and resourcefulness, and you left me behind to clean up the mess, and . . . and you stupid—!" and she pounded on Kalinda's chest as if she were thumping on Si Cwan's, except, of course, Si Cwan would have been taller and his chest a good deal harder. Kalinda staggered back, clutching at her bosom, gasping for air and wincing in pain. "I'm a widow and a mother left with no father for her child, and it's *all your fault*!"

"You're not being rational," said Kalinda, grimacing from the ache where Robin had punched her.

"I don't feel like being rational. I feel like finding my son and trying to move forward with my life!"

"And I'm trying to help you."

"With finding Cwansi, yes, I know. And if this . . . this flight of fancy, against all reason, is successful, then I'll be grateful to you. But not so grateful that I'll acknowledge you as my husband. Because either I would be taking advantage of a deluded young woman or a dead man. Either way it's way out of the range of anything I feel comfortable with. Do you understand?"

Kalinda had stopped rubbing where Robin had struck her. She sighed heavily. "Yes. Of course I understand. I just—" She cleared her throat. "You have no idea what it was like, Robin. The loneliness, the emptiness. The feeling of being here and yet not. My love for you, for our son, for Kally . . . my determination to see things through . . . it all held me here. I—"

"I can't listen to this. Lift, resume movement."

"All right, Robin," came Morgan's voice, and the turbolift promptly began to move once more.

Robin sagged against the side of the lift and closed her eyes in pain. "The two of you. You're going to drive me insane. The omniscient, all-seeing mother and the dead husband in my sister-in-law's body. This isn't a life. It's insanity."

"Then I shall do whatever is within my power," said Kalinda softly, "to mute the insanity. My apologies for making things difficult for you, Robin. Believe of me what you will, but I ask only that you believe this absolutely: I would not hurt you for all the world."

The doors slid open and Kalinda exited, quickly, noiselessly as a ghost.

iii.

Soleta knew there was every reason that she should remain confined to her quarters, as Calhoun had made clear was to be the case. Despite all that she had once meant to the *Excalibur,* the circumstances—especially considering the involvement of her vessel and her partner in the disappearance of Cwansi—required that some degree of security-oriented decorum be observed. Calhoun had stopped short of putting her in the brig, or even posting a guard outside her quarters. "The honor system," was what he had said to her, willing to take her on her word that she would stay put.

It was not a hard promise for Soleta to keep. What *was* hard was for her to walk the corridors of the ship she had called home. She suspected that Robin Lefler felt much the same way, but then again, the circumstances were quite different. Robin had departed Starfleet with her chin held high, embarking on a grand adventure of love. Soleta had practically been called a traitor, simply because she had been less than candid about the nature of her birth, as if she had any control over such a thing. The various former crewmates whom she had encountered hadn't seemed to know how to address her, particularly attired as she was in Romulan garb. Despite the current thawing of relations with the Romulans, there was still no love lost, and much suspicion, between the two civilizations.

In the end, it was better that she remained in her quarters until such time—presuming it ever came—that she could somehow serve the *Excalibur*'s needs.

Then she heard the sound of footsteps just outside the door. "Come," she called.

The doors slid open and she was mildly surprised to see Robin Lefler standing there. "Sorry," Robin said. "I was just—I didn't realize that you'd hear me. Which, I suppose, was foolish of me, considering the . . ." and she touched her own ears.

"Think nothing of it," said Soleta mildly. "You need not be hesitant in coming to see me."

"Yes, well, I just—" She remained in the doorway, not entering. "It occurred to me that I hadn't been by to thank you for trying to prevent Selar from taking Cwansi. And I'm very sorry that you were harassed for it, and arrested and, well—"

"Think nothing of it."

"Except I do think of it," said Robin sadly. "I think of the old days when we served together, and how the galaxy seemed so full of possibilities."

"It's still full of possibilities, Robin. It's just that, the older you get, the less attractive many of them become."

"I suppose so. Anyway, again—thank you for the help, and sorry about the inconvenience."

"You are welcome."

They remained there looking at each other for a time, until Soleta said, "Do you wish to come in and talk for a while?"

"Desperately," said Robin.

And she did, and they did.

iv.

Xy had lost track of how long he had been sitting in sickbay. He had been in the quarantine section—now vacant except for him—and currently in the chair that his mother had occupied for so long. He looked up, though, when he heard a throat loudly being cleared in what was a transparently obvious attempt to get his attention.

Mackenzie Calhoun was peering in through the door. He smiled politely. "Is it safe for me to come in?" he said with mock concern.

"You mean is there a possibility you'll catch something? Not unless being depressed is contagious."

"I hear it can be, but I'll take my chances." He walked into the quarantine section and stood in front of Xy, his arms folded. "So what are you doing down here, Lieutenant?"

"Filling in for my mother as needed."

"This isn't your shift."

"I subsist on far less sleep than is required by most. An hour or two a day. I can afford to—"

"What *I* can't afford," Calhoun interrupted him, kindly but firmly, "is to have a science officer who's so eaten up by guilt that he's letting it distract him from what needs to be done."

"What makes you think I'm being eaten up by guilt, Captain?"

"Because in so many ways, you are your father's son, and I've spent the last hour in my ready room talking hir down off the ceiling."

Xy frowned. "S/he's on the ceiling? Why is s/he—?"

"It's vernacular. Ever since this happened, s/he's

been spending every waking hour second-guessing how s/he should have handled hir relationship with your mother. S/he keeps trying to figure out how s/he could have seen all of this coming. Maybe averted it."

"There's no way s/he could have—"

"That's what I've been saying, and I think I've got hir about eighty percent believing it. I'm hoping to get to at least ninety percent with you."

Xy looked down, abashed. "Our situations—my father's and mine—are a little different, as are our perspectives."

"Not all that different. You're both trying to dissect the past, to figure out how you could have changed it."

"Respectfully, Captain, that's not what I'm doing at all. I am neither dissecting nor second-guessing. I am merely wallowing in guilt."

Despite the gravity with which Xy had spoken, Calhoun chuckled, low in his throat. "Well, I have to admire someone who knows himself quite that thoroughly. What do you have to feel guilty about? The circumstances of your birth?"

"More the nature of my physiological makeup."

"You were dealt a bad hand, Xy. No sense in blaming yourself for that."

"Well, my father was the dealer. Is there any sense in hir blaming hirself?"

"Not really. At least that's what I've been trying to tell hir."

"Then where do we place the blame? On my mother?"

"Well," said Calhoun, "she *is* the one responsible."

"Except she's not," said Xy firmly. "She was fine before all this happened. Before *I* happened. If it were not for me, and for my condition, then she would be right here, on the ship, serving her fellow crew members. She wouldn't have run off. She wouldn't have taken the infant. She did it for me, Captain. All for me."

"You don't know that. Why would you think that?"

"I've been studying her medical logs. Her journals. Reading between the lines. I think," he said indicating the table where Rulan had been lying, "I think she believed that Rulan somehow held a promise of a cure for me. That there was something about hir that could be applied to my condition and save me."

"But how does the baby tie into this?"

"I don't know," Xy admitted. "Perhaps because he's a half-breed, like me. I haven't figured that part out yet. Nevertheless, they are linked. I'm certain of it."

"Whatever it is, it will be revealed in the due course of time," said Calhoun. "Most things are. In the meantime, stop blaming yourself for your genetic makeup. None of us has any control over how we come to be here, and we have only limited control of how we ultimately depart. There are, however, far too many things we do have control over, and must answer for, to be wasting time on the things that are simply beyond our abilities to affect."

"You're saying I should get over it."

"More or less."

"Is that an order, Captain?"

"More of a suggestion."

V.

They are running through the corridors of a ship. It is hard to determine what ship it is. She reaches out and yes, there . . . the Trident. *It is the* Trident *under attack, from thunderous beings in cobalt-blue armor, and they are wreaking havoc and destruction wherever they walk, and one of them is walking right toward her, stretching out his hand, and it is glowing, blinding, and the force is being unleashed and she feels her body frying . . .*

Tania Tobias awoke with a startled cry. She sat up in bed, in the darkness, breathing heavily. "The *Trident*," she whispered.

A voice next to her in the darkness said groggily, "What?"

"The *Trident* is in trouble. It's under attack. Some sort of . . . of armored beings. The crew members are fighting, running, dying . . ."

"Well, then you've got to tell someone. Tell the captain."

Tobias shook her head firmly. "No. No, I can't. I don't want him to—"

"To what? Know what you can do?"

"I want to be normal."

"Tania—"

"I want to be normal!" and then she dropped her voice to a whisper, as if worried someone might overhear. "You don't understand. I was the Starfleet washout. The one who was too unstable to be trusted. I am not going to have 'occasionally has visions' added to my Starfleet docket. I just am not going to. We should be arriving at the planet in," she said, checking her chronometer, "three hours. I have no idea if what I saw

actually happened, or is happening, or will happen, or maybe never happen. That does occur, you know. That I see something that I could swear is genuine and it never transpires."

"Not to your knowledge, anyway."

"I pray the *Trident* is all right, and if it isn't, there isn't a damned thing I can do about it until we get there. I'm due back on duty soon. In fact, I should get up."

"Tania." Tania felt a warm hand upon her shoulder. "I wasn't expecting this to happen. I—"

"Wanted to feel less lonely. I totally understand." She leaned over, drew Kalinda to her and kissed her gently. "We live in strange times."

"Everyone always does. There's no such thing as normal. Just different degrees of abnormality."

"I've heard that." She rolled out of bed, leaving Kalinda to roll back over and drift back to sleep in a haze of warmth.

?

Selar did not remember lapsing into unconsciousness or falling asleep. She realized with a distant surprise that she didn't remember anything after the image of her son had presented itself to her in the brig of the *Spectre*. One moment she had been looking at that smiling visage that was so much like Xy's, and the next moment, she wasn't.

She slowly opened her eyes. Rulan was looking at her.

Instantly Selar sat up so quickly that she could have sworn her brain rebounded within her cranium. "Oh, I should not have done that," she said, touching her fingers to her temples. "That was ill-advised."

Rulan leaned forward, regarding Selar with open curiosity. "Who are you?"

"I—" How best to summarize it? "I am your doctor."

"Oh." Rulan clearly didn't comprehend, and at that moment, Selar did not remotely care.

Instead she was looking around the room that they were now in.

The first thing that she did was to listen carefully. It took her mere moments to discern that they were no longer aboard the *Spectre*. Any space-faring vessels made constant little noises as they moved. Ambient noise, none of it particularly distracting individually, collectively gave one a sense of the environment. She heard none of that now, so she was convinced they had not been relocated to some small room in the ship that she had not seen earlier.

Instead what she heard was a rushing of air, a very distant howling. It was hard to perceive because the walls of the room were extremely thick. But with her hearing, she was able to do so. There was no doubt in her mind that she was on a planet's surface. They could be anywhere, but given the circumstances, the likelihood was that they were on AF1963.

Fully expecting the door to be locked, or—at the very least—that there would be guards making sure they weren't going anywhere, she got to her feet and moved to the door. She winced, feeling a stabbing pain in her chest. She touched herself tentatively and ascertained a rib had been broken. That didn't surprise her. Considering the pounding she had taken, she was fortunate to be walking at all. She made her way to the door and placed her hand against it. It felt cold to the touch. Rather than sliding, it had a large handle on it. She pulled on it experimentally. The door swung open slightly.

"I wouldn't do that if I were you," said Rulan.

Feeling it would be best to decide for herself what she should and should not do, Sclar pulled the door wide.

A blast of frigid air slammed into her. She felt as if a thousand needles were stinging her face, and she instantly went numb. Quickly she shoved the door closed, pushing it as hard as she could with her shoulder. Her broken rib ached terribly and it was all she could do not to cry out in pain. She tried to take a deep breath to focus, and inhaled air so cold that she was certain her lungs were going to freeze up and shatter in her chest.

Rulan came to her side and pushed along with her. Within moments, as if staggering uphill, they managed to get the door closed once more. She leaned against the door, giving the pain time to subside, while Rulan said laconically, "I see you're not someone who takes advice easily."

That much was true, but she didn't appreciate hearing it from hir. It was obvious to Selar that the beings who had boarded the ship must have brought them here. She had no idea why they would do so, or what they wanted with her and Rulan . . .

Rulan, who had been lying unconscious, was now standing there, awake and alert and obviously ready to respond to any questions she might have.

"How long have you been conscious?" she said.

"I have no idea. I don't exactly have any means of keeping time. A while, I guess."

"I mean, did you wake up here?"

S/he nodded. "Yes. I came around and saw you lying there. I tried to awaken you, but you weren't responding. So I figured that you would come around when you were ready to."

"A reasonable assumption."

"How did you become my doctor? I've never seen you before." S/he looked her up and down. "You're wearing a Starfleet uniform. How did I wind up getting a Starfleet doctor?"

"It would help me to answer your question if you answered mine: How did you come to be in the vessel where we found you?"

"Vessel? What vessel?"

"You were discovered by the *Starship Excalibur,* floating in a small derelict ship in a remote region of space. Are you claiming that was not your ship?"

"No! I've never owned a ship in my life. I—" Then s/he stopped. "Oh my gods."

"What?"

"I . . . I thought I was dreaming. Dreaming that I was on a ship. That I was dying in it, but it all happened so quickly, and it felt so surreal. I didn't think it was real."

"Believe me, it was. Tell me your last memories before you were discovered in the vessel."

"That was real? Are you sure? Is it possible it might have been a dream?"

"No. Tell me the last thing you remember. Anything that can explain your connection to these beings . . ."

"I didn't know they were 'beings' of any kind. I was approached by a group of Hermat scientists. At least that's what they said they were. They claimed that they wanted to try to expand the Hermat lifespan, and that I was an ideal candidate for their experiments."

"Did they give any indication as to why you, specifically, would be suited to their experiments, or for that matter what the experiments were exactly?"

"No, to both. But the treatments were injections of some kind. They didn't tell me what it was."

"You let individuals whom you have never met inject unknown chemicals into your body?"

"Looking back on it, I suppose it was ill-advised."

"It should have seemed ill-advised to you without the benefit of hindsight." She had spent so much time thinking of Rulan as a potential asset for her son. She had given no thought to Rulan as a person. It was becoming evident that Rulan was not one of the deep thinkers in the galaxy. "Did they limit their activities to the injection of chemicals?"

"No. They also placed me in some sort of large device. I have no idea what it was doing."

"If I had to hazard a guess," she said, "it was subjecting you to radiation poisoning."

For the first time, Rulan actually appeared disconcerted. "That's . . . not good."

"On the surface of it, no. However, as near as I can determine, your cellular structure is completely healed."

"Oh!" s/he said and looked relieved. "Well, excellent, then. Obviously you're a qualified doctor who knows what she's doing."

"I did not do it. Your body did it. Or, more precisely,

they did it. Their treatments of you enabled you to recuperate. I cannot determine precisely how they accomplished it. I had you in my sickbay for days and still was unable to discern just how your cells were regenerating. I was hoping that you would be able to provide me answers or that, ultimately, these beings would be able to do so. But you know nothing of the specifics, obviously, and they have been—uncooperative. What is the last thing you recall?"

"Being inside one of those machines of theirs? It was"—s/he paused—"it was the fifth visit to their facility. The fifth time I was there, they rolled me into this larger machine that I hadn't seen on any of my previous visits. I was lying flat on my back on a sort of rolling table, and they slid me into it, and the next thing I knew, I was here."

"Any dreams?"

"Not that I can recall. I wasn't even aware of the passage of time. When I opened my eyes, I was fully expecting to be in the facility. I thought I had simply dozed off during the procedure. I was stunned to wake up here, wherever 'here' is. Do you have any idea?"

"I believe we are on a world called AF1963."

"Why do you think that?"

She hesitated, and then realized that there was

nothing to be gained from withholding information. "Because that is the world I was in the process of transporting you to, along with an infant."

Rulan didn't understand. For once, she couldn't blame hir. "Was it an assignment that Starfleet gave you?"

"No," she said flatly. "It was something I did in violation of Starfleet regulations, and in violation of my trust as chief medical officer of the *Excalibur.* I did it at the behest of unknown alien beings who promised me that they would provide me a cure for a cellular degeneration disease that is in the process of killing my son."

"I see." To her silent astonishment, s/he looked amused. "So you basically trusted people you never met in exchange for something that you thought might be a good idea because, really, you didn't have anything better to do."

"Yes."

"I guess we're well matched to be prisoners here together."

"Perhaps we are at that. That does not mean, however, that I am inclined to accept matters as they are."

With that she headed for the door again.

"What are you doing?" Rulan called after her.

"Leaving."

"You can't! I mean, it's obvious why there aren't any guards there. Walking out into that wasteland without proper protective gear is suicide!"

"So it would seem."

And with that she pulled the door wide, brought her arm across the lower half of her face to provide minimal shielding, and threw herself out into the darkness and cold.

Starship Trident

The armored intruders went through the corridors and various rooms, seeking out and destroying any crew members they could locate. With every passing minute, however, it was becoming more problematic. The crew could quickly be divided into two groups: those who were dead, and those who simply couldn't be found. The majority of the crew fell into the latter group.

The one advantage the ship's crew had over the invaders was their knowledge of the ship's layout. The crew members had hid in the inner recesses of the ship: circuit junctions, Jeffries tubes, and the like. From their places of concealment, they attempted acts of guerilla warfare on the invaders. The armored figures never knew when they would suddenly be subjected to phaser fire coming at them from random directions.

They even had two fatalities, as sidelong phaser blasts nailed with pinpoint accuracy the vents in the right sides of their helmets. In both cases it was remarkably satisfying for the crew to see their attackers staggering, clutching at their necks as blood would ooze out of its confinement and trickle down their armored bodies before they'd pitch forward and land with a resounding crash.

But those triumphs were rare. The armored beings were far more accurate, pinpointing the angle of attack, and returning fire with lethal results. The bodies of *Trident* crew members tumbled out of concealment or simply lay there, forcing their frustrated crewmates to abandon their smoldering corpses.

On the bridge, Kat Mueller was living and dying with the deaths or imagined deaths of every one of her crew. Outwardly, however, she displayed no emotion. She stared at Gold's body, thinking of all the times when he had annoyed her with his arrogance and his insufferable pride in his family's Starfleet record. Gold had never married, never sired an offspring. His older sister, Leanne, had gone missing and was presumed dead during a Borg altercation. His death had ended a service to Starfleet that had spanned ten generations.

Not that these bastards cared about any of that, of course.

M'Ress had nearly slipped into unconsciousness from pain, but she had fought it off and instead was tending to Arex. Arex was a study in stoicism. Insanely, he had picked up the dismembered arm and was holding it close to him, fixing a glare upon the armored figures. Mueller suspected that, were he able to do so, Arex would come at them with the stray limb and try to beat them to death with it.

"How long do you intend for this to go on?" asked the fake Calhoun. "Order your people to surrender."

"Sorry," she said tightly. "It's drilled into us in the Academy: Never give up. Never surrender."

"Well, that certainly seems pointless."

"*Surrendering* would be pointless. We have no guarantee that, as soon as we did so, your friends here wouldn't just kill my crew."

"That is true. Indeed, they might well do so. They are sometimes a little difficult to control in combat situations."

"I find it difficult to believe you can control them at all. I look at them, and I look at you, and I frankly think the odds favor them if they should decide that you're of no use to them."

"That will never happen. I am quite confident."

"Overconfidence tends to lead to a precipitous fall."

"Were you schooled in that at the Academy as well?"

Despite the gravity of the situation, she smiled slightly as her finger touched the scar that adorned her cheek. "No. Earlier."

"Why don't you use the captain as a bargaining chip?" said Takahashi.

Mueller fired him a look. "Be quiet, Lieutenant."

"Come on, Captain," said Hash, all trace of his laid-back attitude gone. "I'm not suggesting anything that wouldn't have occurred to them already. Why don't they just inform the crew that if they don't stand down, they'll kill you?"

"Because they know that my crew will not give in, any more than I will."

"Actually, they very well might," said the fake Calhoun. "But that is not the way of the D'myurj."

"The D'myurj? Is that who they are? Who you are?"

The fake Calhoun put his hand to his lips in a mocking gesture and said, "Did I say that aloud? Oh my, did I inadvertently slip and provide you with a piece of information that will ultimately do you no good at all? In the final analysis, it is merely a name. Nothing more. Use it if you wish."

"Very well. What is the way of the D'myurj, then, if not negotiation or employing leverage against opponents?"

"Crushing them entirely," said the fake Calhoun. "Annihilating them through force of arms. Forcing them to rise to their greatest heights and see if they can, in fact, survive. It is all about survival, is it not? Survival of the fittest? Accomplishments that you previously would not have dreamed possible?"

"In that case," said Mueller, "why am I still alive? Why is the rest of my bridge crew still alive?"

"No reason," said the fake Calhoun with a shrug. "No reason other than that I find you interesting to speak with."

"Just that arbitrary, is it?" said Hash.

"Yes, Lieutenant. Just that arbitrary. If you'd like, I can prove it by asking my associates here to kill you where you stand. What would you say to that?"

Hash looked warily at the armored figures. "Don't feel any need to provide a demonstration on my account."

"Very well. In that case, we shall wait," said the

fake Calhoun. "And we shall see. And then we shall kill you all. No offense."

"None taken," said Mueller.

The one option left open to her was to trigger the ship's self-destruct protocol. She could have done so. The invaders appeared to have taken no steps to impede her interaction with the ship's computer. She did not, however. Suicide wasn't in her nature. Furthermore, there was no reason to think that doing so would simply prompt the invaders to remove themselves from the ship the same way they had arrived, thus leaving her crew to perish in the explosion and accomplishing precisely nothing.

Where there was life, there was hope. And at that moment Kat Mueller's hope was to find a way wherein the fake Calhoun's throat would wind up between her fingers.

?

Four minutes, thirty-seven seconds . . .

   Thirty-eight seconds . . .

   Thirty-nine seconds . . .

   Selar counted off mentally as she staggered unprotected through the brutal environment. The skies were inky black above this barren wasteland. The ground was frozen and uneven, and a range of mountains loomed in the distance. Every step she took was torturous, and her body screamed in protest and begged her to simply lie down and wait for death to overtake her. That would certainly be soon enough, because she had mentally calculated just how long she could survive under these sorts of conditions. She had arrived at approximately eight minutes, nineteen seconds, give or take. She hated to be imprecise, but it was the best she could do under the circumstances.

   Five minutes even . . .

Five minutes, one second . . .

She went to her knees yet again, shielding her face as best she could under the pummeling wind. After having gotten a basic mental picture of the lay of the land, she kept her eyes closed, for there were millions of grains of dirt blowing around at high speed. With her eyes open, she would have been instantly blinded.

Five minutes, fifty-nine seconds . . .

Six minutes . . .

Her breathing was becoming more labored. She felt as if a sword had been driven through her chest and remained there, causing her unending agony. She cried out briefly and then her practiced stoicism kicked in. Gritting her teeth against the brunt of the brutal weather, she continued moving. She had no idea where she was moving toward. Even if the mountains might provide some form of shelter, she was never going to make it. But she did not once consider turning around and making her way back to the small room in which she and Rulan had been imprisoned.

Seven minutes, eighteen seconds . . .

Seven minutes, nineteen seconds . . .

She became aware that her knees were giving out completely about two seconds before they actually did. She hit the frozen ground and remained there for a moment on her hands and knees, trying to find the strength to keep moving. Selar forgot what it was like not to hurt. Then again, she had been in mental anguish for so long because of her son's condition, pain had become part of her day-to-day existence.

If you die, then you die. A small enough price to pay for the sins you have committed, and even then it will do nothing to truly balance the scales.

Seven minutes, forty-five seconds . . .

Seven minutes, forty-six seconds . . .

"What do you think you're doing?"

She did not require her eyes to know who was standing in front of her. She would have recognized the voice anywhere.

Selar was unable to move, her body having completely given out. Her face was flat upon the frozen ground, and her body temperature was dropping rapidly. She didn't have much longer until hypothermia overtook her. She wondered if she would lapse into a coma and die, or go straight to death. Her thoughts were wandering so far that it didn't even occur to her that the false Xy who was standing directly in front of her—apparently unbothered by the horrific surroundings—had not issued a rhetorical question.

"I said what do you think you're doing?" he said again. "How much longer do you expect to last out here?"

"Thirty-seven seconds," she managed to say between cracked and bleeding lips. Particles of whatever the hell was blowing around worked their way into her mouth. She paid them no mind. It didn't matter anymore.

"Is that what you want? Do you want to die?" he asked.

She wouldn't have thought it possible, but she actually managed to raise her head. "No. And I do not think you want me to die, either. If you did, you would have killed me by now."

"So you are expecting me to save you, is that it?"

"That is . . . my plan."

"And if you have guessed wrong? Then you will die."

"That is my . . . alternate plan."

He made a *tsk* noise as if disappointed in a stubborn child. "What do you want, Selar? What do you hope to achieve?"

"Answers," she said as she sensed her heartbeat slowing down. "Answers . . . or . . . or . . ."

"Or what? You'll die in ignorance? There's a threat to conjure with. Besides," he continued, "my people value the free will of all races. If it is your desire to die, then I will not stop you."

It is my desire to find answers . . . dying is my default position . . .

"Even with death hovering over you, you embrace the sardonic," he said, and she realized he was responding to what had gone through her mind rather than anything she had articulated. "I applaud that. I applaud you, Selar. To be honest, I would far prefer that you lived. You are very important and I would hate to see you removed from the equation of life."

How . . . ? She forced herself to speak. "How . . . am I important? Important to what? Tell me what . . . this is about . . . at least tell me where I am . . ."

"No," said the image of her son. "No, I'm afraid I'm not going to do th—"

Then she heard a thud—a scuffling. She couldn't fathom what it might be and forced herself to open her eyes and see what was going on.

To her astonishment, "Xy" was on the ground, and crouched on top of him, hir claws poised and a feral, infuriated look on hir face, was Rulan 12. "Answer her questions!" s/he snarled at Xy. "Tell her! Tell her or I swear I'll gut you!"

"Xy" struggled to get out from under Rulan, and

failed utterly in the attempt. The sight buoyed Selar's hopes. Until that moment, she hadn't been sure if the creature before her had had any substance at all. Now she saw that, whatever he was, he was very real, and obviously could also be injured.

Eight minutes, nineteen seconds . . . twenty seconds . . . twenty-one seconds . . .

Her rational mind told her that she was out of time, that she should be dead. She refused to allow her knees to give out. She acknowledged the stabbing pain in her chest and then pushed it aside and to the back of her mind where it would not bother her.

As she staggered to her feet, she was pleased to see a look of utter fear on the face of the creature pretending to be her son. Then she shielded her eyes against the pounding of the wind and dirt.

"Fine," said Rulan. "If you're such a big believer in free will, then it's my free will that I kill you." S/he started to swing down hir claws.

"You are on AF1963!" screamed "Xy." "We are the D'myurj! And we just wish to help. We have always just wanted to help."

"Help who?"

"All of you! None of your races would have

survived were it not for us! Don't you understand? *You owe us your existence!*"

"What are you talking ab—?"

Suddenly a blast of energy ripped through the freezing air, catching Rulan in the side. It knocked hir clear of "Xy" and s/he hit the ground, unconscious.

Selar saw the same armored figures that had invaded the *Spectre* advancing upon them. She turned to face them, having no more an idea of what she was going to do now against them than she had had earlier. Yet she was determined not to back down. She began to advance upon them, and then the adrenaline that had managed to propel her to this point ran out. She crumbled, striking her head on the ground. She saw armored boots advancing toward her, and the last thing she had time to think was, *I am getting sick and tired of lapsing into unconsciousness,* right before she lapsed into unconsciousness.

Starship Trident

i.

Kat Mueller was mildly surprised to see a change of expression on the fake Calhoun's face. Until this point, he had simply had that superior, smug look to him. Now, though, he appeared to be listening to something, looking off into the distance and with his head tilted slightly.

"Problem?" she said sarcastically, as if she actually cared about whatever difficulties he might have.

The Calhoun imposter appeared to plaster a smile back onto his face as he said, "As a matter of fact, it would seem so. The Brethren are becoming impatient."

"The Brethren? I thought they were . . ."

"In the interest of clarity, my people are the D'myurj. We simply refer to our armored associates as the Brethren. They have another name, I am quite sure, but they have never seemed inclined to share it with us. And from what I can discern, the Brethren are not particularly happy at the moment."

"Why would that be?"

"Well, because several of them have perished thus far," he said as if it should have been self-evident. "They are not accustomed to dying."

"I see. How tragic for them."

"You have a streak of cruelty to you, Captain; that is most unseemly," said the fake Calhoun in a scolding tone. But there was something else that she perceived, an uncertainty . . . perhaps even . . . fear? Yes. Yes, there was fear within him. "I think you fail to comprehend how serious this can become."

"My crew is under attack and they are fighting for their lives. I fail to see how the stakes can escalate."

"There is much that you do not understand."

"Since you've been explaining nothing, then that's something of a hazard."

"Order your people to stand down, Captain. You are running out of time."

"And you are running out of control," she said. "I can see it in your eyes. The Brethren aren't as much on your side as you wish to believe."

"That is a ridiculous notion," he said. "They are merely the brawn. We are the brain. They were helpless, hopeless before we found them and raised them up into the fighting machines they have become. They know that."

"What they know is that my people are showing that they're not invincible. I think you convinced them that we would be easily cowed, and that their invincibility would remain intact. For someone who claims to be 'the brain,' you must be coming across as extremely stupid right about now."

"You are speaking about things of which you know nothing," he said dismissively.

"Am I? I'm starting to think that's not the case, especially considering the way the Brethren are looking at you right now."

It was, of course, impossible for anyone to discern how the Brethren were, in fact, looking at the D'myurj, but looking in that direction they most definitely were.

The fake Calhoun's face remained inscrutable. "It is the Brethren's desire," he said, "that you order your crew to surrender immediately."

"We've been over this."

"Yes, we have. However, what we have not been over is what will happen when the Brethren kill your bridge crew, right in front of your eyes, one by one, unless you order a total surrender."

No one moved. No one reacted. Mueller's gaze never wavered from the fake Calhoun's. "That would be ill-advised," she said.

"I agree. The D'myurj cherish free will, and I am loath to compel you to do something that is so clearly anathema to you. But the Brethren's feelings on the matter must be honored as well."

"The Brethren, whom you claim are totally obedient to you."

"They honor our wishes, yes, but that is—"

"Then tell them that you refuse to allow my people to be executed."

"I do not have to prove anything to you."

"No, you don't. But perhaps it might be wise for you to prove something to yourself."

"Choose someone," said the fake Calhoun.

"No."

"Choose the first among your bridge crew to die or a choice shall be made for you."

"Tell them you won't do it!" said Mueller. "Tell them you refuse to do as they order you to!"

"They are not ordering me! They do not issue orders."

"Then tell them!"

"Choose someone to die!" said the fake Calhoun again, his voice rising.

"Aren't *you* the superior race!" said Mueller, her clipped voice dripping with contempt. "Honoring our right to free will, except when you find it inconvenient! Allied with your so-called Brethren, except it seems to me that they're the ones calling the shots! If we die, at least we die knowing who and what we are. We don't disguise ourselves as others, and we don't compromise our principles!"

"Your history is filled with nothing but compromised principles and people pretending to be something they're not."

"Then set an example by showing us you really *are* superior. Rein in your so-called Brethren, if you can."

"For the last time, choose someone to die!"

"*You* choose!"

"Fine! Him!" He pointed at Hash.

One of the Brethren advanced upon Hash. Hash backed up, maneuvering so that the corpse of Mick Gold was between him and the oncoming armored figure. Seemingly oblivious of Gold's presence, the Brethren warrior's foot slammed up against the corpse and the Brethren almost tripped over it. It stumbled and righted himself just before falling, a lapse that Mueller noticed and filed away for later—

Later . . . as if there's going to be any later . . .

The Brethren raised its armored hand, aiming its palm weapon at Hash. Hash, his back against the far bulkhead, had nowhere to run.

Mueller lunged toward the Brethren, trying to grab at its arm, and another of the Brethren came forward and grabbed her, yanking her back. She screamed Hash's name, certain that she was about to witness his death, knowing she could have stopped it, telling herself that, no, she could have only stalled it for a short time, that it was hopeless, that she was hopeless . . .

"Stop! It is my desire that you stop!"

It had been the D'myurj who had spoken. The Brethren turned to face him, lowering his arm as he did so.

The fake Calhoun looked at her with calm regard, his hands folded in front of him in a relaxed manner. "You see?" he said. "The Brethren respect *me,* and attend to my—"

The armored warrior raised its arm again, except this time the target was fixed upon the D'myurj.

Genuine surprise appeared on the fake Calhoun's

face, and then before he could·say anything, an energy bolt erupted from the Brethren's hand. It lanced through the D'myurj, who threw his arms wide and cried out something incomprehensible. With a shriek he vanished from existence.

"Yeah, that's not good," muttered Hash.

The three Brethren brought up their hands, palms out, pointed straight at Mueller and the crew. And for the first time, one of them spoke.

Its voice was male—astoundingly soft, even gentle, a stark contrast to its appearance.

"Surrender," it said. "You have no more options."

Mueller flipped an obscene gesture at them.

Their weapons began to charge, and Mueller knew without question that this was it.

And suddenly there was the crackle of transporter beams and, once again, three Brethren vanished in a haze of molecules.

The bridge crew looked at one another in confusion, and then all eyes turned to Hash. But he was exactly where he'd been before, and he shrugged.

"Wasn't me," he said.

Then the transporter beams hummed yet again, and Mackenzie Calhoun appeared, along with several *Excalibur* security guards. Mueller could scarcely believe it, and then she saw the mighty starship appearing on the main viewscreen, dropping into orbit around the planet below.

Oh, thank God, you wonderful man.

"You took your own sweet time getting here," she said sharply.

"I had a feeling you'd say that." He looked around. "Our sensors detected unknown beings on the bridge and energy bursts being discharged around the ship. We guessed invasion."

"You guessed correctly. They're all through the ship, and their armor's invulnerable to almost anything we can throw at it."

"We have a few things we can throw that they might not have expected," said Calhoun.

ii.

Down the third-level corridor stampeded Zak Kebron.

Brethren warriors turned and fired at him. Kebron staggered under the assault, but the blasts were unable to penetrate the incredible thickness of his Brikar hide. They did, however, hurt like hell, a fact that

Kebron acknowledged with a furious roar. They hurt, they slowed him, but they did not stop him, and then he was upon the Brethren. He picked up one in either hand and simply started slamming them together repeatedly. Their armor made deafening *clanging* sounds with every impact, and the Brethren waved their arms about in frustration, unable to prevent themselves from the humiliating beating they were receiving at Kebron's huge hands.

"And there's a hundred more like me right behind me!" Kebron said in his rumbling voice. A blatant lie, of course, but he was reasonably sure that the Brethren would be unaware of that.

Suddenly the two armored figures he was holding in his hands vanished. A third warrior backed up and disappeared as well, popping out of existence. Kebron was confused. Perhaps it had been some manner of transporter in action, but he had never seen the like. No energy buildup, no nothing. Just there one moment, gone the next.

"All right," he said. "*That* was unexpected."

iii.

Like a bad dream passing out of consciousness with the advent of the morning sun, the Brethren vanished from the decks of the *Trident.*

At first crew members were hesitant to come out of hiding, suspecting it was some sort of trick. Even Mueller's preliminary announcement that all was clear didn't overcome the reluctance of a number of the crew to make themselves potential targets. Mueller's follow-up announcement of, *"Get back to your posts!"* was, however, enough to get the job done.

On the bridge, Mueller turned to Calhoun and said, "That was easier than I possibly could have hoped."

"It's been my experience that when things get easier, it's typically right before things get monumentally difficult."

"True enough," she admitted.

A medical team from the *Excalibur* had beamed over and was in the midst of doing triage, necessary since most of the medtechs on the ship had been killed by the invaders. Arex and M'Ress had already been beamed over to the *Excalibur* for immediate treatment, and Mick Gold's body had been removed as well.

Mueller had brought Calhoun up to speed on as much as she knew about their attackers. She wished there had been more information that she could have provided him. He had not heard of either the D'myurj nor was he experienced with the Brethren that had served as their shock troops.

"Why would they just back off from a fight so quickly?" said Calhoun.

"That," said Mueller, "I think I can answer. It would never occur to you, Mac, because you never met a fight that you weren't prepared to see though. Some individuals, though, are quick to back off if they think that the people they're attacking can actually hurt them."

"Or," said Hash, "if they figure that it just ain't worth their time to keep fightin'." As he spoke, though, he wasn't looking at either Calhoun or Mueller, but instead at the vacant navigation chair. As soon as matters were stabilized, a new conn officer would be assigned. In the meantime, the ship's computer was keeping the vessel on a geosynchronous orbit with AF1963.

"So we weren't worth disposing of," said Calhoun. "I'm not entirely sure whether to be relieved or offended."

"At least we can hope that they won't use this opportunity to beam attackers onto the *Excalibur* as well. The question is, now what? We're here at AF1963, but there's still no sign of the *Spectre*." She saw a shift in Calhoun's expression. "What? What are you thinking?"

"I'm thinking that perhaps there's another reason we haven't considered that the Brethren broke off the attack," said Calhoun. "That reason being that it served its purpose."

"Served its . . . ? " Her voice trailed off, and then her eyes widened as she realized what he was getting at. "*Scheisse*. A distraction."

"Exactly," he said. "They could have done anything while you were fighting for your lives. Flown in the *Spectre*. Used one of those ultrapowerful transporter beams they apparently own to bring Selar, Lucius, and the baby to them over a vast distance, undetected by your ship. *Grozit,* Kat, a Borg cube could have parked itself on the far side of the planet and you wouldn't have noticed it rolling in because you were all on the defensive."

"And now?"

"Now," said Calhoun with mounting concern, "the *Spectre* could be anywhere. Down on the planet's surface, hidden away. Blasted into a million pieces. We have only one option left. Sensor sweeps of the entire surface of the planet. See if we pick up any readings from Selar, Lucius, or the baby."

"That's going to take a long time."

"True. We can, however, shorten it somewhat. I'll take the northern hemisphere, and you take the southern hemisphere."

"Sounds like a plan," said Mueller. "Oh . . . and Captain . . ."

"Yes, Captain?"

"Thank you for saving our lives."

He smiled and said something that a Federation ground pounder he'd once met had said in such circumstances: "All part of the service."

AF1963

Selar had the oddest feeling of déjà vu as she came to, only to discover herself in the same small hut she had been in earlier, the one from which she had hoped to escape. Here she was, right back where she had begun.

Rulan was seated a few feet away, hir legs drawn up, hir head resting on hir knees. S/he appeared to be dozing lightly, but when Selar awakened, s/he instantly came awake as well. "Are you all right?" s/he said.

She flexed her fingers, stretched her toes within her boots. She was pleasantly surprised to feel all of them, which was fortunate. There was something to be said for Vulcan durability, even under environmental circumstances that were markedly dissimilar from the arid world in which she was born. "I appear to be whole." Then she turned her attention to hir. "And you?"

"I'll live."

"That was most foolish of you, coming after me the way you did."

S/he shrugged. "I tried to tell myself to stay put. Finally I decided that it wasn't an option, so I went after you. Who was that who was talking to you?"

"He was one of the beings who encouraged me to—"

"Betray everyone and everything you know?"

"Yes," she said flatly.

"He looked extremely strange, if you ask me."

She fired him a faintly annoyed look. "That was not his normal appearance. He assumed the image of my son."

"Oh," said Rulan, faintly chagrined. "Well, by 'strange,' I mean that it seemed strange to see him here under such circumstances."

"Of course that is what you meant," said Selar.

"So . . . now what? Are you going to go out into the cold again and probably die unless I come after you?"

"I did not require your intervention," she said.

"Okay, then, just be aware that if you plan to go out there again, then we're both likely going to die, because I can't say for sure we're going to make it back this time. So there are two lives you have to factor into your calculations."

"I am not responsible for you if you choose to intrude in my affairs."

"To intrude?" S/he was incredulous, and stabbed a finger at her for emphasis. "You're the one who pulled me into *your* affairs! From what you said, I was safe and sound on a space station! I'm here because you dragged me here, so I don't think you get to choose what I decide to concern myself about! You understand?"

Selar knew that s/he was right. She had no real response to it, and so instead she simply looked down and contritely said, "Yes. I understand."

Something about her tone prompted Rulan to back off. "Look . . . I didn't mean to upset you."

"I am not upset," she lied. "I am simply acknowledging the truth of your words. I will . . ." She hesitated. "I will do as you request. I will stay here for as long as is required. I will stay here until I die of thirst or starvation, if that is your wish. I have . . . I have no desire to cause any more difficulties for anyone else. I—" She couldn't think of anything else to say, so she simply stopped talking and stared straight ahead.

Rulan approached her uncertainly. "Look . . . maybe we . . ."

The door flew open suddenly and the alien who had assumed the shape of her son—the being who had referred to himself as a D'myurj—was standing there with a look of consternation on his face.

"You have to go," he said urgently. "Both of you—and me. We have to go now."

"Go? Go where?" said Rulan.

"Away from here."

Rulan and Selar exchanged looks. "You cannot be serious," said Selar after a moment.

"I am completely serious." He entered the room, then braced his back against the door and pushed it shut. The moment it was securely shut he advanced upon them. "You have to come with me, immediately."

"Why?"

"The Brethren are proving . . ." He seemed to be struggling to find the right word. ". . . uncooperative. This has never happened before, not in all the time that we have worked together."

"The Brethren? Who are the Brethren?" said Rulan.

But Selar's mind was racing. "The armored beings? Is that what you call them?" When he nodded in response, she said, "It would appear, then, that your goals and theirs are not exactly in accord."

"This is a serious, even dangerous situation," said "Xy." "How can you sound so dispassionate about it?"

"A lifetime of practice."

"I don't think that you fully grasp the situation," said "Xy." "The Brethren are lethal, and they vastly outnumber us. If they have turned against us—"

"Then you will die, as will we. I will take some measure of satisfaction that you will share our fate," said Selar.

Rulan looked at her uncertainly. "Is that fate definite? Because, honestly, I was hoping for a different fate if at all possible. One that didn't involve dying anytime soon."

"This is not a joking matter," said "Xy."

"I don't tend to joke about my own death."

"Listen to me," "Xy" said impatiently. "I did not have to return here for you. I am doing so out of compassion."

"I do not believe you," said Selar. "You have forfeited all of your credibility. If you are interested in aiding Rulan and me, it is out of self-interest, not generosity. What is it that you require of me?"

"I cannot leave you here! If I do, they will likely destroy you, and you are—"

"I am what?"

"Too important."

"Ah. Now we are getting somewhere," said Selar, speaking so calmly that one would never have guessed destructive, murderous armored beings were heading their way. "Why am I important? To whom?"

"Come with me now and I will tell you later."

"You will tell me now," said Selar. "Unless you believe you can make me come with you by force. And since every application of force that you have employed thus far has required the assistance of the Brethren, I would not expect you to be capable of forcing me to depart on your own. Besides, that would not exactly be in keeping with your philosophy of free will, would it?"

"Free will is fine to a point," said "Xy" with growing urgency. "But if you see a child sticking its hand into a flame, you wouldn't honor its right to free will. You'd snatch its hand away from the danger."

"An apt comparison, were I a child. Tell me what I want to know or on your way with you."

"Xy" looked to Rulan. "Do you share this suicidal position?"

"Well, I—" Rulan looked ready to say that s/he was,

in fact, completely prepared to throw in hir lot with the D'myurj. But s/he hesitated and looked to Selar. Something unspoken passed between them, and then Rulan—never taking hir eyes away from Selar—said, "Yes. Yes, we do."

"Xy" shook his head. "Unbelievable," he said in a low voice. And then he said more loudly in exasperation, "All right! Fine! You know of the Borg, I assume."

"Of course," said Selar.

"Think of us as their opposite. Whereas they move from race to race, assimilating technologies and taking it for themselves, we go from race to race changing them. Improving them. My people—our branch of the D'myurj—oversee the progression of races to the next level."

"What next level?" said Selar.

"The progression that inevitably leads to a stage where they are predominantly beings of the mind. The Organians, the Thasians. You Vulcans," he said, "have the potential to be such as they. So do humans."

"How could you possibly know that?" Selar said, thinking the entire thing sounded dubious.

"One of the markers of that is the ability to cross-breed with other races. We wanted the infant—the child dubbed Cwansi—to study him. We wanted you, the mother of a half-breed, to study you as well. But it is our way to move with subtlety. To not draw attention to ourselves. On occasion force of arms is required, and at such times, the Brethren have always served us well. But we prefer to allow others to do as we require of them, typically by convincing them that it is their idea. We appear as visions . . . as voices in their heads. Why be the crushing fist when you can be the helping hand?"

"You call what you did to me—what you moved me to do—*helping*?"

"What about me?" said Rulan. "You wanted to study me as well—?"

"You were simply the means to the end. We manipulated your fellow Hermats in the same way that we did the good doctor here. We have arranged it all to bring us to this point. We did not count, however, on the Brethren taking this moment to turn against us. They are unaccustomed to suffering casualties, apparently."

"Casualties?" said Selar. "How? From where?"

"Two star vessels. Yours and another. They arrived shortly before you. More powerful engines, greater speed, I would imagine."

"The *Excalibur*? Here? How?"

"I do not know. We sent the Brethren in to distract them while your vessel was brought here. We did not anticipate that they would provide any sort of credible resistance. We were . . . wrong. And now the Brethren are forcing us to pay for our miscalculations. We had no idea they were so . . . vengeful."

"Perhaps it has nothing to do with vengeance," said Selar. "Perhaps all this time, when you believe you have been using them . . . they have, in fact, been using *you*. And they simply decided that now was the time to dispense with you."

"But why now?" said the bewildered D'myurj.

"Because," said Selar, "you may have something they want more than they want you. Where is the infant? Where is Cwansi?"

"In a stronghold below the surface of this planet. A stronghold that some of my fellow D'myurj scientists run."

"I am beginning to think," said Selar, "that you may not be running it anymore. What you may need to do—"

She did not have the opportunity to complete the sentence. She was suddenly surrounded by a familiar humming. Rulan appeared equally as startled, and then the room around them dissolved away. The next moment, she was standing on a transporter platform, and the moment after that, she was knocked off her feet.

Starship Excalibur

i.

In retrospect, Calhoun couldn't believe how easy it had been.

Here he had been discussing involved sensor searches of the planet's surface that could have taken many hours.

It had never occurred to him that Selar might simply still be wearing her combadge. As a result, it had taken Morgan mere minutes to get a lock on her badge, even though she wasn't actively using it. The moment she had her locked in, she informed the captain. Robin Lefler, however, had been up out of her ops station and heading for the turbolift door before Calhoun even had the opportunity to tell the transporter room to beam her up.

"Robin."

Robin Lefler had spun to face him and was expressionless as she said, "Captain, with all due respect—and you know my respect for you is boundless—don't even *think* about telling me that I can't be there when she beams up."

"Promise me you'll let me handle it."

"I swear," she said.

"Fine. Kebron, you're with me. Burgy, you have the conn."

"But, Captain—!" the startled Hermat began to protest. S/he had been up, out of hir chair, clearly believing that s/he was going to be coming along.

"There's only so many people who Selar betrayed that I want with me. Stay here. You too, Xy."

"As you wish, Captain," Xy had said. It seemed to Calhoun that Xy didn't seem particularly broken up over the prospect of not seeing his mother immediately.

Calhoun, Kebron, and Lefler had gone down to the transporter room, where Calhoun had instructed Transporter Chief Halliwell to beam up everyone in the immediate area of the combadge. This presented a calculated risk; if there were several of the Brethren with her, Calhoun would be bringing them directly into their midst. Halliwell would have to be prepared to act quickly to send them back out of the ship before they could start wreaking havoc.

"All right," Calhoun said coolly. "Energize."

The transporter beams had whined into existence and, seconds later, the familiar form of Selar appeared on the platform. Standing directly behind her was Rulan, obviously up and around.

Before Calhoun could say a word, Robin had bolted across the room and tackled Selar just as she finished materializing. Selar appeared startled and then she went down beneath Robin's tackle, and Robin straddled her back and started pounding her fists into Selar's head. *"Where is he? Where's my son, you bitch!"* she screamed.

"Robin! Get off her! Kebron—"

"I'm on it, sir," said Kebron, walking over to Robin and grabbing her by the back of her uniform. With no effort at all, he picked her up, pulling her clear of Selar who had offered no resistance to the pummeling.

"You promised me, Robin," he said sternly. Kebron was dangling her in the air.

"I lied! Courtmartial me!" she shot back.

Calhoun sighed and cocked a thumb toward the door. "Kebron, get her out of here."

"No! Let me stay! I'll keep my hands off her! I swear—!"

He put his face right up to hers and there was no trace of sympathy in his voice. "I don't make deals with liars. Either you're going back to the bridge or to the brig. Your choice. Don't trifle with me on this, Lefler, I'm not in the mood."

She looked as if she were prepared to say something else, but wisely she held her tongue. Kebron took the precaution of taking her straight to the door and depositing her in the hallway. She looked with burning fury at Selar as the doors hissed shut, blocking her from view.

"Who was that?" said Rulan.

"A former patient," Selar said as she got to her feet and brushed herself off.

Calhoun walked up to the edge of the transporter platform. Selar squared her shoulders and stood at attention. "Doctor," he said with surprising calm—indeed, he was surprised himself at the restraint he was displaying—"would you care to tell me where Cwansi is?"

"I do not know," she said. She was looking straight ahead, remaining at attention, not looking him in the eyes. "Perhaps the D'myurj with Xy's appearance knows."

"What the hell are you talking about?"

She looked around and mild surprise appeared to register. "He is not here. I had assumed you had transported all life-forms within the vicinity up here."

"We did."

"There was a being there . . . he called himself a D'myurj . . ."

"That is the name of the being that Captain Mueller said appeared on her bridge," said Kebron.

"She's telling the truth," said Rulan. "I saw him myself. He was standing right near me."

"If he was down there with them, why didn't he come up when we beamed them here?" Calhoun said to Halliwell.

Halliwell double-checked her readings and shook her head. "I'm not getting a reading of any other life-form at that transport site, Captain. If there's someone or something else down there, it's invisible to my instrumentation."

"I suppose anything is possible with these beings," said Selar. "They are able to convey a—"

She let out a startled gasp as Calhoun suddenly

reached out, grabbed her by the wrist, and yanked her off the platform. He then pushed her backward, keeping his arm crosswise across her body, forcing both of her arms down. The next instant he had slammed her up against the wall with such force that she cried out.

"If we were back on Xenex and I was your warlord," he said with barely contained fury, "I would take my sword and cut your head off right now. No discussion. No trial."

"A very efficient justice system," Selar whispered back. "I commend you on your alacrity. If it is of any consolation, I am in tremendous pain right now."

"I'm not holding you that hard."

"That is true, but my broken rib is threatening to puncture my lung. So if killing me is your desire, then by all means, keep right on pushing. I will offer no resistance, if that will help."

The muscles in his jaw clenched and unclenched several times, and then he stepped back, lowering his arm, and releasing his hold on her. Selar straightened her jacket as if she had been merely discommoded. "I should have contacted you as soon as I was aware of the ship's presence," she said. "But I had no desire to return until I could find the child and make up for, in some small measure, my actions in this matter."

"You can't make up for it," said Calhoun. "You cannot possibly think that you will return Cwansi to his mother and everything will go back to the way it was, simply because you were seized by some . . . some Vulcan madness."

She raised both eyebrows, which was typically the most surprised look she allowed herself to display. "How did you—?" But then she answered her own question. "Soleta. She must have told you. She sensed it. I—"

"You what?"

"I am shamed," and she lowered her eyes. "Perhaps fetching your sword from your ready room and beheading me would be the best way to proceed."

"The hell with that. You don't get off that easily. Kebron. Bring her. And hir," and he indicated the Hermat.

"Where to, sir? The brig?"

"The conference lounge. Alert command staff, and have Captain Mueller join us as well. Also tell Soleta that her presence would be appreciated. And let Lefler know that if she tries something again, I'll put her in restraints."

"Aye, sir."

ii.

There had never, in the history of the *Excalibur,* been a more tense gathering in the conference lounge than there was at that moment.

Doctor Selar was seated at the far end of the table. Representing the divide between them were Burgoyne and Xy at the opposite end. Robin Lefler was seated halfway, smoldering, glaring, apparently ready to kill Selar with a look. Standing just behind Robin, her hand resting supportively on her shoulder, was Morgan Lefler. Tania Tobias, Kalinda, Soleta, Xy, and Kat Mueller rounded out the assemblage, with Calhoun seated near Burgy and Kebron preferring to stand.

Rulan had departed the room after telling them everything s/he knew, which admittedly was not much. S/he had been dispatched to sickbay for them to give hir a physical and work-up. Able to discern the mood in the room rather easily, s/he appeared glad to be given the opportunity to depart.

Morgan had then, with Mueller's permission, tapped into the visual logs of the *Trident.* Images of the Brethren annihilating crew members who tried to stand in their way played across the screen. Mueller had told them about the vent vulnerability, and there was much speculation as to the makeup of creatures whose blood was so hot that it actually melted sections of their armor.

At that point, Calhoun had turned to Selar. There was a heavy, ominous silence, and then he simply said, "Tell us everything."

She did, not sparing herself any blame nor offering excuses. She spoke of her mentally destructive obsession, of the visitation she had received, her assault on Robin, and her subsequent flight. She was interrupted only once: when she spoke of what she had seen outside the brig of the *Spectre* just before the Brethren had shown up.

"Lucius is dead?" It was Soleta who spoke. She looked stunned upon hearing the news. "He . . . are you sure?" When Selar nodded, Soleta said, "How?"

"I believe Rulan killed him. That s/he came out of hir coma briefly, at precisely the wrong time, and attacked Lucius without even realizing what s/he was doing. I . . . am sorry, Soleta."

"No. No, it's all right," said Soleta, who appeared to be fighting to keep her emotions in check. She nodded, shaking off the rampant feelings within her, and said harshly, "It saves me having to kill him myself. I am . . . grateful to Rulan. I must be sure to thank hir. Soon."

"And the whereabouts of my son?" Robin's voice was brittle. She was clearly barely keeping herself together. Morgan's hand squeezed tighter on her shoulder, signaling solidarity.

Selar repeated all she knew of what had transpired on the planet's surface, including the comments from the fake Xy regarding an underground facility.

"Kalinda," said Calhoun. "You got us this far. Can you sense where the child is?"

All eyes shifted to Kalinda. Robin appeared extremely uncomfortable looking to Kally for guidance. Most of them did. The only one, Calhoun noticed, who seemed okay with it was Tobias, who actually appeared eager to hear what Kalinda had to say.

Slowly Kalinda shook her head. She closed her eyes. "I sense that he is down there," she said. "But I cannot get anything beyond that. Not his precise whereabouts."

"Why not?" said Robin, annoyed. "Why the sudden limits?"

"They were never sudden, and everything has limits," said Kalinda, not matching the irritation in Robin's voice. "I'm not a cosmic locator device. I have a sense of Cwansi's whereabouts. I know that he's down there. But that is as far as I can take you."

Selar looked puzzled at Kalinda. No one had brought her up to speed on Kalinda's status, and apparently after considering inquiring, she obviously decided it would be wiser not to ask.

"How do they see?"

The change in topic caught them by surprise. Xy was staring at the screen, studying the images of the Brethren stomping across the picture. "Look at their helmets. They're solid. Blank."

"Kat, you had the most time to study them up close and personal. Did you notice anything that could pass for eyeholes?"

"There was a horizontal ridge in the face plate. I thought—"

"No," said Xy. "I don't think so. That may be related to the structure of the suit's ventilation system. But I don't think there are any eyeholes."

"Morgan, can you give us a magnification?" said Calhoun.

Morgan's sullen face did not so much as twitch as the image of the Brethren warrior on the screen grew larger around the face. Even though it made no difference in their ability to study it, they all reflexively leaned forward. "He's right," Soleta said after a moment. "There's nothing there."

"Then how do they see?"

Soleta sat back, scratching her chin thoughtfully. "There's a warrior race in Sector 27, the Danoob. They live in a world that's perpetually dark. So when they go off world, their eyes would never be able to adjust. They have very similar helmets."

"Could it be the same race?"

"Considering the Danoob average seven feet tall with four arms, I'm thinking not. However their helmets are rigged with what are essentially onboard scanners. A sort of sensor array. They see electronically, basically. Outlines. Shapes."

"Thermal readouts?"

Soleta turned to Mueller, who had just spoken. "Yes. Why?"

"Because they killed one of my men. Mick Gold. And then, when his body was on the floor and one of them approached me, he almost tripped over it. It was as if Gold had become invisible to him, or at least harder to see."

"That would be consistent with the type of sensory apparatus that the Danoob possess, especially if they count on such things as bodily metabolism to perceive living beings. Body temperature, pulse, and such."

"So how do we find them?" said Robin with growing urgency. "How do we find my son?"

"When we first arrived, there was an energy spike from the planet's surface," said Mueller. "It was the origin for the transmat device that flooded our ship with those things."

"Got it," said Morgan instantly. "I've downloaded it from your ship's database. It's here." The image on the conference lounge monitor shifted from the frozen picture of the Brethren's helmet to the planet's surface with one particular section highlighted.

"Scan it," said Calhoun.

"Already doing so," said Morgan.

Mueller glanced around the room. "Am I the only one who finds this disconcerting?" she said, indicating Morgan. There was shaking of heads from most of the people grouped around the table.

"It's at the edge of a mountain range," Morgan said, apparently oblivious to the uncomfortable way in which the others were reacting to her. "I think there's something there."

"Why do you think that?"

"Because I'm not getting anything from it."

There were confused looks. "What's that supposed to mean?" said Calhoun.

"It means that I'm getting sensor readings from the surrounding area, but not from there. It's almost like a hole in the planet's surface. A sensor hole. It's rather sophisticated, actually. For an ordinary shipboard sensor array, it would work. It's a way of tricking a standard shipboard computer. The computer is told that there's nothing of interest there, and the computer in turn informs the human operator that that particular scanning section has drawn a blank and it's time to move on. A normal ship's computer wouldn't be able to process that it's actively being fed wrong information. But I, on the other hand—"

"Am hardly normal?" Robin said with a rueful smile.

"It can't fool a seamless blending of technological development and human consciousness," said Morgan, taking some pride in saying so. Then she added with a slightly rueful tone, "Unfortunately, I can't perceive much beyond there. The area is shielded too thoroughly. There is definitely something there, but whatever it is, I cannot provide any details."

Calhoun leaned back against the wall. "I'm not exactly thrilled with this situation," he said. "The odds could be insanely skewed. I'd like to know more before sending my people there on a rescue mission."

"Then don't send in your people," Soleta said quietly.

All eyes turned to her. Calhoun knew immediately that this was not some random comment. Soleta already had a plan. It was just a matter of her laying it out. "If these 'Brethren' see via electronic means, I can rig up tricorders to create localized scrambling fields. It wouldn't fool any one of them indefinitely. Just long enough that, if someone wearing the scrambler drew near them, they would experience difficulties with their 'sight.' They wouldn't have reason to think that there is someone there, however. They would likely ascribe it to some sort of temporary technical malfunction. It would pass so quickly, as the wearer keeps moving, that they probably wouldn't give it any thought."

"That's a lot of likelies and probablies," said Tobias.

"I would estimate a ninety-three percent chance of success." Soleta said primly.

"I like the odds," admitted Calhoun. "But what did you mean by not sending in my people?"

"You send in me. And you send in Selar. I assume she's not your person anymore—?"

Voices raised in protest and confusion, but Calhoun silenced them with a preemptive wave of his hand. Selar had not reacted in the slightest in hearing her name brought up for what might well be a suicide mission. "It makes sense," she said.

"How in God's name does it make sense?" said Robin angrily.

"There is a chance that, even with the scrambling field generated by the tricorder, they will still be able to pick up some metabolic cues," Soleta said, acting as if she were oblivious to the skepticism and even outright hostility in the room. "Vulcans have greater control over their metabolism than just about any other race in the Federation."

"Don't you have faster pulses?"

"Yes, Captain, we do. But we have the ability to slow our pulses through meditation and concentration. In an emergency situation, we can slow our hearts and pulses nearly to nonexistence."

"And you can function that way?" said Mueller.

"No, we collapse. But we can bring ourselves out of it. So we have the best chance of eluding detection. The worst-case scenario: We are able to relay information to you of what we've seen before we are found and killed. And if we are killed, what have you lost? A former member of Starfleet and," she glanced toward Selar, "a traitor who doesn't have a friend on this vessel right now."

"Shut up," said Xy. The calm in his voice was a stark contrast to the vehemence of his words.

"I am simply saying—"

"I know what you're simply saying, but you're saying them about my mother, and you will shut up or I'll shut you up."

"All right, that's enough," said Calhoun sharply. "Soleta, you're only half Vulcan . . ."

"That is irrelevant. Romulans remain a Vulcan offshoot species. There are only some surface dissimilarities."

"The planet's surface is extremely hostile to life," said Selar. "Furthermore, if they have transmat beams, there is every likelihood that there is not a direct means of access from the surface to the underground location."

"That is not a problem," said Morgan calmly. "I've been probing the area further with ship's sensors. I have detected what I believe to be the underground facility. It is shielded against sensor probes, but I am able to triangulate a safe beam-down point."

"Captain," said Robin, "you're not actually considering this . . ."

"No. I'm not considering it. I've decided. Soleta, do whatever needs to be done to the tricorders to enable you to avoid detection. Xy, provide her whatever help is necessary. Selar, you are cordially invited to partake of our facilities in the brig until such time that your presence is required."

"Captain—!"

Calhoun glanced toward Robin. "May I remind you, Lady Cwan, that you are not a member of this crew. You serve because I am allowing you to serve, but I can and will revoke that privilege at any time. Your opinion is not being solicited in this matter. Is that clear?"

"Yes, Captain," was all she managed to say.

"Mr. Kebron, escort the doctor to the brig. Xy, take Soleta to the technical support bay and get started on the tricorders. The rest of you, to your posts."

They did as they were instructed immediately, although Robin hesitated long enough to fire what she no doubt thought was an angry glance Calhoun's way.

As Calhoun headed for the door, the last to leave, Morgan appeared in front of him. "I thought you were with Robin," he said.

"I am. I just needed to ask you, Captain. Are you sure of what you're doing?"

"Always."

"But how do you know it's the right thing to do?"

"I never am. That's always judged after the fact."

"That's a hell of a way to live."

He nodded grimly.

iii.

Selar had known that Burgoyne would show up sooner or later. In this case, it happened to be sooner. Indeed, it was at least three minutes sooner than she had expected.

Burgoyne stood just outside the brig, on the other side of the force field. "Are you all right?" s/he asked solicitously.

"I am becoming accustomed to residing in brigs," Selar said. "This one is, at least, more hospitable than the one aboard the *Spectre*."

"That's not what I meant."

"I know what you meant. You mean: Am I still insane?"

"I wouldn't have phrased it quite that way."

"No. You never would have. You would not have wanted to hurt my feelings. It is . . . a rare individual who worries about a Vulcan's emotions. Most assume we simply do not possess any."

"I know better." S/he stepped closer to the field. "Let me talk to the captain on your behalf."

"What?"

"To the captain. To the crew. I can convince them that you weren't in your right mind."

"I do not believe that will require much convincing."

"I can fix this, Selar. I swear I can. Stop shaking your head!" s/he said angrily.

"It would be an exercise in futility. After what I did, no matter what the reason, it is ludicrous to think that I can simply pick up where I left off."

"Around this place? Stranger things have happened."

"A doctor must engender trust in her patients. How can anyone in this crew trust me, knowing what I am capable of?"

"They'll understand . . ."

She got up and walked to the edge of the force field screen. "What is this truly about, Burgoyne? Why such fervency in your demeanor? Are you concerned about me? Or about yourself?"

"Don't be ridiculous. What does this have to do with me?"

"Everything," she said. "I know you. You have been drowning in guilt for months now. You have seen my downward spiral, my attitude toward you. I have treated you terribly, and yet you keep coming back. You tell yourself that our relationship is salvageable, and that if you can only conceive of the right thing to say, the right approach to take, then somehow you can repair it. You have taken the weight of the world upon your shoulders and you are cracking under the strain."

"Selar—"

"This is not about you, Burgoyne," she said, but she did not have any of the typical, cold arrogance with which she had addressed him so frequently in the past months, when she deigned to speak to him at all. "This is not about failure on your part to save our relationship. To save me. You did all you could, and more than any reasonable being could have expected. This is entirely about me, and the decisions that I made, and my taking responsibility for my actions." She paused and then said, "Lower the force field."

Burgoyne glanced around. There were no guards, and s/he was clearly apprehensive.

"It will be all right," she said softly. "I give you my word."

S/he reached over and shut off the force field generator. Selar didn't move from the spot. They gazed at each other, and then Selar extended two fingers of her right hand and held them out to Burgoyne.

Burgoyne reached out with hir two fingers and lay them across Selar's. It was a gentle, loving caress.

She reached out with her other hand and rested her fingertips on Burgoyne's forehead. She closed her eyes. "So much pain," she whispered. "So much pain. And I am the cause."

"I welcome it. It makes me feel alive."

"Yes. But there is such a thing as quality of life. And I can ease the pain."

"Don't . . . please . . ."

It was too late. She lowered her voice and, barely audible, she said, *"Forget."*

S/he shuddered slightly and then stepped back, looking at Selar in wonderment. "What did you do?"

She reached over, took Burgoyne by the back of the neck, drew hir head forward to hers, and kissed hir gently. It was long and lingering and full of promise that would never be kept, and then she released Burgoyne and stepped back. "You will want to reactivate the force field now."

Burgoyne did so. "Can I get you anything?"

"I am quite fine, thank you. And you?"

"I am . . . quite fine as well," said Burgoyne. "It was . . . good to see you again, Selar."

"And you, Burgoyne. And you."

Burgoyne walked away with a bit more spring in hir step than Selar could recall having seen in quite some time. Selar watched hir go, and then walked over to the far side of the brig and sat. Her hands rested on her legs and she stared straight ahead.

A single tear rolled down her right cheek, but she quickly brushed it away before anyone could notice.

iv.

Soleta nodded in approval and lay the tricorder down on the worktable. "It works."

"Are you certain?" said Xy.

"As certain as I can be without field-testing it."

"Except you'll be putting your life, and my mother's life, at risk in the process of doing so."

She saw no reason to sugarcoat it. "Yes. That is correct." She paused and then said, "I can complete work on the second one by myself. Perhaps you would like to go see your mother?"

"I would. Yes. But I . . ." He shook his head. "I do not think it would be advisable."

"As you wish."

He looked at her. "You don't want to know why?"

"I don't consider it my business, no. My assumption is that you are concerned you will become over-emotional and believe that such a display will make Selar uncomfortable. You are probably correct in that regard. Besides, there will be plenty of time for you to speak to her after we return with the child in hand."

"You truly believe that you will succeed?"

"It is not my intention to die, if that is what you mean."

"Good."

She sensed that there was something else he wanted to say. She waited.

"If you get my mother killed, I will kill you myself."

She stared at him and, to his annoyance, seemed more amused than threatened. "Believe me, Xy, if we are in a position where we're being killed, your wrath will be the least of my concerns."

V.

Selar and Soleta stood on the transporter platform. They were both armed with phasers, although based upon all that had transpired, it seemed to them that the phasers would be of minimal use. But Calhoun simply couldn't see his way to sending them down unarmed.

Morgan had materialized, her holographic form standing next to Transporter Chief Halliwell. Halliwell was looking a bit puzzled at the coordinates that Morgan—in her computer state—was feeding into her panel. "Are you sure?" Halliwell said. Morgan nodded.

"Are you going to be able to communicate with us once you're there?" said Calhoun.

"My supposition would be that we won't be able to," said Soleta. "Presuming we find the child, we will have to find a way to either reach the surface— in which case, you will be able to detect Selar's combadge—or else we will find some means of contacting you."

"What sort of means?"

"I do not know. But we can be resourceful if we have to."

He nodded. "I know that is very true. All right, then. Good luck."

"Thank you, Captain," said Soleta. Selar did not reply. She looked stone-faced, in the midst of unimaginable pain, but unwilling or unable to even acknowledge it, much less deal with it.

Calhoun said "Energize" with the same feeling as if he had just said "fire" to a firing squad that was aiming at two condemned prisoners standing against a wall. Sparkles enveloped Soleta and Selar, and just as they vanished, Xy charged into the transporter room so quickly that he banged his shoulder on the door because it hadn't slid open quickly enough.

"Mother!" he shouted. "I know you did it out of love for me! I know you—!"

Selar smiled.

He had never seen her smile in his life. Not ever. But she did so now, a broad and genuine grin that lit up her face, just before it dissolved into molecules and then vanished. The last thing he saw go was the smile, giving Selar a resemblance to the Cheshire cat.

Xy sagged against the wall and pulled his roiling emotions together. Calhoun walked over to him and stood in front of him, hands draped behind his back.

Xy looked up at him and said, "She has a lovely smile, doesn't she."

"Who knew?" said Calhoun. He patted Xy on the shoulder and then walked out of the transporter room.

vi.

Robin Lefler stepped into the turbolift, hoping that no one would try to jump into it with her and discuss something deeply emotional. Her nerves were strung so taut that she didn't think she could handle much more. "Bridge," she said.

The turbo lift started moving.

She paused and then said, "Mother? Are you there?"

"Of course I am, dear," came Morgan's voice.

"Just tell me: Where do we stand on Soleta and Selar's . . ."—she couldn't bring herself to say "rescue attempt"—"expedition," she finished.

"They have just been beamed down to the planet to the coordinates I provided. The ones I informed the captain I was able to discern by detecting subterranean activity."

"Yes. It was a good thing you were able to do that."

"I did not say I was able to do it. I said that is what I told the captain."

Robin felt a chill working its way down her spine. "What are you saying?"

"I calculated a point underground several meters below the energy spike that Captain Mueller's ship recorded. And that is where I instructed they be beamed to."

"But . . . you don't know for sure?"

"No. It does seem a reasonable guess, though."

"Reasonable *guess*? Mother . . . !" Robin was stunned. "Are you saying you may have just provided coordinates that beamed two people into solid rock?"

"Not two people, Robin," said Morgan, sounding chillingly indifferent. "One person who kidnapped my grandson, and one person whose poor choice of lovers provided an escape vehicle. The worst that happens is they die far more quickly and mercifully than they deserve."

Robin felt her throat starting to close, and then the doors to the turbolift slid open. The bridge lay before her. Her legs moved her forward, practically on autopilot. She felt as if she were viewing the world through a distorted lens. Calhoun turned and looked at her curiously. "Robin? Is something wrong?"

My mother is insane. Drunk with power. Unlimited machine power with no human conscience. A danger to everyone on this vessel.

"Nothing, Captain. Nothing at all. Just . . . a headache."

"Do you need to go lie down?" he said solicitously.

"I'll be fine," said Robin, taking her seat at ops without really being aware that she was doing so. "I'll be just . . . fine."

AF1963

I've never seen anything like it before.

The phrase had become something of a cliché. It had worked its way into so many science logs and recordings of encounters with previously unknown phenomena that students at Starfleet Academy laughed about it.

Soleta was not laughing. Not now. For she truly had never seen anything like it before. The closest she had come was the inside of a Dyson sphere.

It was a vast underground facility that appeared to go on forever. Vast stretches of alien machinery were working away at tasks that she couldn't even begin to guess about. She felt like an insect looking up at the accomplishments of higher life-forms and trying to fathom them; she was that outclassed, and she knew it. It was humbling. It was also annoying.

Selar was standing next to her and looked just as

disconcerted, although naturally she managed to cover it extremely well. They had both activated their tricorders as soon as they had materialized. "Which way?" said Selar in a low voice.

Soleta didn't have the faintest idea.

They were standing on a rampway that seemed to run the length of the place, although it was difficult to tell for certain considering how big it was. "This way," said Soleta, hoping to overcome her uncertainty by speaking in as authoritative a manner as possible.

"You do not actually have any idea, do you."

That didn't deter Soleta from firing Selar an imperious look and heading off as if the very notion were too ridiculous for her to discuss. Selar hesitated only a moment and then fell into step behind her.

Two of the Brethren emerged from a side corridor.

The women froze where they were, Soleta's hands resting on the tricorder. The Brethren walked toward them and then began tapping on the sides of their helmets in what was obvious confusion. Seizing the opportunity, Soleta and Selar sidled past them, gracefully moving to either side and not coming into contact with them despite the narrowness of the passage. Seconds later they were past them. Soleta watched over her shoulder as the Brethren shook their helmeted heads and then kept walking.

It worked, Selar mouthed to Soleta. Soleta shrugged back as if to say, *Of course. Did you expect anything else?* Inwardly, though, she felt extremely relieved.

Then she realized an opportunity had presented itself. She turned quickly, aimed the tricorder at the Brethren, and used it to lock in basic life readings. Her eyes widened at some of the stats she was receiving. The Brethren were like miniature volcanoes on two legs. She didn't understand how they weren't simply spontaneously combusting.

Selar stepped in close to her and said, "Now what?"

"Now," whispered Soleta, "I set the tricorder for any non-Brethren life-forms. And we see what we've got."

Moments later she had multiple readings. They appeared to be clustered about five hundred meters ahead and ten meters straight down.

Tentatively they continued on their way. Every so often they would encounter more of the Brethren, and they would avoid detection through the same process. Soleta's concern was that they would start to notice it as a recurring pattern, realize it was a coordinated deception of their detection devices, and take offensive action the very next time it happened. The two women might have been "invisible," but if the Brethren just started firing away, even blindly, there was every chance that they'd get lucky and the women would get unlucky.

They reached a ramp that angled steeply downward. They followed it, gripping the handrail to make sure that they didn't fall. Moments later they reached the bottom level. Soleta looked up. The ceiling of the place stretched high above like a vast cathedral.

"There," whispered Selar, and pointed. Soleta saw where she was indicating and led the way. She had no idea why she did so, but she pulled out her phaser and kept it at the ready, proceeding one step at a time.

For a heartbeat her mind was torn away from where she was and she could "see" Lucius lying unmoving on the floor of the *Spectre*. She had no idea where her vessel was and, by this point, she wasn't entirely sure she ever wanted it back. Then she refocused her attention on the problem at hand. She certainly didn't need to let herself get distracted.

There was a glow ahead of them, accompanied by a steady hum. They weren't going to be able to see it clearly until they were practically on top of it, which didn't particularly thrill Soleta. But there was no way around it.

They stepped around a huge column that was lined with what appeared to be circuitry and then Soleta blinked in amazement.

There were rows upon rows of clear canisters lined up. Even though they were elevated about ten feet off the floor, Soleta could still easily make out the contents.

There were bodies in each of the canisters.

The bodies were enveloped in thick, bubbling liquid that appeared to be preserving them, even nurturing them, and then Soleta saw the bodies twitching ever so slightly even as their eyes remained closed. They were alive. Every damned one of them. It was like a living mortuary. There were all different races represented, except . . .

Not just races. Half-breeds. With some it was barely detectable, and with others it was extremely obvious. She had trouble believing that all of them had occurred naturally. The Klingon with the light blue skin and white hair of an Andorian; a human with the piggish snout and mane of a Tellarite, on and on.

But it did not end there. Each of the canisters had

elaborate arrays of tubes attached to them, and the tubes apparently ran to another point entirely. That point was easily discerned: It was a vast ring of more tubes, upright rather than horizontal, surrounding them. There were bodies in there as well, but whereas most of the bodies in the horizontal tubes were fully grown, or at least fully developed, the bodies in the upright tubes looked as if they were being . . .

". . . grown," said Selar, completing the thought that was going through Soleta's head. "They're being grown. These—" and she indicated the bodies in the horizontal tubes, "are serving as source material for those."

"Clones? They're growing clones? My God, why?"

Selar was using her tricorder to get readings on the developing creatures. "This is . . . it makes no sense. They have no brain activity. How can they have no brain activity? Why would they be growing brain-dead bodies? Why—?"

Instantly they became silent, having both heard it at the same time. Soleta froze where she was, unmoving.

Three Brethren strode into the area as if they were moving with a purpose. They took a position, stood back to back, and stayed right where they were.

One of them was looking directly at Soleta.

She didn't move. Didn't breathe. She rapidly began to slow her heart rate. It spiraled downward at breathtaking speed; a human would have collapsed. Soleta managed to remain on her feet. It was as if she was willing herself to blend with the shadows in order to avoid detection.

He didn't look away from her.

She slowed her heartbeat further. She was beginning to feel light-headed. She should really have been sitting, but she willed herself to remain on her feet.

Still he remained focused on her. He didn't see her. She knew he didn't see her. But he was trying to. He suspected she was there, but could not be absolutely certain. And obviously he didn't want to start firing blindly because he would hit some of the bodies in storage and cause all manner of damage.

A few feet away, she could see Selar doing the exact same thing. Their eyes met briefly and then both of them descended into themselves, stopping just shy of a total self-induced trance lest they topple over.

Time slowed to a crawl and then, finally, the Brethren resumed their march. The women didn't know whether they knew that someone was in the complex for sure or if they just had vague suspicions; either way they moved on leaving Soleta and Selar behind.

It took the women a full minute to restore their bodily processes to normal. They did not exhale in relief or trade comments about how lucky they were. They remained focused on their situation.

They began moving along the rows of canisters, trying to find some trace of Cwansi. There was no doubt in Soleta's mind at this point they would find the child there. It was just a matter of being patient.

She also studied the control panels that were monitoring the various canisters. She continued not to recognize a good deal of the technology, but some of it looked vaguely familiar to her. She had to hope that she would be able to operate it when the time came.

"There."

She had spoken so softly that Soleta almost didn't hear her. Then she turned and saw where Selar was pointing, and her heart skipped a beat.

It was Cwansi. He was floating in a canister the same size as any of the others, sleeping peacefully.

"Now what?" said Selar.

"Now we get him out."

She studied the edges of the canister, circling it, trying to find some means of opening it. There was nothing. No visible latch, no unlocking mechanism. Deciding to take a different approach, she went over to the computer array and began studying it, looking for some means of opening it in that manner.

"Well?" said Selar.

"If I had about three days to study this, I might be able to make some headway," said Soleta impatiently. "No promises, though."

"Then perhaps the best way to proceed would be—"

"What?!"

They turned as one, and Soleta saw an astounded Lucius looking at her.

Her first impulses were to demand to know what he was doing there and how he had survived when Selar had said he was dead, to struggle with her sense of betrayal over what he had done to her. Had she allowed herself to give into those impulses, she would have landed herself in even deeper trouble. Fortunately she was able to follow her second impulse, which was to move so quickly that Lucius didn't have time to react as she swung her phaser around and caught him squarely in the jaw with the butt end. Lucius stumbled backward over his own feet and fell against Cwansi's canister. She caught him just before he slid to the floor and, turning quickly, slammed him against the computer console.

Selar stepped in and, to Soleta's shock, placed the business end of her phaser against the side of Lucius's head. "Stop impersonating my son."

"Your son is Lucius?"

"He looks like Xy. And he is going to permit us to see him as he really is, right now." The phaser amped up in power audibly.

Instantly the area was suffused with a blue glow, and a bizarre creature with translucent skin appeared beneath Soleta's grasp. He was looking up at her grimly and he said, "You have run out of time. I have already summoned the Brethren. They will be here within moments."

"Don't be an idiot. They've turned against you."

"No. They've turned against the others. My fellow D'myurj," he said tightly. "I wanted to take the D'myurj to the next level of development. Of greatness. Why should we shepherd others along and never follow that path ourselves? None of them understood. The Brethren understood, but they were reluctant to listen to me. But then you showed up, with your barbarism and your murderous ways. Your actions helped convince the Brethren where my words could not."

They heard the tromping of feet heading their way. The Brethren were seconds from reaching them.

"Time for a new plan," said Selar, and she brought her phaser up and fired at the canister at point-blank range.

The canister shuddered for a moment, then cracked, and then shattered. Fluid gushed out, surging around their feet. Soleta moved quickly and caught the infant as he tumbled through the gaping hole. The baby startled awake, his arms thrashing about, and he looked panicked. He started howling.

I don't have time for a squalling infant, thought Soleta, and she brought her fingers down gently upon his shoulders. Instantly the child's head lolled and he went right back to sleep.

Selar had one arm around the D'myurj's neck and her phaser against his head. He was squirming fiercely but was no match for Selar's strength. "Now," she said tightly, "we get out of here." She tapped her combadge. "Selar to transporter room! We have the child. Emergency beam out."

"Locking on," came Halliwell's voice.

Soleta looked surprised. "I'll be damned," she said. "Sometimes it's just that easy."

Just as three Brethren advanced into view, with the

sounds of thundering boots indicating that more were on the way, the two women and the sleeping infant began to shimmer out of existence . . .

. . . and then shimmered right back in.

Their backs against the console, Soleta and Selar found themselves surrounded.

"Then again, sometimes it's not," said Soleta.

Starship Excalibur

"I lost them, sir!" came Halliwell's frustrated voice over the comm system. "One second they were there, and the next, bam! Some sort of scrambler field came up and blocked the transport beam!"

Robin Lefler's heart was pounding. They had her son! They had found him! Yet the relief she felt over that warred with the relief that her mother had not dispatched Soleta and Selar to their deaths inside the substrata of a planet.

Either way the fact that they had found him meant nothing if they couldn't get him back to safety.

Calhoun was already up and out of his command chair. "Alert the shuttlebay," he said briskly. "Muster as many shuttles as we have ready to fly. If we can't beam them out, then we go down and get them ourselves. Mr. Kebron, with me. Burgy, you have the—"

"Belay that, Mr. Kebron," said Burgoyne. "You're with me."

Calhoun turned and looked with astonishment at Burgoyne. "You are not authorized to countermand my orders, Commander."

"I *am* authorized to prevent the commanding officer from needlessly exposing himself to risk."

"And the fact that it's Selar, the woman you love, down there wouldn't have anything to do with it."

"Love?" Burgoyne looked puzzled. "No, sir."

There were confused looks exchanged by everyone on the crew, except for Xy. Xy regarded his father thoughtfully for a moment, and then simply looked saddened.

Calhoun noticed, as he tended to notice everything that went on on the bridge of his vessel. But he decided it was a matter that was best pursued later. "Get going, Burgy," he said, stepping aside, and Burgoyne followed Kebron out the door into the turbolift.

"Be careful!" called Robin after them.

"Save your concern for the bad guys. They're going to need it," Kebron said as the doors hissed shut behind them.

AF1963

i.

They remained frozen there for a moment, like a tableau. The D'myurj was not attempting to break free of the hold Selar had upon him, but he did not seem especially perturbed over the situation. "You may not have noticed this," he informed her, "but you are slightly outnumbered." More Brethren were moving in from all directions.

"There may be many of them, but there is only one of you. And if they do not step back and allow us to leave, then there will be none of you."

"Do you truly think we will allow that? After all that you have seen?"

"You cannot prevent it. There are two starships in orbit around this world. They know we are down here. They are going to come after us."

"And we will be prepared for them, and they will die. Hundreds of Brethren will be sent up to the ships, and this time they will not simply remove themselves once the point of a distraction has been served. This time they will remain and finish the job."

"Perhaps. But you will not be alive to see it." She shoved the muzzle of the phaser tightly against his head.

"Go on," said the D'myurj. "Kill me. Lose the last shield between yourself and the Brethren. Kill me in cold blood. Watch me die the same way that you watched him die . . ."

And the face of Voltak was looking at her.

Selar was momentarily shaken as her dead husband stared at her with eyes that were accusing, as if to say that she should have somehow found a way to save him; then Voltak slammed an elbow into her face. He pulled away from her, retreating to the safety of the Brethren, and shouted, "Now! Kill them now! But do not hurt the child!"

Soleta didn't hesitate. She swung her phaser up and opened fire, not on the Brethren, but on the tanks overhead.

She blasted two apart in as many seconds, and liquid gushed from within. It cascaded down upon the

Brethren and, as Soleta had hoped, seeped in through the narrow vent slots in their helmets.

The Brethren staggered, their arms flailing, as steam billowed from within. Instantly there was a vast haze hanging over the area, and she even thought she heard choking noises from within the helmets. *Good. Suffocate, you bastards.*

Then Selar was grabbing her by the wrist. "Come on!" she shouted and Soleta was following her, sprinting as hard as she could. She could only imagine what it must be like for the beings who were suddenly finding themselves coming around as the fluids that had been supporting them were spilling away. But she couldn't stop to worry about that now. She had to get Selar, Cwansi, and herself the hell out of there.

The tricorders had done nothing to hide them from the Brethren moments before because the D'myurj had been looking right at them and, due to his obvious mental link with his armored cohorts, was able to be their eyes. Now that they were on the run, however, they were able to use the tricorders to scramble their appearance once more. They did not, however, attempt anything approaching stealth. Instead they ran as fast as they could, sprinting toward oncoming Brethren and then past them before the Brethren could fully process that they were there.

"This way!" gestured Soleta, even though the truth was that she didn't have any idea which way to go. Nothing changed the fact that they were underground, and they needed to find a way to get to the surface. It was obvious that somehow the D'myurj had interfered with their ability to use the transporter. Now the only option was to get clear of the underground facility and hope that, once above, the *Excalibur* could lock on to them once more.

They rounded a corner and hit a dead end: a massive series of conduits were humming with power. She turned to Selar. "Energy generator. Their power source. Perhaps if we could shut it down somehow . . ."

"Look out!"

A lone Brethren stepped from the shadows and opened fire with his palm weaponry. His presence caught them off guard because before they had been moving in groups of three, so they weren't expecting to find one on his own.

Clutching the baby, twisting her body to avoid the blast, Soleta was only partly successful. Having zeroed in on her voice, the Brethren's blast struck her a glancing blow across the ribs. Soleta went down, still holding the baby, and the tricorder tumbled away from her.

She looked up as her death hovered directly in front of her eyes.

ii.

Selar saw Soleta lying there helpless, the unconscious baby still upon her, and the Brethren aiming his weaponry directly at her head. Within the next second her skull would be nothing more than a mass of protoplasm.

Before she had time to contemplate what she was doing, she dashed forward and hurled her own tricorder directly at Soleta. It landed on her stomach, effectively causing her to disappear from the Brethren's sight.

She kept moving, stopping only long enough to grab up Soleta's phaser. Her mind was already racing, thinking several steps ahead. She yanked off her combadge and slapped it on Soleta's chest. "Run in the opposite direction from here and then find someplace to hide," was all she said and then she fired off a fast phaser blast at the Brethren. It didn't slow him, as she expected it would not, but it was more than enough to draw his attention away from Soleta.

He lumbered after her and, with no tricorder and no means of hiding her presence, she was an easy target. Or at least that was the theory, for she darted between the throbbing generators that provided power for the entire complex. She gambled and won in one regard. Her pursuer had no desire to fire upon her and risk hitting one of the generators. That indicated to her that they might be vulnerable to a phaser blast.

But one generator wasn't going to do the job.

Farther and farther she moved, gliding as noiselessly as she could from shelter to shelter, and she heard the pounding footsteps of the Brethren all around her. They were converging upon her, and she was running out of directions and out of options.

From around one of the generators came the D'myurj, and he was still wearing her late husband's face, which infuriated her. She brought up one of the phasers, aiming it squarely at him, and he was simply looking at her sadly. "Put it down," he said. "You cannot get away." She looked upward toward the ceiling, many feet above. "No, not that way either. We are completely underground. You cannot get out of this place."

"I do not intend to," said Selar. With an abrupt twist, she jacked up the power level on her phasers, first one and then the other. A slow, steady humming sound, a building up of power began to emanate from the phasers.

"What do you think you are doing?" he asked, sounding only mildly curious.

"I have removed the safeties that typically manage the power flow of the phasers. It is causing energy to be transferred from the power cell to the prefire chamber and back again faster than the cell can absorb it. In short, it is causing the phasers to overload. The damage will be considerable."

The D'myurj no longer looked mildly curious. Instead he was genuinely concerned. "Get those from her!" he ordered. "Get them and shut them down!"

Still unwilling to shoot because of their proximity to the generators, the Brethren moved toward her. They came together, grabbing for the phasers, trying to wrestle them away.

Selar darted between them, bending over, clutching the phasers tightly with as much fervency as if they were an infant she was trying to protect—

—*and she is in her marital bed with her husband, and he is dying*—

—and the D'myurj was shouting at them, bellowing, even as he was backing up with wide eyes, the expression of terror looking comically wrong on the face of her husband—

—and she is in a cave on a storm-torn world giving birth to her son—

—and she darted between two oncoming Brethren, getting distance, banging up against one of the generators as they turned as one to face her—

—and Burgoyne is looking at her with infinite love, how could she have kept hir at bay? How foolish she had been, how illogical she had been, how glorious it is to be loved, not in spite of one's failings, but because of them—

—and the phaser reached critical mass, and as they rushed her, trying to grab at them, she drew back her powerful arm and slung one skyward as hard as she could. It arced through the air, toward the ceiling, and lodged in a crossbeam, and then she spun away from them, dropped to the ground and shoved the other phaser against the nearest generator, holding it there . . .

—and love washes over her, true love, and this time when the tears come she welcomes them as if old friends whom she has missed terribly have arrived and is happy, at the last, to have the chance to see—

—and the phaser above and in her hand erupted

at precisely the same time, as a massive burst of light enveloped her—

I'm sorry, Xy, I tried, I tried so hard, and his voice comes back, I know, you did your best, no one could have done better, I forgive you, we all forgive you, and she takes that forgiveness to her and smiles, and she is content—

iii.

Soleta was running and running, sprinting past Brethren who were running in the other direction. *Just survive, Selar, that's all I ask. Just survive long enough for me to figure out a way to—*

She spun upon hearing the distant eruptions and saw a massive explosion from the area of the generators while, at the same time, another detonation erupted in the ceiling. Supports crumbled away overhead as exactly at the same moment a fireball blasted upward from the generators, a fireball that kept building upon itself as one generator after another detonated. The concussive force of the two slammed into each other and recoiled in opposite directions. A huge hole was ripped in the ceiling, and quickly widened as more and more debris began to fall from it.

The place was erupting all around Soleta, and the only thing she could think of was to go up, because if she stayed where she was and it all came crashing down, they would never find her.

She got to a ramp and started running up it. At the same time, she was pounding on the combadge shouting, "*Soleta to* Excalibur! *Soleta to anybody! Is anybody reading this? Beam me the hell out of here!*"

Soleta kept on going even as flame tore through the facility below and debris rained down from on high. Higher and higher still she ran, to the uppermost ramps in the place, and suddenly she skidded to a halt. One of the Brethren was approaching, her shouting drawing him like a beacon. He was clearly locked on to her. She spun, started the other way, and there was another one coming right at her. Both of them had their energy weapons up, and both of them looked ready to fire at her. The gaping hole in the ceiling was twenty feet above her, but it might as well have been twenty miles.

To hell with you. Nobody chooses the way I die except me. She looked down regretfully at Cwansi, who was sleeping blissfully and would never awaken. Then she sprinted toward the edge of the ramp, a sheer drop yawning beneath her, and she threw herself into the abyss.

She closed her eyes so that she would not have to see the flames and the floor coming toward her. Consequently, she was thoroughly surprised when she landed on something hard, much sooner than she could have expected to. She looked down and discovered that it was the top of a shuttlecraft.

The jolt of the impact almost caused her to lose her grip on Cwansi. At the last second she managed to pull him back and clutch him to her. He continued to snore softly.

A blast of energy ripped just over her head. She twisted around and saw the two Brethren, both standing there on the ramp, firing at her. They fired again as the shuttlecraft angled around, and Soleta grabbed desperately onto the top. She skidded halfway down before snagging a protruding handle. One blast went past them and the other slammed the shuttle sideways, rebounding off the ship's armor. The shuttle whipped around, facing the Brethren, and before they could fire again, the craft's phasers lashed out at the ramp under the Brethrens' feet. It gave way and the Brethren tumbled down and out of sight. Then with a roar of thrusters, the shuttlecraft rose through the hole above.

Immediately she was hit by such vicious winds that

Soleta was knocked right off the top of the shuttle. Fortunately it had moved to the side, so rather than falling into the hole, she instead landed on the frozen ground. She desperately tried to shield the baby from the freezing air.

The shuttlecraft angled down, and Soleta saw that there were other shuttles moving in as well. The hatch slid open and Burgoyne's face peered out from within. She could spot Kebron at the helm as Burgoyne reached out toward her. Getting to her feet, she stumbled forward and into the shuttle just as her legs gave out. She started to crumble to the floor of the shuttle, but Burgoyne caught her and eased her over to a chair. Then s/he crouched and looked into the face of the unconscious baby. "He can sleep through anything."

"I knocked him out with a nerve pinch."

"You could make a fortune as a nanny. Where's Selar?"

She didn't answer immediately, and Burgoyne repeated the question with greater urgency.

"Down there," she said finally. "She was responsible for the detonation . . . for blowing the hole in the ceiling so you could find us. She . . ." Her voice trailed off.

Burgoyne processed the information. "She didn't make it," s/he said.

Soleta shook her head.

"But she was responsible for you surviving."

She nodded.

"Well . . . she died as she would have wished to. Making amends."

Soleta stared at hir for a long moment, and then reached out with her fingers. She touched Burgoyne's forehead lightly, closed her eyes, and then shook her head. "That bitch," she said softly.

"What?"

She withdrew her fingers. "Never mind. It doesn't matter. It's what she wanted, and I'm not going to question it. And neither should you."

"Question what?" said Burgoyne.

"Exactly."

Starship Excalibur

i.

Robin Lefler sat in her quarters, clutching her child to her breast. He was happily suckling, and did not seem the least bit affected by everything he had endured.

"I am never going to let you go. Not ever," she told him softly. "You'd better get used to having me around all the time. When you go to school, I'll be there with you in the classroom. When you marry and go off on your honeymoon, I'm going to be in the room right next to yours."

"Don't you think you may be overcompensating?"

She looked up. Kalinda was standing in the doorway.

"A little, I suppose," said Robin. "Look, Kalinda . . . I want to . . . I suppose I should . . ."

"Thank me?" Kalinda walked over to them and let her finger caress Cwansi's face. Cwansi reached over and wrapped his tiny fingers around Kalinda's single one. "This is thanks enough."

"Still . . . I had trouble believing this wasn't all some mad diversion, and I was nasty to you, and I shouldn't have been—"

Kalinda leaned over, tilted Robin's chin back, and kissed her gently.

Robin returned it, reaching up, touching her cheek, and she whispered, "Cwan . . . ? "

"Good-bye, my love," whispered Kalinda.

"Cwan, wait—!"

Then Kalinda's head pitched back and her eyes opened wide. She twisted and convulsed, and Robin cried out to her in confusion, first Cwan's name, then Kalinda's, and she wasn't sure what to say or what to do.

Kalinda sagged down onto the floor, caught herself before she fell over completely, and then looked up at Robin with confused eyes. Bewildered eyes. Kalinda's eyes.

"What happened?" she said.

Robin didn't quite know where to start.

ii.

Xy stood in the viewing bay, looking down upon the planet that was slowly turning beneath them. Soleta was standing next to him on one side, and Calhoun was on the other. Xy had already learned what had happened to his mother, but Soleta—at his request—had provided him a blow-by-blow description.

"Are you sure she was—?" He couldn't finish the sentence.

Soleta looked to Calhoun, who said softly, "We found the blast site. Enough of her DNA in the remains to verify that she was there. Nothing else left of her, I'm afraid. Considering she was at ground zero, it's not all that surprising."

"I suppose not."

"I'm sorry, Xy," said Calhoun. "I'm sorry it ended that way."

"She deserved better," Xy said. "All anyone is going to remember of her is that she betrayed her friends, her colleagues . . . endangered her vessel . . . all in some fruitless and pointless quest to save me."

"Not pointless. Not to her." Calhoun glanced at Soleta and then said, "And not exactly fruitless."

Xy frowned. "What?"

Soleta handed him a data chip. He took it and looked at it, uncomprehending.

"Your mother may have done a good job blowing the place up, but she didn't take out all of it. Their information banks were damaged but intact. With Morgan's help, I was able to study the contents."

"Did it tell you who these beings were? What their overall plans were?"

"No, they didn't leave a detailed memo about their backstory or their goals," she said dryly. "Mostly it was records of their research data, including the work they did on Rulan. They made remarkable progress on the slowing of cellular degeneration. It's doubtful that it will be of much use to Hermats, but it could well be of use to you."

Slowly he took the chip. "Are you serious?"

"Always. If my initial impression is correct, you can use the research to synthesize a drug that would slow the aging process considerably. You'd have to take it for the rest of your life, probably on a weekly basis. That's a small price to pay, though—"

"What are we talking about here? How 'considerably' are we talking about?" Xy was trying to repress his growing excitement, scarcely able to believe what he was hearing.

"Well, not as long as a Vulcan. Give or take—" She shrugged. "A century?"

He couldn't believe what he was hearing. He stared at the chip as if he were staring at the Holy Grail.

"Congratulations, Xy," said Calhoun.

"She did it," he whispered.

Calhoun knew to whom he was referring. "Yes. She did. I can't say that I agree with the methods that she employed, but she accomplished her goal. She saved the one person she loved in the universe."

Xy's hand was trembling, and perhaps it was the Vulcan aspect of him kicking in, but it was suddenly incredibly important to him that no one see him having an emotional breakdown. "Captain . . . Soleta . . . I would . . . I would very much appreciate it if you left me alone right now."

Calhoun seemed a bit puzzled, but Soleta understood immediately. "Of course." She looked to Calhoun and somehow from her unspoken cue he immediately understood. He nodded and the two of them walked out of the room.

Once they did, Xy sank to his knees and, clutching

the data chip to his chest, rocked back and forth and whispered thanks to his dead mother, who had sacrificed everything so that he could live the life she had dreamed of for him.

iii.

"*What* did she do to him?"

Calhoun and Soleta were walking down the corridor toward the transporter room, but he had stopped in his tracks. She looked at him with an arched eyebrow as he repeated, "*What* did she do?"

"Captain, you're the one who brought it up. You're the one who mentioned how well you thought Burgoyne was handling Selar's passing. Would you rather I hadn't told you?"

"I'm starting to think it would have been preferable, yes. Are you telling me she . . . ?" A couple of crew members were passing by, and Calhoun quickly pulled Soleta into the closest room, which happened to be the armory.

Soleta glanced around. "I can't say I'm enamored of these surroundings. If you don't like what I have to say, how do I know you won't shoot me?"

"Soleta—"

"All right, all right. At some point, Selar brushed hir mind and took away—"

"Hir memories?"

"No. S/he remembers well enough. But Selar excised the hurt."

"That's appalling."

"Appalling?" Her elegant eyebrows knit. "Perhaps she simply thought she was doing the decent thing. Perhaps she was tired of hurting people and thought that, for once, she might be able to spare someone."

"She lobotomized hir!"

"Oh, don't be so melodramatic, Captain. The memories are there. They simply don't sting."

"S/he has the right to hir feelings. How could Selar possibly think that was the right thing to do?"

"I doubt she thought it was. But she probably thought it was the logical thing to do."

Calhoun shook his head. "To the end, she remains a mystery to me."

"I think she would prefer it that way," said Soleta. "Are we done here? We wouldn't want to start rumors."

He gave her a mildly annoyed look and walked out of the armory. She fell into step behind him.

"So my ship is undamaged?" she said.

"As near as we can tell. We found it abandoned on the planet's surface. The recovery crew looked it over and it appears to be in working order. We can't get it started up, though."

"I wouldn't think so. It's computer locked to respond to me. Well, to a Vulcan."

"If you have any problems with it after we beam you down to it, contact us and let us know."

"Will do."

There was something in her expression, though, that concerned Calhoun. "What's on your mind, Soleta?"

"What's on my mind, Captain, is that the D'myurj had plenty of time to go over every aspect of my vessel and determine how she works. The cloaking device, the ion glide. If they're resourceful—and I think we have to assume they are—they might now have the ability to make a fleet of undetectable vessels."

"Thank you, Soleta," said Calhoun. "Now I have one more thing to worry about."

"Glad I could help, Captain." She stood at the door to the transporter room. "This has been fun. We should do this more often."

He smiled. "For what it's worth, Soleta, I miss you."

"It's worth a lot, Captain. Believe me."

"Oh. Our team . . ." He paused, not quite sure how to say it. "Our team found the remains of Lucius on the ship. They cleaned up the mess and put the body into a photon torpedo shell. You can do with it what you wish."

"I know just the place for it," she said. "Alpha Koneri IV."

"Isn't that the planet that Alpha Koneri III uses to dump its pollutants and toxins?"

"That's right, Captain. I think it fitting to dump him with the other garbage."

There was a hardness in her eyes that she seemed determined to maintain, although it might well have been for his benefit as much as hers. "Were I able to," Calhoun said softly, "would you want me to take the pain away, as Selar did with Burgoyne?"

"No need," she said. "I'm doing fine with that on my own." And she turned and strode into the transporter room.

Starfleet Headquarters

Admiral Alyanna Nechayev had become accustomed to giving Mackenzie Calhoun incredulous stares, and yet somehow it always seemed a new experience. "And you simply allowed Soleta to depart. In her spy vessel."

"It is her vessel, Admiral," said Calhoun over the viewscreen in her office. *"I had no grounds upon which to confiscate it."*

"How about on the grounds that it is, in fact, a spy vessel?"

He shrugged.

"That's it?" she said. "Nothing else to say?"

"I've been working long hours since we uncovered the existence of the D'myurj, Admiral. I regret that my repartee is not up to its usual standards."

She leaned back and shook her head. "Fine, Calhoun. Fine. How is the recovery process at AF1963 coming?"

"The Trident *is doing an excellent job of handling it. Most of the victims who were found in tubes are recovering from the experience. From what I understand, though, none of them is able to offer much in the way of explanations as to how they got there. They all have holes in their memories."*

"What about the other things? The bodies that were being grown?"

"Most of them were destroyed in the explosion."

"Do you have any idea what intentions these D'myurj might have had for them?"

"I've been thinking about that," said Calhoun, *"and consulting with my people. We have a theory . . ."*

"I'm all ears."

"Well," said Calhoun, leaning in slightly toward the screen, *"our initial question, of course, was why they would have all these bodies being grown with what were essentially blank slates for minds. But if you walked into a large warehouse and saw uniforms hanging there with no one in them, you wouldn't wonder what the purpose of them would be, correct? Wouldn't wonder what they were designed for?"*

"Not especially," said Nechayev. "I would assume that they were designed to be . . ." Her voice trailed off. "Truly? You think they were designed—"

"To be worn. Yes. Something in the genetic makeup of half-breeds enables either the D'myurj, or their associates

the Brethren, to transfer themselves into these bodies, once grown."

"But, good Lord, why?"

"Any number of reasons. Infiltration. Manipulation. Passing themselves off as members of the Federation in disguise. They might be creating wars in the hopes of 'testing' us to see if we rise to the occasion. According to anyone who has had contact with them, they keep claiming that they want to advance us. Soleta told me about something that happened some months ago, during the Paradox incident. She encountered an alien vessel that appeared to be upgrading the Paradox. Advancing it. Outfitting it with improvements."

"Are you saying that it might have been the D'myurj?"

"It fits the pattern. A race dedicated to evolution of what they see as lower species, no matter what the cost. Individuals purporting to be beneficent when they're really destructive. Who knows how far back it goes? There was an incident I studied involving a probe—I think it was called Nomad— that became upgraded and advanced when it encountered another, more advanced entity."

"I know of that incident, yes. We had theorized it was the Borg."

"But why would the Borg upgrade something else? They just take. They don't give. That might well have been con-

nected to the D'myurj as well. That means we're talking at least a century of their getting involved in Federation affairs."

"It sounds to me, Captain, as if you're treading on very thin ice here. Pulling together disparate strands and trying to weave together a whole that doesn't quite work. Still." She drummed her fingers on her desk. "This merits further investigation, at the very least. It would probably be wiser to keep this quiet, at least for the time being."

"I'm sure you're right, Admiral."

"All right. And Mac . . . my condolences on the loss of Doctor Selar. A tragedy all around."

"Thank you, Admiral. Calhoun out."

The screen went blank.

Nechayev leaned back in her chair, her thoughts racing.

Calhoun knows. Something is going to have to be done . . .

About the Author

PETER DAVID is the *New York Times* bestselling author of more than sixty books, including numerous *Star Trek* novels, such as *Imzadi, A Rock and a Hard Place, Before Dishonor,* and the incredibly popular *New Frontier* series. He is also the author of the bestselling movie novelizations for *Spider-Man, Spider-Man 2, Spider-Man 3, The Hulk, Fantastic Four,* and *Iron Man,* and has written dozens of other books, including his acclaimed original fantasy novels *Tigerheart, Sir Apropos of Nothing, The Woad to Wuin, Tong Lashing,* and *Darkness of the Light.*

David is also well known for his comic-book work, particularly his award-winning run on *The Hulk,* and has written for just about every famous comic-book superhero.

He lives in New York with his wife and daughters.